What Comes After One
A Cornwall Lesbian Romance
By Sabrina Kane

Thank you!

I want to extend a special thank you to my England-based UK consultants for helping make sure this book reads "British."

Catherine
Katherine
Lauren
Sarah
Sian

Chapter 1

Tamsin smiled at her clients, Deborah and Millicent.

It was hard, but she did it.

"So…ladies," she began. Her voice was pleasant. That too was hard…but she did it. "You are all set. I have you booked for two weeks in a lovely private bungalow in…" She swallowed. This part was going to be extremely difficult to say. "…in Carlsbad, California."

"We are *so* excited!" Deborah jumped in. She was thirty—Tamsin knew this from having had to make all the travel arrangements—with stylishly short curly hair. Her girlfriend, Millicent, also thirty, was sitting next to her. In contrast to Deborah's, Millicent's jet black hair was very long—like, Morticia Addams long—and she was the taller of the two.

"I heard the beaches there are amazing!" Millicent added. "And that it's such a cool town, especially for gay women."

Again, Tamsin forced a smile.

"You're going to have a wonderful time," she said cheerily. She decided she really ought to look into acting. Who knows? She might be the next Jessica Chastain.

In addition to Carlsbad, the women would also be going to Disneyland and Universal Studios, both of which were in the Los Angeles vicinity. Tamsin had managed to secure them good rates at both amusement parks thanks to her connections as a travel agent. If she was being honest with herself, this trip sounded fantastic. Well, mostly fantastic. She could do with a holiday, and Disneyland would be amazing. Although, Disney World would probably be more to her liking. Technically, it *was* closer to England, and it had the added benefit of being in Florida, rather than bloody California.

She explained some more details about the trip to her clients and then told them they were all set.

"Thank you!" Millicent said. "This was *so* much easier than booking everything ourselves!"

"And cheaper," Deborah added. "You have no idea how much this was costing us back when we were planning it ourselves."

Tamsin had some idea, yes.

The internet may have made travel planning more accessible for people, but the truth was that for certain voyages, a travel agent was not only an easier choice, but a more economical one. She was willing to wager that she had saved Deborah and Millicent close to seven-hundred quid by using her insider knowledge and industry connections.

She stood, wanting this interaction to be over. She had given the two women everything they needed, they had paid their final instalments, and now all that was left for them to do was get on a plane, hurry off to Cali-bloody-fornia and enjoy their holiday.

Deborah and Millicent hugged her, and she wished them a safe voyage one more time.

Once they had exited the agency and were back out on the street, Tamsin scowled.

"Bloody Carlsbad!" she muttered between clenched teeth.

"What's that, luv?" a voice said from the back of the agency, where the office was.

Tamsin rolled her eyes.

"Nothing, Uncle Richard!" she called out cheerily.

Her uncle Richard owned the agency, and he would not understand her disdain for Carlsbad, California. Especially since she'd never been there. He would not understand *that* at all! Uncle Richard took travel seriously, and for someone to tell him that they did not like a destination they've never visited, would be anathema to him.

There were exceptions, of course. Uncle Richard would excuse one from visiting countries currently undergoing a coup, for instance. The same went for any nation which actively and publicly oppressed people, such as Afghanistan or Iraq.

But Carlsbad, California?

No coup going on there, and as far as she could tell, the Carlsbadians—or whatever they called themselves—didn't oppress anyone. Although, Tamsin secretly suspected that the Amazonian lesbians who lived there probably looked down—literally and figuratively—on anyone shorter than 5' 10". Such as herself, for instance.

Carlsbad was currently in her bad books because it had beaten her village of Tremont as the "Most Lesbian-Friendly Travel Destination in the World."

The loss particularly stung because until *she* had suggested it to a top travel website, the designation "Most Lesbian-Friendly

Travel Destination in the World" hadn't even existed! Which meant, not only had she invented a travel industry award, but her own town came in second place!

Now, she often had to spend her workday planning trips to Carlsbad for traitorous Cornish lesbians who wanted to visit that apparent sapphic Shangri-la.

Which reminded her…

Using the computer at her desk, she input the dates of Deborah and Millicent's trip into the agency's Google calendar. She then instructed Google to remind her one week prior to their holiday. It was customary here at Xplr to send a gift to their clients, specifically a lightweight drawstring travel bag bearing the Xplr logo. It was perfect for tourists walking around a new town, picking up the odd souvenir here and there, or for carrying a small travel book or things like that.

In Deborah and Millicent's case, Tamsin imagined that they could use their bags for bringing bloody sunblock to the bloody gorgeous beaches in bloody gorgeous Carlsbad, and for carrying vials of pheromones to attract all the bloody Amazonian lesbians there.

This idea for sending gifts to Xplr's clients was hers, implemented when she started working for her uncle fresh out of uni. Back then—three years ago—the gift had been a ceramic mug, also bearing the Xplr logo, but after a year or so of that, Tamsin had decided it would be best to give their clients something they could take *with* them on their trips. After all, no one packs their favourite mug with them for a journey to Amsterdam or New Zealand.

The drawstring bag, however, was something a person *would* bring with them. And…score! As they walked around Amsterdam, New Zealand, or bloody Carlsbad, they'd be doing some guerilla marketing for the travel agency which got them there!

Uncle Richard had come to rely on Tamsin for ideas like that. In fact, he had come to rely on her for completely modernising the business he had started back in the 1970s—an era Tamsin couldn't even *imagine* being alive in.

To begin with, she had rebranded the agency, changing its name from Explore Travel to just Xplr.

"No vowels in *Explore?*" Uncle Richard had asked, dubiously, when Tamsin had written her idea down on a Post-It Note and showed him.

Tamsin had rolled her eyes.

"Vowels are so twentieth century," she had told him. "Trust me, this looks much more hip and much more now!"

"No *Travel* either?" he had then asked.

That had earned another eye roll from Tamsin.

"Redundant word," she had replied. "Let's allow the concept of *explore* to speak for itself."

It was also Tamsin who designed—herself—Xplr's first-ever website, using skills she had learned in the software development course she had taken at uni, and thus bringing Xplr into the modern age. This widened Xplr's reach. No longer was it just a Newquay travel agency, relying on customers who lived in Cornwall. After Tamsin was done, Xplr was able to handle the travel plans for clients *no matter* where they lived in England, Scotland or Wales.

Furthermore, it was she who had introduced her Uncle Richard to the monetary potential of LGBTQ+ travel, devising and marketing gay-friendly travel packages for the rainbow community. He had never even considered that as an untapped market. To him, people were people, which was wonderfully egalitarian and unprejudiced of him. However, when she pointed out that gay people—no matter where they were on the rainbow—appreciated when businesses made it known that they were not only queer-friendly but were willing to cater specifically to such customers, he began seeing the monetary potential. It also helped when she pointed out that she was a lesbian who did a lot of travelling and that there were plenty of other gay women just like her.

Tamsin also created the social media accounts for Xplr, and posted on each one several times a day, usually with travel tips or funny memes. The Instagram account alone had over 35,000 followers, thanks to the amazing photos Tamsin posted of places she had visited.

And being no dummy, she made sure that when she did take photos in a fabulous city or other locale, the photos often included herself.

Only 25-years-old, she was young and pretty, with blazing natural red hair and a killer smile. Her slender figure made her seem taller than 5' 6", and this was helped, in part, by having long legs.

Oh, and she had boobs. Boobs which looked great in bikinis, crop tops and tight sweaters. The kind of boobs, in short, which could have their own social media accounts.

It was shameless, she knew, and as a woman she ought to be outraged with herself, but it was business. Uncle Richard's business now, but one day it would all be hers. Her uncle was planning on retiring within the next year or two—he often changed his mind about which it would be—and when he did, he was going to hand Xplr over to her.

The day that happened, she wanted to be handed the keys to a thriving enterprise.

And cleavage helped with that.

***

As soon as she finished adding the reminder about the gift to send to Deborah and Millicent, her phone chirped with a text message.

I'll be there by six.

It was from her girlfriend, Kendra. They'd been seeing each other now for five weeks. Tamsin had met her here in Newquay. She worked as the manager for a bar inside one of the nicer hotels in town, a place where Tamsin often stopped in for a quiet drink.

She checked her watch. It was nearing four-thirty. She had no more appointments for the rest of the day, and if someone walked in between now and when Xplr closed at five, Uncle Richard could handle it. This would give her plenty of time to get home to Tremont, shower (including doing some shaving maintenance she needed), and then await Kendra's arrival.

"Leaving, Uncle Richard!" she called out, putting her computer to sleep.

"Fine, luv!" he called back, unseen. "I'll hold down the fort. See you tomorrow!"

"Right then, bye!" she replied, putting on her jacket, and then picking up her handbag and umbrella. It was spitting outside, had been off and on all day, which meant she'd need to be careful on the roads back home and not get too distracted while singing along to Florence + the Machine.

As she walked to the car park, shielding herself from the rain with her umbrella, she considered the night ahead of her…

Kendra, sure…

They hadn't seen each other for three days—something her girlfriend was making seem like the plotline of a Greek tragedy—due to Kendra having been in Falmouth this past weekend for a cousin's wedding. Therefore, Tamsin knew she needed to be sure to give Kendra an appropriate amount of attention before doing any one of a number of other things…

Updating her travel blog, *Ginger On the Go*, for example, with a funny anecdote from her recent trip to Hungary, taken just before she met Kendra.

She also needed to post on Xplr's Facebook page about some new travel deals to America she had learned about. Nobody really used Facebook anymore, except geezers, but then again, it was the geezers who did most of the travelling, so maintaining the page actually accounted for a good portion of the travel agency's business.

Additionally tonight, she wanted to start posting—on Facebook, Twitter, *and* Instagram—teasers about an exciting opportunity for more adventurous travellers. She wasn't going to reveal much yet—in fact, she planned on teasing about it for at least a week—but she knew many of her followers would totally be excited for this one.

In other words, there was quite a bit she expected to get done while at home. She'd definitely be looking forward to some sexy time with Kendra—after all, three days *was* a long time to go without—but…well, she just hoped her girlfriend wasn't expecting one of those all-night marathons lesbians seem to think was eternally de rigueur. So, of course she wanted to have sex this evening, but once it was done, she needed to crack on with other things.

Getting into her Renault Clio, she shut the door, sealing herself in from the rain. A few moments later, she was heading home to Tremont.

Chapter 2

Done!

Robyn sighed as she placed the last box taken from the Enterprise hire van down on the floor, in what would eventually become her office in this cottage she was renting.

Sitting down on the box—it contained art books, thus it wouldn't collapse as she settled on it—she felt a sense of accomplishment.

And why shouldn't she?

This had been a shite day to move!

Gloomy and rainy, it had ruined the excitement she had been feeling over the past few days about moving to Tremont. She knew that excitement would return once the rain stopped and the sun returned, but today it had gone. The rain and low ceiling of grey clouds in the sky had made moving feel even more like the odious, exhausting task that it was.

It didn't help that it was also a lonely task this time around.

Professional movers had already brought over the bulk of her belongings yesterday, emptying her old flat in Barnstaple. Today, after spending the night at her best mate Erin's place in that town, she had emptied her storage unit, using the hire van. But as it was just boxes and some other small items she owned, she had done all of this work today by herself, feeling there was no need to bother any of her friends with helping her.

She regretted that decision now. It would have been nice to have Erin or Bebe—or both—with her now. It would have provided some welcome brightness on such a drab and dismal day.

All in all, between the rain and the lack of friends helping, she decided she ought to feel as if she had done a great job.

She blew out a breath.

Of course, unloading the hire van had only been part of it. She still had a lot to do, and she was determined to get started on it…

Robyn had just taken a job as the general manager of the Linden Gallery Cornwall, the newest location in the Linden Group's collection of art galleries in the UK.

This was a big deal for her. She was basically charged with setting up this new location from scratch, turning an empty storefront in Newquay into yet another premier Linden gallery, just like the ones in London, Manchester, and Edinburgh.

Linden had recruited her based on her work running a much smaller gallery in Barnstaple. Realistically, no one should have expected the Henwith Gallery to amount to anything. When Robyn had taken it over, it was simply a local art spot which showed some interesting pieces, but nothing of particular note. It even had a gift shop—an abhorrent addition which had been the first to go once Robyn started running things. Art galleries *do not* have gift shops.

However, with Robyn at the helm, she managed to turn Henwith into a place worth visiting. She accomplished this using her keen eye for talent, as well as her savvy marketing skills.

Within six months, Henwith had its first ever vernissage—a word none of the staff she inherited had even heard of. It was for an artist Robyn had discovered in Sheffield, and thanks to her promotional efforts, that artist's work began gaining notice well beyond England.

This was followed by other showings, all of them featuring artists Robyn had discovered. Pretty soon, the Henwith Gallery, in tiny Barnstaple, in Devon of all places, was getting attention in the art world at large.

She sustained that for two years, until finally, at another invite-only vernissage for a sculptor from Wales—a sixty-year-old man whose works combined the surrealism of Giacometti with the kitsch of Koons—a woman with silver hair, dressed entirely in black, approached Robyn.

Victoria Linden.

Robyn had been inviting Victoria Linden, and others associated with the Linden galleries, to Henwith showings ever since taking over management of the gallery, the same way she invited all the artworld bigwigs in Britain. As time passed, several of those bigwigs had started showing up. But this was the first time anyone with the Linden name had actually deigned to make an appearance, let alone *the* Victoria Linden herself.

"I've been following your career," Victoria said to her, without introducing herself or even saying *Hello*. "I'd like to discuss with you an idea I have…"

Thus, at the ripe old age of twenty-nine, did Robyn find herself challenged with creating a Linden Gallery in Cornwall, and renting the most darling cottage on Penhallow Lane, in a place called Tremont.

***

An hour later, Robyn knew she *must* have accomplished something, although she couldn't tell exactly what.

Despite the number of boxes she had unpacked, it still seemed as if there were countless more, both downstairs and here, upstairs in the bedroom.

She sighed.

Standing next to her bed, she closed her eyes and took several deep breaths.

I have accomplished something! she chided herself silently.

She did this whenever she felt as if she hadn't done enough during a particular space of time. If she *didn't* do this, she was prone to going into a tailspin of self-doubt and worry, which would then lead into another tailspin of her losing focus and having her mind jump from one thing to the next.

Therefore, keeping her eyes closed, she reminded herself of what she had done so far...

Everything for the en suite is unpacked and put away, including towels.

I've made the bed with clean sheets. I found the box with my pillows.

A good number of my clothes are now hanging in the wardrobe.

All of this means I can take a shower, have a comfy bed to sleep in, and get dressed tomorrow.

Yes, she still had *a shit-ton* of work to do, but that was why she had arrived nearly a week early. It was Tuesday, and she didn't need to be at the gallery space until Monday, when she would walk in and determine what she wanted to change.

Feeling better, she opened her eyes and then stretched her five-five frame, to work out some of the stiffness from her exertions. That done, she redid her light-brown hair into a new ponytail.

Her eyes caught some movement just as she finished.

"Ooh!" she cooed. "Feeling brave now, you little coward?"

She bent and scooped up her cat, Empress. A fluffy white Persian, Empress had run away and hid as soon as Robyn had opened her carrier when they arrived here in this new place, and Robyn hadn't seen her since. Apparently, Empress was finally feeling courageous enough to begin exploring.

"This is our new home," Robyn told her, stroking the super soft fur of her pet.

Empress looked up at her, as though to ask what the problem had been with their *old* home, but Robyn ignored her.

A nearby sound from outside caught her attention. It was a car engine.

Curious, she stepped over to the bedroom window and looked down and to the right.

A blue Renault had just pulled into the driveway next door. Robyn watched the driver's door open, immediately followed by an umbrella opening.

"Oh my," she said softly as a pair of spectacular female legs emerged from the Renault, green high heels on their feet.

From this angle, the umbrella hid the driver from about the waist up, but from just seeing her lower half, Robyn could tell the woman had a nice figure. Hips which flared from a small waist, and long legs, which were partially encased in a midi-length pencil skirt.

Once out of the car, the woman stood there in the rain, facing Robyn's driveway, evidently noticing the hire van parked there. After a few moments, the woman turned and headed towards the front door of her own cottage. As she moved, and Robyn's angle of view shifted, Robyn saw a flash of fiery red hair peek out from beneath the umbrella.

"Oh my," she told Empress, raising both eyebrows. Empress knew she had a thing for gingers. And legs.

"If she has boobs, Empress, I'm in trouble," Robyn told her cat.

She then chuckled at herself.

Her neighbour might very well turn out to be a very attractive woman, but shit lot of good it would do her if the woman wasn't even gay!

"I could try turning her, of course," Robyn told Empress, knowing the cat would remember Vivian, "but that's *so* much work!"

Putting Empress down, Robyn resumed unpacking her clothes, putting thoughts of the ginger next door out of her mind.

She didn't know how much later it was when she heard another car engine close by. Again, she went to the window and looked down. She wanted to be annoyed at herself for acting like an old busybody, but she consoled herself with the fact that she was simply curious about her neighbours. Besides, it gave her a diversion from the chore of unpacking.

By now, it had stopped raining, and therefore when the driver's door of this second car—a Ford Puma—opened, an umbrella did not hide anything.

This driver was also a woman!

Blonde and shorter than the ginger, she was wearing jeans and a light-blue jumper, with cute ankle boots to finish off the outfit. She opened the back passenger door of her car, extracted a small handbag, and then an oversized tote bag.

Robyn cocked an eyebrow. She had a bag just like that tote. And the only reason why a woman would carry a smaller handbag along with a larger tote was if the larger tote contained a change of clothes as well as anything else she might need for when she woke up at someone else's house.

She shook her head briskly. Now she really *was* acting like an old busybody.

She stepped away from the window, feeling ridiculous.

She had better things to do than speculate on why the blonde was visiting the ginger. And even if the blonde ended up spending the night, it still didn't mean the ginger was gay. After all, Erin and Bebe used to spend the night at her old flat in Barnstaple quite frequently.

She huffed and rolled her eyes at her own stupidity.

That was an idiotic comparison because—drumroll, please—she, Erin and Bebe *were* gay. Just gay *friends*, however, but still…

So, to recap…

The ginger next door may or not be gay.

The blonde who is visiting her may or not be gay.

Even if the ginger is gay, the blonde may not be, and vice versa.

Even if they are *both* gay, they could just be friends.

Robyn rolled her eyes again.

It was time for a glass of wine.

All she had to do was remember which box had the wine glasses in it.

And also which box had the wine.

Chapter 3

Tamsin clutched the bed sheets tightly.

"Bloody hell, Kendra!" she grunted.

Her clit was positively begging for it now, but Kendra was doing an expert job of keeping her centre skating on the edge of the abyss.

Kendra was on fire tonight, practically pouncing on Tamsin as soon as she walked in the door.

Recognising her girlfriend's need, Tamsin had decided to give her what she obviously wanted. Therefore, things began right there, just inside the closed front door. Tamsin pressed Kendra up against the entryway wall, priming her further by grabbing her crotch with one hand over the skinny jeans she was wearing as they kissed hungrily, while with the other hand, she squeezed one of Kendra's breasts over the jumper she had on.

Minutes later, Kendra's clothes had been taken off in the living room, and Tamsin had fucked her with her fingers on the sofa, amazed at how wet her girlfriend already was. When Kendra came, Tamsin eased her down from the orgasm by licking her quaking pussy, catching her streaming arousal with her tongue, and planting gentle kisses on her folds.

Then, since she was down there…

As soon as Tamsin detected Kendra's breath beginning to even out, it took less than five minutes to make her come again, her swollen clit captured between her lips, being sucked on.

They went upstairs after that. By then, the knickers Tamsin had put on post-shower were soaked. Yet following a completely nude Kendra up the stairs—her full bum tantalisingly close, seeing the evidence of her two orgasms streaming down her thighs—had made Tamsin top her again on the bed as soon as they entered the bedroom, this time with Kendra laying facedown.

When Kendra started coming again, screaming into a pillow, Tamsin brought her mouth down to her arse, giving it little nips with her teeth until her girlfriend finally stilled, breathing hard, recovering.

Now, the pyjamas Tamsin had put on after her shower were discarded, and Kendra's face was between her legs, the tip of her tongue drawing circles around her clit but not touching it, building up the anticipation even more.

Tamsin released the sheets and grabbed both her breasts, mewling as she squeezed them, her diamond-hard nipples pressing into her palms, the sensitivity of the two buds feeding the storm building up in her mound.

"Oh god!" she uttered. Her eyes, which had been closed, popped open in surprise. She might actually come *without* Kendra touching her clit, she was that fired up now! Her centre had just warned her that there was only so much more teasing she could take before it took matters into its own hands. It was now on the tipping point, and the inevitable was at most seconds away.

However, perhaps Kendra sensed that she was letting this play out too long, because suddenly, Tamsin felt a tremendous burst of pleasure when her clit felt a warm tongue swiping across it.

"*Oh...fuuuuuuuuuuck!*" she cried out as her release was finally granted.

It trembled through her pussy, making her inner walls quake with contractions of ecstasy which then dissipated throughout her entire core.

She pinched her nipples now, wanting some pain with the pleasure. She smiled as her orgasm continued to spill from her, further fuelled by the twin aches at the tips of her breasts.

Whimpering, she felt herself plateau, her pussy downshifting back to a less excited but still energised state.

Between her legs, Kendra was humming contentedly, and Tamsin could feel her tongue moving all over her sex, licking up the results of her climax.

As her orgasm faded, Tamsin released her breasts, and then that familiar feeling came over her.

What's next?

Kendra had given her a good orgasm, and Tamsin was satisfied. She had been horny, and...well, now she wasn't. As a result, her mind had chosen to ruminate on that list of things she wanted to get done tonight before bedtime.

She and Kendra still needed to eat dinner, for example.

Also, there was that blog post she still wanted to write for *Ginger on the Go*. She figured it would be less than a thousand words, and therefore something she could bang out quickly.

Then there were the posts she wanted to make on Xplr's social media accounts. At times, that in itself felt like a full-time job. But her efforts in that arena were paying off, so she needed to keep on it and not get lazy. When Uncle Richard finally handed over the reins, she wanted them to be attached to a thriving travel business.

Once she was done with all that…well, she would then want to just relax and unwind before starting another day tomorrow.

However…

Kendra's face was still between her thighs, kissing her vulva, licking her folds, every now and then poking her tongue inside her sensitive opening to probe.

It felt good, it truly did, but now Tamsin was getting a bit frustrated. Instinctually—as a gay woman—she knew she should just want to give over this night completely to fucking with Kendra, but really…

She had given Kendra what she had come here for—sex after not seeing each other for three days—and Kendra had reciprocated. As far as Tamsin was concerned, she was good until next time. So why couldn't they just close this chapter of the night, and move on to other things?

"Let me guess," Kendra suddenly said, "you're done?"

Tamsin, her reverie interrupted, looked down at her.

"No!" she said, blushing, wondering why she was lying. "I mean, I loved what you were doing…"

Kendra sighed and glared at her.

"You were staring at the ceiling, Tams!"

With another huffed-out sigh, Kendra removed herself from between Tamsin's legs. In a moment, she was beside her on the mattress, sitting up against the headboard. However, she slipped under the covers on that side of the bed, pulling them up over herself and hiding her nude form.

Tamsin took this as a bad sign.

She rolled over and propped herself up on her elbows, kind of leaning over her girlfriend. She was still on top of the sheets on her side of the mattress, meaning her body was still on display. Lying like this pushed her large breasts together, creating the kind of cleavage that were like magnets for the eyes.

She may be ready to stop having sex and get out of bed, but she also wanted to mollify Kendra somewhat. They could still have a very pleasant time tonight, after all.

Sure enough, Kendra stared at her chest and licked her lips. She then raked her eyes over Tamsin's back, and Tamsin could then feel them settling on her arse.

"I had a great time," Tamsin told her.

Kendra took her eyes off Tamsin's bottom and looked at her.

"And we could have even more of a great time, Tamsin," she said, with a bit of an edge to her voice. "But no…as always, you put the brakes on things too quickly."

"I'm done, Kendra!" she exclaimed. "You did your job, now I'm ready to do something else!"

She winced immediately.

That did not sound good…

Kendra's eyes widened.

"Job?" she spat. "Is that what you think I'm doing? A *job?*"

Fuck!

"Hun, of course not!" Tamsin said quickly. "You know that's not what I meant! I just meant that, you know, you made me come—and it was *massive*, like wow!—and now I'm ready for us to do other things."

Kendra gave her a dubious look.

"You mean, you're ready for *you* to do other things," she stated.

This was true, Tamsin conceded.

She chose her next words carefully.

"Okay, listen," she began, "I do have things I want to get done tonight, *but*…I love the idea of you being here in the house with me while I do them."

Kendra opened her mouth say something, but Tamsin quickly spoke again before she could.

"I mean, I can even work on one or two of the things while we watch some telly!" she pointed out.

Honestly, why was this such a point of contention? She wasn't telling Kendra to get out of her home, nor was she telling Kendra to not speak to her the rest of the night.

They'd *had* sex! Fantastic *I've-missed-you-while-we-were-apart* sex!

Tamsin had loved pleasuring Kendra. She had loved getting reacquainted with her body and hearing those special noises her girlfriend makes.

But right now…she was simply done!

"Tams," Kendra went on, "I know you have this and that which you like to stay on top of, but I *like* having sex! Sex is fucking amazing! And—news flash—we're women! The blokes blow their load and—*pffft!*—they're done! *We*, on the other hand, can keep going!"

Tamsin huffed and rolled over onto her back, staring at the ceiling.

Which got me into trouble in the first place.

"Why do lesbians feel like they *have* to have sex all night long?" she asked. "Why is that the default expectation?"

She really wondered about this and had for years.

She blamed the bloody *L Word*.

Oh, and the bloody lesfic writers! Chapter after chapter of women starting to have sex at bloody lunchtime, and not finishing until bloody sunrise.

Next to her, Kendra sighed.

"It's not the default," she said, "but it would be nice from time to time."

Tamsin was irritated now.

"I may not want to have sex all night," she began, "but unless I've lost my ability to count, you came three times tonight!" Tamsin replied. "Or were you faking?"

"*Excuse me?*" Kendra spat out.

Fuck!

This was going from bad to worse. The ironic part, Tamsin knew, was that as many times as she'd had similar conversations with plenty of other women, she should be better at it.

"Sorry," she began, "that was…just a heated comment. I should have thought that through. I'm sorry it upset you. I'm just…frustrated."

"You know what," Kendra said, "forget about it, okay? Just remember this conversation when you're seventy."

Tamsin blinked.

"What do you mean?" she asked.

Examining her fingernails and looking for all the world like a woman who had lost any and all interest in Tamsin, Kendra shrugged.

"It's just that one day, you'll be seventy, and you will *not* be having sex all night long…" She turned her head to look at Tamsin. "*If* you even get any sex at all." She resumed examining her nails. "And when you're sitting in the care home, knitting a cardi or whatever, you'll remember these days and think, 'Gosh, I wish I would have fucked Kendra all night long when I had the chance.'"

Tamsin felt a pang of sadness pierce her heart at Kendra's hypothetical scenario. Partially because it seemed so very possible. Partially because if she ever got to the point where knitting a cardi was the highlight of her day, she'd rather be euthanised.

"Look…" she said.

"Tams, just forget about it, okay?" Kendra interrupted. "We're good. You *did* get me off three times…" She turned her head and glared at Tamsin again. "…*genuinely*, you bitch, so I guess I have no right to complain."

She crossed her arms over her chest, though, and to Tamsin it looked as if Kendra felt she had every right to complain…she was just choosing not to.

"Anyway," Kendra said after a moment, "I saw the van next door. Who's moving in?"

Tamsin had noticed the van also when she arrived home this evening, though she hadn't seen anyone.

Old Mrs. Burberry-Foster's cottage next door had been vacant since the biddy ran off to Israel to join a kibbutz two months ago. Tamsin had actually started getting used to the idea of not having a neighbour to her north.

"I don't know," she answered. "Mrs. Arrington-Maffin popped 'round yesterday evening to tell me that movers and a BMW had been next door while I was at work, but that she didn't get a chance to see who the new tenant was."

Mrs. Arrington-Maffin was one of Tremont's biggest gossips, so undoubtedly she had come by to find out if Tamsin could shed some light on who the village's new resident was.

"Ooh, BMW," Kendra said. "Posh."

Tamsin hoped not. Okay, fine…she herself *presented* as posh. She dressed really well—especially for work—and she wasn't averse to spending a few extra quid for designer labels. Whenever she went out, even if it was just to the Ladle & Spoon, Tremont's local, for a drink with her best mate Rylea, she made an effort with her appearance. She made sure her hair looked nice, that she was had on at least some makeup, and that she was wearing something cute.

She hadn't gotten around to affording a BMW or, even better, a Merc yet, but that was on her list.

However, with all of this being said, Tamsin felt confident that she didn't *act* posh. She wasn't a toffee-nosed twat, walking around thinking she was better than everyone else, and she hoped the new neighbour wasn't either.

Her brow furrowed.

She didn't even know if it was a woman or a man who moved in. Or…(shudder)…both! A straight couple.

She rolled her eyes.

Well…whereas it wasn't that she didn't have anything against the straights in general, if it *was* a Mr. and Mrs. next door now, they'd better be cool about gay people, especially gay women. Tremont was teeming with them. In particular, a posh-but-not-posh ginger living next door to them.

Chapter 4

The sound of a car door shutting woke Robyn up the next morning. It was followed immediately by the sound of an engine starting.

Robyn rolled over in her bed and shut her eyes again. Whoever it was leaving next door—the ginger or the blonde—it was too early. It was still dark out, and as Robyn wasn't planning to start her drive back to Barnstaple to return the hire van until eight or nine, she planned on staying in bed.

But sleep—having been set free—proved elusive to catch once again, and after twenty minutes of struggling to send her brain back to unconsciousness, she gave up with a huff of frustration, feeling mildly resentful of whoever it was next door who needed to start their day so early.

However, she chided herself. If the ginger or the blonde needed to go—presumably to work—she needed to go. That was life. Robyn knew she'd eventually get used to it. Eventually, she wouldn't even notice such early starts from next door.

Getting out of bed, she cursed England and its blasted cold mornings, even in May. She also cursed old Cornish cottages like this, with their less-than-modern insulation. She was wearing fleece pyjamas—with a long-sleeved top, no less—and she was still feeling the bite in the air.

Rubbing her arms, she started for the en suite but then stopped. Curiosity got the better of her again, and she padded over to the window on bare feet that were definitely feeling the cold of the stone flooring. It reminded her to purchase an area rug for the room soon.

Which one of you woke me up?

Pulling aside the drawn blackout curtain, she peered at the driveway next door, which was illuminated by a streetlamp.

The Puma was gone.

Wait…which one was the Puma again?

Initially, she thought it was the ginger, but then quickly remembered that was wrong. The blonde was the Puma, which meant the ginger was still home.

Okay, so the blonde was the early riser. Having discovered this, she hoped her brain would remember the fact so that if it happened again tomorrow morning, she would sleep right through it.

In the en suite, she peed, swished some mouthwash, and brushed her teeth. Then she turned on the shower, waiting until the water was very hot before stepping under the spray.

While washing her vulva, her clit responded strongly each time her lathered-up bath pouffe passed over it. So much so, that it was impossible to ignore.

She let out a slow breath as the tiny button became swollen, demanding attention quite insistently.

This made her realise that it had been a while since doing any DIY down there. The past fortnight, in particular, had been rather busy preparing for this move, paying for this move, and then executing this move. Add to that the attendant stress which comes with moving—and starting a new job—and every sexual impulse had been siphoned out of her.

Now, however, the move at least was over, and her pussy was practically begging for mercy.

She could do it here in the shower, of course, but by now her vagina was letting her know that this was going to be a big one, and in these cases, Robyn enjoyed more than just a quick rub in the loo.

She hurried with the rest of her washing, her skin tingling with anticipation. When she reached to turn the shower off, she noticed her hand was even trembling.

After drying off, she decided not to bother putting on her plush bathrobe because it was just going to be taken off momentarily anyway. Whenever possible, she preferred masturbating in the nude.

But as soon as she stepped out of the steamed-up en suite, she cried out, "Bugger!"

The air in the bedroom was still chilly, and on her damp skin it felt as if she'd just stepped outside in December, wearing nothing more than a smile.

She scurried to the bed, pulling the covers and duvet over her immediately. But then…

"Bugger!" she exclaimed again. She had forgotten one important thing.

During last night's unpacking session, she had discovered the box-within-a-box which contained her sex toys: three vibrators, two dildos, a butt plug and the mistress of them all, a Magic Wand.

She had placed her toy box in the bottom drawer of her dresser, as usual, but right now that did her no good.

And she had just started feeling warm!

However…she needed a toy! She had neglected herself down there for too long and thus wanted more than her fingers could provide. Inside her vagina, her walls were already swollen, lubricated, and pulsing. Fingers—it was telling her—were not going to do.

Gritting her teeth, she threw off the covers, the cold air assailing her nude body once more. Hurrying to the dresser, she crouched, opened the bottom drawer and extracted the two items she needed quickly.

Getting back into bed, and back under the duvet, she didn't waste any time. Pulling her knees up and laying her feet flat on the mattress, she spread her legs, her knees tenting the heavy fabric over her.

Item number one was her favourite dildo, one of those hyper-realistic jobs with a large head and a veiny shaft. It never bothered her that it looked exactly like a bloke's penis, all that mattered was what it did to her…filled her passage entirely and deeply, forcing her vagina to really stretch to accommodate it.

Guiding the head of it to her opening under the bedclothes, she gasped at how easily it slid it.

"Ohhhhhh…" she murmured, closing her eyes, "…this is what I needed!"

She wanted to get to Item Number Two right away, but she knew once she utilised that, it would all be over, and she wanted to spend at least a few minutes enjoying the sensation of being *stuffed* with this dildo first.

She pushed it all the way in, until the suction cup base pressed against her spread-apart folds.

"Oh my god…" she whimpered, loving the weight of the toy in her passage, loving also how her walls throbbed against it, and how her arousal trickled out of her opening to run down her perineum and coat her rear opening.

She closed her legs, brought her knees up to her chest, and wrapped her arms around them. Then she rocked her hips from side to side, breathing hard at how her movements made her hyper aware of how *large* the dildo inside her was.

Spreading her legs again, she grasped the suction cup base with her right hand, and fucked herself with the toy, being sure the base of her hand slammed against her clit with each inward thrust, her grunts providing the soundtrack to her actions.

Fuck!

She needed to come!

She ruthlessly shoved the dildo all the way back in, knowing she could take it, and then reached to her left…

Item number two was her clitoral stimulator. A suction vibe that was one of the best purchases she had made in her life.

Ever.

Switching it on, its humming noise both familiar and arousing, she guided its tip to her clit, her breathing becoming more ragged as she positioned it just so over her swollen bud and the device started sucking on it.

She expected to last a little longer than she did, but no…she came instantly.

"*BloodyfuckingHELLLLLLLLLLLLL!*" she screamed, arching her back and lifting her arse off the mattress.

A fortnight of stress, a fortnight of worry and angst…all of it melted away as her pent-up and neglected pleasure exploded in her core. Her spasming pussy clutched at what was filling it, Robyn loving how the rigidity of the dildo pushed back against her walls. Meanwhile, she concentrated on keeping the suction vibe on her clit, wanting it to pull out every iota of ecstasy her little button had trapped in it.

She began shaking on the bed, the waves of this climax completely owning her. Her pussy started pushing the dildo out, and Robyn let it. When it eventually fell from her opening, plopping onto the mattress, her come streamed out also. Feeling that, she started coming again, another massive orgasm pummelling her from the inside out.

"*GAAAAAAAAAAAHD!*" she shouted. "*Oh my fucking GAAAAAAAAAAAHD!*"

She pulled the suction vibe away now, her clit too sensitive to take it any longer. Rolling over under the duvet, she buried her face in the nearest pillow to ride out the climax, but she also brought her right hand down to palm her sex, wanting to feel and play with her wetness—and perhaps get herself primed for number three.

***

When she was finally done, she was very much wide awake. So much so that she decided to make her drive to Barnstaple earlier than originally planned. It was just past seven a.m. Given it was a nearly two-hour voyage to her former hometown, she should arrive just as the Enterprise branch was opening. Then, she could pick up her car from where she had left it at Erin's and be back here around midday.

After cleaning herself up, she started getting dressed. As she pulled on her Nike trainers, she smiled.

Christ, she had just treated herself well! In less than twenty minutes, she had made herself come four times. She supposed going a couple of weeks without would do that to a girl. She swore that during the last one, she had temporarily lost her vision. Her pussy—now put away behind cotton hipsters and skinny jeans—was still tingling, and she was still very much aware of her sensitive clit. She hoped things down there would settle down soon, though. She had a lot of driving to do and would prefer not to do it with soaked knickers.

Before she left, she checked the forecast on her phone, for both Tremont—well, Newquay—and Barnstaple. Thankfully, though Barnstaple was predicted to be about five degrees cooler than here, it was still going to be a lovely and sunny day in both locales. Nonetheless, she brought her umbrella with her, her father having insisted ever since she was a little girl that a true Brit doesn't get caught out unprepared in the rain.

Outside, after locking her front door, she looked to her right.

The Clio was still there.

Well, whatever it was the ginger did for a living, she certainly didn't leave as early as the blonde, which made her wonder what kind of work the other woman did.

She shrugged, putting it out of her mind.

She'd find out soon enough, she supposed.
They were neighbours now, after all.

Chapter 5

The alarm on Tamsin's Alexa went off, as usual, at 6:55 a.m.

Groaning, she opened her eyes reluctantly, blinking at the bedroom light, which Alexa had also turned on. Why Tamsin had thought programming Alexa to do that when she had first bought the thing, she had no idea, because she really preferred to open her eyes to a darkened room. The problem now was, she couldn't remember how to tell it *not* to do that.

"Alexa, stop," she ordered, and the smart speaker fell silent.

She looked to her left, expecting to see Kendra next to her, but the bed was empty.

Maybe she's downstairs already.

Unlike herself—who could sleep through a nuclear explosion—Kendra was a terrible sleeper and would often awaken in the middle of the night, unable to fall right back to sleep. In those cases, she would either go to the living room in her flat—if that's where they were staying—or go downstairs to Tamsin's sofa here.

In her en suite, Tamsin brushed her teeth while peeing. Once done, she set about bundling up her shoulder-length hair into a messy bun atop her head, prior to getting into the shower, when she heard what sounded like a door being pulled shut outside.

The new neighbour! Or neighbours!

This was a chance to get a look at them!

She spat out the three remaining bobby pins that she had been gripping with her lips, disentangled her fingers from her hair and ran to the bedroom window, pulling aside the curtain.

Too late! The new resident of Tremont was already in the hire van. She knew it was only one person, because she had only heard one of the van doors close, but because the driver's side was furthest from her, Tamsin couldn't even get a peek inside the vehicle to see who was driving. Woman or man. Old or young. She was still in the dark.

Disappointed, she had turned away from the window to return to the loo when she stopped.

Belatedly, her mind was telling her that something was missing outside.

Pulling aside the curtain again, she examined the scene in front of her home, seeing the problem right away.

Kendra's car was gone, and as car thefts were not a particular problem in sleepy Tremont, that meant Kendra was gone as well.

Now, Tamsin was confused.

Okay, yes, they'd had a bit of a row last night following sex—a row *about* sex, as it turned out—but in Tamsin's mind it didn't even really count as a row! It was more of a…slight difference of opinion. And they'd been fine afterwards!

As a kind of olive branch, Tamsin had opted not to write that blog post, after all, deciding to do it today at the agency. Instead, she had spent time with Kendra on the sofa, watching *Schitt's Creek*.

Yes, she had still done those social media posts she had planned to do, but that task had been quickly dispatched, and once she had put her phone away, she and Kendra had snuggled together watching the travails of the Rose family before going to bed.

Phone!

Picking up the device from the nightstand, she activated the screen. Sure enough, there was a text from Kendra.

Left early. Talk later.

Tamsin blinked.

That was it? No further explanation? No follow-up text stating that she had reached home safely?

As a woman, that last bit bothered her, and so she called Kendra's phone. She would be fine not getting the full story of why Kendra left without a word, but she at least wanted to know she was okay.

"Hey," Kendra answered.

After five rings…

"Hey," Tamsin said. "You made it home?"

"Yeah, a while ago," Kendra told her.

Tamsin scoffed.

"Okay, well next time you abscond in the middle of the night like that, at least let me know you made it home safely!" she said.

There was a pause, but eventually Kendra said, "You're right, of course. I should have sent another text. Sorry if you were worried."

"Is everything alright?" Tamsin asked, knowing already that it wasn't.

She heard Kendra sigh, and Tamsin steeled herself.

"Can you come by the bar today?" Kendra asked. "Maybe around lunchtime, before my shift starts?"

Tamsin shifted her weight to her other leg.

"You want to break up with me while you're at work?" she asked snidely.

Another sigh from Kendra.

"Well, I don't want to do it over the phone, Tams," she said quietly.

Tamsin clenched her jaw, trying not to feel the sting of this one, but failing.

Five weeks…

They had lasted five weeks.

Even worse…

That pathetic number was actually a record for her.

"The sex thing," she stated.

"Yes, the sex thing!" Kendra confirmed. "Call me petty, call me superficial, call me a horny slut, but for fuck's sake, Tams, we hadn't seen each other for three days!"

"And I took care of you, didn't I?" Tamsin shot back. "Twice downstairs, if I recall, followed by another up here!"

"Oh my god!" Kendra exclaimed. She then started chuckling, which Tamsin thought an odd thing to do.

"What are you laughing about?" she demanded.

"You don't get it, do you?" Kendra asked. Even over the phone, Tamsin could detect a note of pity in her voice. "I mean, you simply lack the ability to *get it!*"

"What am I supposed to be getting?" Tamsin prodded.

She heard Kendra take a deep breath.

"Tams, it's not about how many times you get *me* off," Kendra said. "Well, it's *sort of* about that, yes, but that's not what's important here. What's important here is that I have an incredibly beautiful and sexy girlfriend who turns me on, and when we're having sex, I want to spend a lot of time pleasuring her! And that's, like, even if I see you *every day!*

"Last night, I hadn't seen you in *three days*, Tams! I wanted to fucking devour you! I wanted to lick every inch of your body, and I wanted to eat you out until you went insane! But no…one go and that was it! Suddenly, you're staring at the ceiling, probably composing a tweet in your head!"

She took a very audible breath before she continued.

"Maybe it sounds stupid to you, Tamsin, but even if you hadn't given me a *single* orgasm last night, I would have been fucking ecstatic if I could have licked you from your toes to your tits, and then spent hours tasting you. For fuck's sake, I was *dreaming* about that on the train ride home! *That's* what you're not getting. But, you know…whatever! Forgive me for actually wanting to get pleasure from *pleasuring* my girlfriend."

Tamsin stood still, digesting this.

Everything Kendra just told her—being licked from her toes to her tits, being eaten out until she went crazy, being *devoured*—sounded wonderful, and the sexual creature inside her actually responded to those images by making her clit quiver a bit.

So then why, Tamsin wondered, when such scenarios could have been hers for the taking last night, did she tap out after one climax?

Of course, if she hasn't figured that out by now…

The truth was, Kendra was Cora, Cora was Angie, Angie was Micah, Micah was Penny…et cetera.

A long list of women Tamsin had dated, all of whom had complained about this very thing, and how she seemingly had no interest in continuing to fuck past one or—if the planets were aligned—two orgasms.

Kendra was just a continuation of a pattern.

Well, she thought, feeling her eyes sting a little, *at least I'm consistent.*

***

After a very distracted day at work, Tamsin took a detour to Tretherras Road, Tremont's high street, rather than drive straight home. She parked in front of Bean There/Done That, the village's coffee shop.

It was owned and operated by her best mate Rylea. Currently, it had just closed for the day, but Tamsin knew Rylea was still in there waiting for her.

She had called her friend as she left Newquay about twenty-five minutes ago, asking if they could talk privately. She had just been dumped—again—and needed solace and succour.

She would have preferred having this discussion at Rylea's house, so that Darcie, her fiancée, could join them. Darcie was several years older than her and Rylea, and Tamsin thought perhaps those few extra years might provide some much needed wisdom and perspective.

But Rylea had told Tamsin that Cleo, Darcie's niece-but-now-adopted-daughter was at the house also. Tamsin loved the little kid, but this had to be a grown-up conversation.

Getting out of her car, she said good evening to a couple of pensioners out for an evening walk. The Quintrells. Married for over forty-five years, and they still walked holding hands.

Watching them continue along Tretherras Road, Tamsin wondered if such a future was meant for her. Would some young person forty-five years from now get out of their car (or spaceship, or whatever it was they'd be driving then), spot her with the love of her life and think, "How sweet! They still hold hands!"

Rylea unlocked the front door of The Bean—as the locals called it—before she could knock. Her best friend—lithe and fit, with auburn hair—was wearing skinny jeans and a Pet Shop Boys t-shirt. She peeked around the doorframe, in the direction of the Quintrells.

"You're doing that thing again, aren't you?" Rylea asked, standing aside to let Tamsin into the shop.

"What thing?" Tamsin asked, turning to face her.

Rylea quirked an eyebrow.

"That thing where you look at old couples and wonder if that'll be you someday," she said. "You confessed to doing that after Micah—no, wait—Angie called it off with you."

Tamsin blinked.

"Did I?"

Rylea shrugged.

"You were pissed," she replied. "It's also how I know you had a huge crush on me in Year 8."

"I did not tell you that!" Tamsin said, blushing, but knowing that would be exactly the type of thing she'd confess to while pissed. In any case, it was true…she had crushed *hard* on Rylea back then, but thankfully they never got together romantically, as teens or adults.

She sighed and covered her face.

"God, I can't believe I told you that," she murmured.

"It's okay, Tams," Rylea said, approaching her. "I had a crush on you too back then, so we're even. Now, are you okay?"

Rylea opened her arms, and Tamsin gladly melted into a hug from her. Her love life may be shite, but she knew that when she was old, Rylea would walk down the street holding her hand. Sure, it would be just as friends, but Tamsin supposed that once she got to that stage in her life, if she still had friends as amazing as this one, it would be a blessing.

Rylea, still keeping her arms wrapped around Tamsin's back, pulled away just enough to be able to look at her and ask, "Do we need an exorcism?"

Tamsin considered that. A relationship exorcism was a ritual she and Rylea did whenever they needed help getting over someone—and Tamsin often needed help getting over someone.

"We do," she answered Rylea. Vodka was only going to get her so far this time. Fine, she hadn't been in love with Kendra, but up until this morning she had believed that their relationship had legs; that it might last long enough to eventually reach the point of being in love. Therefore, the catharsis from a relationship exorcism would go a long way towards putting this disappointment behind her.

They sat down at one of the tables in the empty café, and Tamsin explained how this latest chapter in her romantic chronicles ended. By now, Rylea was familiar with the primary villain in the story…her own lack of desire to have sex all night long when seemingly every other gay woman on Earth expected that.

"And, as usual, I didn't know what to tell her," Tamsin stated. "I mean, what the fuck do I tell her, Rye Bread?" she asked, using her childhood nickname for her friend. "Whatever bloody gene it is that the rest of you lesbians have that make you Energizer bunnies in bed, I missed out on. But why does that mean I don't deserve a successful relationship with a woman?"

She stopped herself. She was on the verge of tears, and she didn't want that right now. Maybe later, once she was home; although, she couldn't help wondering if she kept crying each time a woman called it off with her, would she have any tears left for other sad moments in her life?

Rylea pursed her lips and stared off to the side, obviously chewing on something mentally.

Finally, Rylea looked at her.

"Have you ever considered that maybe it's not you, it's them?"

Tamsin blinked.

"Say more," she said.

Rylea shrugged.

"Okay, so it's totally possible that this is bollocks," she began, "but what if it's not so much about *you* not wanting to have prolonged sex, as it is about you not wanting to have prolonged sex with *them?*"

Tamsin's brow furrowed as she processed this. If she understood what Rylea was getting at, this was something she had never considered before. It was a new perspective on things. She felt as if she had always believed the Earth was flat but was now being shown one of those Apollo photos taken from space, showing that the bloody thing was in fact, round.

"Okaaaay," she said slowly. "But I really liked some of these women, Rylea. I could have been happy making a go of it with them, even with how things were in the bedroom."

"I get that," Rylea told her. "But they were unhappy with how things were in the bedroom and, to be fair, I can see their point. Sex may not be the most important thing in a relationship, but it's pretty fucking important, Tams, and your girlfriends weren't getting what they wanted."

"So, we're back to this being about me having a problem again," Tamsin said.

"No," Rylea said reassuringly, placing her hand on Tamsin's arm. "All I'm saying is, there had to have been a reason why things in the sex department with these women was…lacking. And who knows? Maybe that's just you! And if that's the case, fine, because you're wonderful! *Buuuut*…maybe the reason was that you didn't feel that kind of…motivation, if you will, for those *particular* women."

At first, Tamsin was liking where this conversation was going, but now she quirked her eyebrow dubiously at her friend.

"Rylea, you've seen these women. Cora, Angie, Kendra…They're fucking hot!"

"I didn't say they weren't!" Rylea insisted. "I'd fuck them all night long! Don't tell Darcie I said that! But so what? Maybe for you, a woman being hot isn't enough. Maybe you need an extra something in order to kick your sex drive into a higher gear."

Tamsin nodded slowly.

"I'm liking this again," she said thoughtfully. "Primarily because it makes me sound better than the rest of you lot who will shag anything with ovaries until you pass out from exhaustion."

"Hey!" Rylea shot back.

***

By the time Tamsin left about half an hour later, she felt a little better. At the very least, Rylea had given her a different perspective; a different angle from which to view the problem all of her recent girlfriends had broken up with her over.

Maybe she *did* need a woman to have an extra *something* in order for them to have nightly shag-fests, like seemingly every other lesbian couple.

"Either that, or I'm just not all that into sex," she muttered, as she turned her car onto Penhallow Lane, her street. "In which case, I'm back to square one."

Well, that was something to consider another day. Right now, all she wanted to do was get home, pour herself a drink—specifically vodka—and wallow for a bit on the sofa.

Turning into her driveway, she looked to the right, at Mrs. Burberry-Foster's old cottage which was now…someone else's cottage.

There was the BMW Mrs. Arrington-Maffin had told her about. A black coupe with alloy wheels.

Posh.

She still needed to lay eyes on this newcomer but figured that it would happen when it happened.

Right now, vodka needed to happen.

Chapter 6

When she woke the next morning, Robyn was surprised at how late it was.

8:37 a.m. She'd had a bit of a lie-in.

She was doing this settling-into-Tremont week without an alarm clock, one of the benefits of not having to resume her professional life until Monday, when she would most definitely be using her alarm clock as she began the work of opening the Linden Gallery Cornwall.

To that end, she reminded herself now to call Sasha Hoffman, the Cornish artist she had chosen for the inaugural showing at the LGC, the vernissage for which, if everything went according to plan, would be happening—as scheduled—in a little more than three weeks, on the twenty-second. Sasha was one of those artists who needed coddling. Unlike many artists, Sasha lacked arrogance and cockiness. She most certainly *did not* believe the solar system revolved around her and her art. This meant Robyn liked to check in with her every now and then, just to be certain she wasn't cowering in a corner of her studio in fright.

Noting the time, she wondered if the blonde had stayed over next door again last night. If she had, and had left as early today as yesterday, then it hadn't disturbed her sleep, which was a good sign.

With her mind now on the blonde, and then by extension the ginger, she started to hope they were a couple. It would be quite the stroke of luck to have chosen a place to live right next to lesbians. Perhaps she could befriend them and learn about the sapphic scene in this bit of Cornwall. It would be nice to start dating again. She had taken some time away from 'putting herself out there' following the debacle with Christine and all her lies but was now feeling she was ready to find someone special to spend her free time with.

Getting out of bed, she opened the curtains to let some daylight into the room, and to check the weather. Clear blue sky greeted her; however, she could tell by the tree in her front garden that it was somewhat breezy, her sixth sense telling her there might be a storm later.

(Well, it was either her sixth sense or the fact that she had checked the weather forecast on her phone yesterday, and she seemed to recall it mentioning some rain for today.)

Glancing to her right, she noticed the ginger's Clio was gone, meaning—presumably—she was off at work. Robyn wondered if she worked somewhere here in town, or in Newquay, which reminded her…

She needed to drive into Newquay today to do a proper shop for groceries at Sainsbury's. So far, she'd been living off of canned and boxed food—including Jammie Dodgers—brought from her old flat in Barnstaple. However, she now had her kitchen here in the cottage set up, ready for her to cook some real food—and to store more Jammie Dodgers.

All in all, she was rather pleased with herself for the progress she'd made over the past two days. On her own, she had managed to make this cottage start to feel like hers, like *her* home, and with the exception of a few remaining boxes—mostly containing seasonal clothes—she was pretty much done, which meant celebrating.

Padding to the bathroom on feet covered in fuzzy socks, she decided she'd make a day of it in Newquay. Lunch somewhere nice, with some wine to go with it, and then maybe some shopping to buy something for her new home. She'd finish up at Sainsbury's, buying the ingredients for a lovely dinner she'd cook tonight, which she would then eat while watching *Gypsy* on Netflix, ensuring she'd have dreams later about Naomi Watts.

She smiled to herself as she stood in front of the mirror in the en suite, swigging Corsodyl before getting in the shower. It sounded like a perfect day.

Therefore, it shouldn't have surprised her when something ruined it.

Hearing her phone ring in the bedroom, she spat out the mouthwash and stepped over to her nightstand. It was an unknown number. Usually, she had her phone set to block those, but because over the past several days she'd had to field many unknown-number calls from the movers, Virgin Media, the local utilities company, and other one-off entities—all related to her relocation—she had turned that feature off for the sake of simplicity.

"Hello?" she answered.

"Mrs. Bedford?" a man's voice greeted her.

Robyn sighed.

"It's *Miss* Bedford," she corrected. It sounded like whoever she was talking to was driving.

"Sorry, luv," the guy said. "Anyway, we're with Sønderborg Interiors. Just wanted to let you know that we're about ten minutes out from dropping off your furniture."

Robyn's heart dropped.

"*What?*" she barked. This wasn't the furniture for her cottage…*that* was already here. This was the furniture for the gallery! *That* wasn't supposed to be delivered until *Wednesday!*

"You're supposed to deliver that on Wednesday!" she told him.

She was met with silence. Then…

"Are you sure?" her new least-favourite-person-on-Earth asked. "I'm looking at a sheet here that says delivery is today."

"Yes, I'm sure!" she insisted. "Just…hang on!"

Her iPad Pro was also on the nightstand. Every single invoice related to the opening of the new gallery had been prudently saved in her iCloud account. With a few taps, she had the Sønderborg document open.

"*I* am looking at an invoice—signed by *Steve* at your store— stating delivery is *Wednesday,* the seventh!" she said. She had known she was right, yet it still felt good to have proof.

"Huh!" the guy on the phone said, as if that was useful. Robyn then heard him sigh heavily, and then begin coughing. She guessed he was a smoker. "Listen, Miss," he began, an apologetic tone to his voice, "someone obviously screwed up, but I swear it wasn't me! I just load the truck and go where they tell me! My mate and I have driven two hours to get this stuff to you in Newquay. Is there *any* way you can accept delivery today?"

Now it was Robyn who sighed (though she didn't start coughing; she'd never touched a cigarette in her life).

The truth was, there wasn't a single reason why she couldn't accept delivery of the furniture today. She had the keys to the gallery space, all she would have to do is let the blokes in and have them drop everything off. She could wait until next week, when she and the staff she had hired virtually would be on site, to move the items around until she was satisfied with their arrangement.

"Fine," she told the guy. "But it will take me at least thirty or forty minutes to get there. I've just got out of bed and need to change, *and* I live in another town."

"Wonderful, luv!" the delivery man said happily. "Take your time. We'll find a place to park and wait for you. Just look for our truck once you get there."

The call ended, and Robyn had to take a few moments to close her eyes and breathe deeply.

This is a first-world problem. This is a first-world problem. This is a first-world problem.

Yes, other people's incompetence was causing a bit of an inconvenience for her, but it was nothing she couldn't handle, and there were people in the world who were far worse off.

That mental talking-to done, she initiated her gotta-get-out-of-the-house-super-quick plan—used for those times when a girl just had to get going.

She'd shower when she got back. Her hair was pulled into a ponytail, and since it was just deliverymen she was going to meet, followed immediately by grocery shopping, she needn't bother with makeup.

She dressed in relaxed-fit jogger pants, a black tee, and white cardi. After she put her trainers on, she went to her jewellery box.

This wasn't in the interest of accessorising.

From the box, she removed a silver ring, placing it on her right middle finger. The ring had a secret. By sliding a toggle switch on it, a small and very sharp blade would pop up on the ring's top, perfect for self-defence. She was going to be alone in a large, empty space with strange men, and wanted to have some measure of defending herself. This was why she also had pepper spray in her handbag, which she'd keep on her person while the furniture was being delivered.

She was ready to leave less than ten minutes after that phone call ended. Walking out to her car, she muttered the same phrase repeatedly.

"First-world problem. First-world problem. First-world problem."

Chapter 7

Tamsin was getting annoyed.

Sitting at her desk, one long leg crossed over the other, she shook her high-heeled foot as a silent manifestation of her annoyance, while staring through the agency's picture window, to the street outside.

For the past 30 minutes—at least—an enormous delivery truck had been parked on the street *directly in front of* Xplr! It was not only blocking the natural light which typically came into the agency, but Tamsin hated that it was blocking Xplr's shopfront from the view of pedestrians on Bank Street. She had a client arriving in less than an hour, who wanted to meet with her in person to discuss an around-the-world cruise for her and her husband, and Tamsin was worried that the old biddy might walk right past this place because heaven knows anybody over sixty has no idea how to use Google Maps.

The truck was from Sønderborg Interiors, which Tamsin knew was a high-end Dutch outfit, meaning that whoever was having furniture delivered was most likely a toffee-nosed twat who felt the world revolved around them.

She suddenly remembered something.

There was a vacant storefront several doors down from Xplr. It had been vacant for months—no surprise, given this economy— and Tamsin suspected that the expensive Dutch furniture would be delivered there.

Well, she wished they would get on with it! Honestly! What was so bloody difficult about their job?

You show up with a truck full of furniture for a toffee-nosed twat...

You unload the toffee-nosed twat's furniture...

You drive the truck away from the boutique travel agency that you've parked in front of—whose humble furniture, by the way, came from Furniture@Work.

Three easy steps. A *child* could do it!

Well...a child might have a problem with the heavy lifting, but it was still a fair point.

"Truck still there, I see," her uncle said, coming from the back of the agency.

"Bloody cheek," Tamsin muttered.

"Relax, Tamsin," Uncle Richard chided. "It's not as if they're planning on staying long. Just some blokes doing their job."

He picked up some papers from her desk and returned to the back.

Tamsin considered his words.

He was right, she needed to relax and to realise that the truck was but a mere temporary annoyance and would be gone soon enough. To that end, she resolved to focus on her work, namely, the spiel she was going to use to sell her next client on that around-the-world cruise.

And she might have done so…had a new player not entered the scene.

A-ha!

No sooner had Uncle Richard vanished, when, through the window, Tamsin saw a woman in a white cardi approach the truck and knock on the cab door.

The toffee-nosed twat!

So, she was the one who had ordered the furniture…

Tamsin rose from behind her desk. She wasn't going to make a fuss, she just wanted to suss out the situation, and find out how fast things would be moving along. Besides, she felt she had a bit of an edge here, wardrobe-wise.

She was dressed in a sleek pencil skirt, a very couture-looking white blouse, and black high heels. Miss Twat (first name Toffee-Nosed, or just Toffee for short), on the other hand, looked as if she were a mum on the way to drop her horrid children off at football practice, with plans to not even get out of her car, lest anyone see what was obviously a hastily put together outfit.

If Tamsin had to guess, in bare feet, she and the woman were about the same size, but since she had heels on, she'd have the height advantage in this little tête-á-tête she wanted to have with her.

By the time she exited Xplr, the driver of the delivery truck, and his partner, were already down from their perches in the cab, talking to the woman.

"Best to keep it right here, Miss," the larger bloke was telling her. "Never find a spot in front of your place now. Me and Neville can easily get the merch down to where you are."

The woman nodded.

"Fine," she said.

Tamsin blinked.

Not so fast…

"Excuse me," she said, "I hate to be a bother, but how long do you think all this will take?"

The woman looked her up and down.

"I'm sorry," she said, "you are…?"

Tamsin put on her best *this-is-my-fake-smile-and-I-want-you-to-know-that* smile and crossed her arms.

"I happen to be one of the co-owners of this travel agency…" She tilted her head towards Xplr's shop window. "…which this very large truck is sitting in front of."

Fine, she was bending the truth a bit by calling herself a "co-owner" at this stage, but it used fewer words—and sounded more impressive—than saying, "I work at this travel agency, that is until my uncle decides to potter off into retirement, when it will then become mine. All mine, bwa-ha-ha-ha-ha!"

The woman in the white cardi closed her eyes and took a breath. Tamsin bristled. She was being sent a message, and the message was, "Why are you bothering me with such bollocks?"

When the woman opened her eyes again, she also put a fake smile on her lips. Tamsin had to admit it was a good one. What made it brilliant was that she knew the two deliverymen had no idea just how insincere it was. This was a woman-to-woman fake smile, detectable only by having a certain amount of oestrogen in one's body.

"So sorry you're being inconvenienced," she said, her voice saccharine-sweet, making her sound like the paragon of innocence, though Tamsin wasn't fooled, "but I do need these gentlemen to get this furniture into my gallery, so if you could just be patient for a little while longer?"

Gallery?

Like, an art gallery?

Despite herself, Tamsin was intrigued. Nonetheless, she had to ensure she did not lose face in this interaction.

Shifting her weight to one hip—her power-bitch stance—she stared at the woman.

"Just try to be as quick as possible, please," she said, her voice also saccharine-sweet, but even more so. It made the woman narrow her eyes. "I have a business to run."

"Well, so do I," the woman said. "Which is why I need this furniture delivered." She paused. "Of course…"

However, she left the sentence unfinished.

Tamsin furrowed her brow, caught off guard.

"Yes?" she prodded.

The woman shrugged.

"I was just going to say," she went on, "that in the time it has taken to have this meaningless little chat, my men could have begun moving some items off the truck."

Bugger!

Tamsin couldn't prevent herself from blushing. The woman had a great point, to which there was no proper retort because a proper retort would only prolong 'this meaningless little chat' even further, during which the men *still* wouldn't be moving items off the truck, thus proving the woman's point.

Well played…

"Just please try to have them hurry," she said, not quite speaking through clenched teeth, but only just.

Her adversary looked at her with the sweetest doe eyes imaginable. It was as if she had morphed into one of those bunny rabbits from a bloody Disney cartoon.

"I promise I will," she said. "And next time I'll be sure to obey that local ordinance prohibiting delivery trucks from parking in front of travel agencies."

Now, the blokes sniggered.

"Nice one, Miss," the larger of the two men said.

Tamsin was fuming. Bad enough Miss Trat had gained control of this interaction, but now the troglodyte men were on her side.

Since saying anything more would only further delay the unloading of the expensive furniture—thus giving its owner even more of a leg to stand on—Tamsin wheeled expertly on her heels and walked back into Xplr.

When the door closed behind her, she stood in the centre of the agency, her arms crossed, her weight shifted onto her left hip, and one foot tapping.

"Bugger," she muttered.

***

The delivery truck was gone about thirty minutes later. Once more, daylight streamed into the agency, making the space seem bright and gay. This was helped by the fact that some time ago, Tamsin had convinced Uncle Richard to have all the walls painted. Originally, the walls had been a depressing beige colour. He had told her that's the way they had come when he originally began leasing this space two centuries ago, and that he'd never seen a reason to change them. It had made Tamsin wonder—not for the first time—how he had managed to stay in business for so long.

She had the majority of the interior painted white. Britain as a nation only gets about twenty sunny days a year, after all, so she felt it was important that the walls maximised the use of any natural light which came in through the picture window, to create a cheery environment for clients to sit in while discussing their dream vacations.

The truck drove off mere minutes before Mrs. Hargitay arrived to discuss her around-the-world cruise. Mr. Hargitay accompanied her, although Tamsin could immediately tell that his presence was merely decorative, and that he was going on this cruise whether he wanted to or not…and he clearly did not.

Tamsin spent an hour with Mrs. Hargitay, presenting to her various options for her desired holiday. The old woman finally settled on a 274-night excursion that would take her and her (reluctant) husband to over 60 countries. She even managed to save the Hargitays quite a bit of money by accessing discounts that were only available to travel professionals.

Booking this was quite a win for Xplr, as around-the-world cruises are not cheap. The agency was going to do very well off commissions and fees for this one. It was made even better when Mrs. Hargitay inferred that her sister and her brother-in-law might want to join them as well. Tamsin wondered if the brother-in-law would be as enthusiastic about this venture as Mr. Hargitay was, but she doubted it would matter. If that were the case, at least poor Mr. Hargitay would have company in his misery.

After the Hargitays left, Tamsin decided she needed to parley this booking into promotional fodder for TikTok and Instagram. To that end, she recorded a vid of herself at her desk telling her followers about the cruise holiday she had just created for "some clients," and how, considering how many countries they were going to get to see, it was actually quite a good deal. Later, at home, she'd edit the vid, adding some images she'd nick from the cruise company's website, and post it. After all, it wasn't as if she had to concern herself with Kendra coming by tonight.

Thinking of Kendra made her tempted to stop by the bar where she worked and make a play at convincing her to give her another chance. However, almost as soon as that thought flitted into her mind, she recognised the futility of it. Oh, she was fairly certain she could convince Kendra to give her another chance…*that* wasn't the problem. She could convince *any* gay woman to do whatever she wanted.

The problem was, what would be the point? Even now, sitting here in the agency, she knew that if Kendra ended up at her place tonight, nothing would change. They'd have sex, but it wouldn't be that sought-after "make-up sex" people seemed to look forward to after having had a conflict with their partners. Tamsin knew she'd simply use Kendra to satisfy this horniness she was suddenly feeling now, but once she'd had that one massive orgasm, she'd want to start editing her new vid about the around-the-world cruise, which meant Kendra would again be left wanting more.

She sighed.

Closing her eyes, she forced herself to remember Rylea's hypothesis from yesterday.

Have you ever considered that maybe it's not you, it's them?

It really did help her feel better, but at the same time, it scared her. After all, it wasn't as if she'd been living a nun's life all these years. She'd been with plenty of women, and those women had all been her type: femme and classically beautiful. So, what was the problem? If after years of dating the type of women she lusted after, she hadn't yet found anyone who could excite her enough to have marathon sex with, what the hell was she looking for then?

In any case, she needed to figure that out, but not now. Besides, she had another pressing matter to consider…

Why the hell *was* she suddenly so horny?

Chapter 8

Robyn, her hands on her hips, surveyed the scene.

All in all, it had gone well. Putting aside that contretemps with the ginger travel agent who apparently thought she owned the bit of road in front of her establishment, the furniture delivery had gone without a snag. Well, except for the fact that the delivery was supposed to happen on Wednesday, six days from now. Other than that, it had gone smoothly, and now Linden Gallery Cornwall had the furniture she had very carefully chosen from Sønderborg Interiors; furniture that was a hybrid between sleek futurism and mid-century modern.

Of course, nothing was in its proper place yet. That would happen once she returned here next week and had the two staff members she had hired via Zoom to help her rearrange it all until she liked what she saw.

With this done, she checked her watch. It was getting close to lunchtime, and she was feeling hungry. She also had to do her grocery shopping, but she refused to do so until she had eaten. The last time she had done a shop for groceries when she was hungry, she had ended up with enough Jammie Dodgers to last a month. She had also gained five pounds because if there are a quantity of Jammie Dodgers in the house, she will always eat them.

Earlier, she had noticed a sandwich shop (or "shoppe" as the proprietors insisted on terming it on their sign) across from the gallery. Upon further consideration, she determined she was in the mood for a good egg and cress sarnie, then she'd hit Sainsbury's.

The shoppe was a basic no-frills fast-service establishment, obviously catering to those who wanted their lunch quickly before having to return to work. Once Robyn had been handed her sarnie and some herbal tea, she located an empty table and claimed it. She then activated her phone's screen to have something to look at while eating.

Now that she was sitting down, with food before her, the crisis involving the furniture delivery having passed, and the gallery locked up, she began to realise something, and it made her brow furrow as she took her first bite of the sandwich (which was quite good).

Crossing her legs under the table, she became aware that for some reason, she was feeling rather horny.

Okay, nothing quite unusual about that, she reasoned. She was, after all, a healthy young woman who enjoyed sexual pleasure. It's just that…well, she'd had quite the masturbation session yesterday morning before her drive to Barnstaple, hadn't she? In fact, she'd gotten herself off four times. Normally that meant she'd be good for a day or two, especially considering all of the work she had to do back at the cottage, settling in. Yet for reasons unknown, her centre was feeling quite energised right now.

Oh well…

Who truly understood the mysteries of human sexuality? If she was still horny once she got back home, she'd take care of it.

A flash of red in the corner of her eye made her look away from her iPhone's screen. Seeing what—or rather *who*—it was, she rolled her eyes and returned them to the screen, where she was using Google Maps to discover if there were any cute clothing shops here in Newquay.

The flash of red was the travel agent, evidently popping in for her own lunch. Either that, or she was here to complain that someone was eating a sarnie in front of her agency, and would the proprietor please be sure, in the future, to either stop selling portable food, or tell his customers to eat their lunch somewhere else?

Cheek!

After a moment (despite herself), Robyn looked back to the ordering counter again. The travel agent had her back to her and was busy chatting up the middle-aged bloke in a white apron whom Robyn had surmised ran the place. It seemed the two of them had quite the rapport, and Robyn guessed that this was one of the travel agent's favourite spots for lunch.

Well…considering how good this egg and cress sarnie was, the ginger would just have to get used to seeing her in here as well, once the gallery opened. In fact, she resolved now that starting next week, she would make a point of having lunch here every day, just to show the ginger that the new girl in town was going to make herself known. Hell, she might even take her sarnie to go, and eat it in front of the agency.

She returned her eyes to her phone, suddenly wanting to distract herself by once again looking for clothing shops. The travel agent was an amazing-looking woman, with an incredible figure, and because Robyn was inexplicably horny—and gingers were her weakness—she didn't need to be spending much time secretly staring at her, especially given that she suspected this particular ginger was most likely more trouble than she was worth.

***

That evening at home, Robyn felt satisfied with the day.

Not only had she handled the unexpected arrival of the gallery's furniture with aplomb, but she had done a massive shop at Sainsbury's, and now had plenty of real food in the cottage, along with other essentials. What's more, she had spent some time arranging things in this new home of hers, and it was now beginning to feel like *her* space.

By five-thirty, she deemed she was due a break, particularly a break which included wine and two—only two—Jammie Dodgers. She hadn't eaten dinner yet, but she had been very productive today, and felt she deserved a couple of biscuits. Besides, she was an adult. If she wanted Jammie Dodgers before dinner, she believed that, by royal decree, she had that right.

Walking from the kitchen to her living room—a glass of white wine in one hand, a small plate with two Jammie Dodgers on it in the other—she noticed something through the window.

The Clio was in the driveway next door. The ginger must have returned home from…work?

Robyn shrugged. That was as good a guess as any other.

Looking out at the car, she bit her bottom lip, considering.

Why not?

It would only take five, maybe ten minutes. Besides, she was getting tired of the tease. If this was a book she was reading, and she and the ginger next door were the main characters, she'd be shouting at the page, "Just have them bloody meet already!"

In the living room, she placed her wine and biscuits on the coffee table and then hurried upstairs. She had taken a shower not too long ago, so at least she was clean. All she needed to do was shuck off her drawstring sweatpants, take off the tee shirt with a Basquiat image on it, and then throw on…

This skirt here…

And…

She selected a white front-clasp, workaday bra from her dresser, and then put the Basquiat tee back on. It paired nicely with the skirt, and it also gave a little hint about who she was, and what she was into.

To finish up, she slipped her feet into plain black ballet flats, but before leaving the bedroom, she did a quick appearance check. She looked presentable, which was all she was shooting for. It wasn't as if she was preparing for a blind date.

As she walked back downstairs, she went over her plan…

"I'll just pop over, say, 'Hi, I'm your new neighbour, nice to meet you, just wanted to introduce myself.' Simple."

It would be nice to put a face to the car, so to speak. Who knows? Maybe the blonde was over there too. The Puma wasn't in the driveway, but that didn't mean anything. How many times had women stayed at her old flat back in Barnstaple while their cars were elsewhere?

And if the blonde *was* next door, Robyn figured, then maybe she could suss out whether or not she and the ginger were a couple.

Of course, what she would do with that intelligence, she had no idea. It wasn't as if she was going to suddenly announce, "Bloody brilliant that you two are together! I'm also a lesbian! Shall we all watch *Disobedience* together?"

She crossed the distance between her cottage and the ginger's in a few moments, needing to go around the hedges separating the two properties, and knocked on the green door.

She heard a voice call what could have been "Coming!" from deep inside the house, and she hoped she wasn't interrupting anything important. The woman had just gotten home—presumably from work—and Robyn tried to imagine what she could be doing. Putting the kettle on? Looking through the post? Deciding what to make herself (and maybe the blonde) for dinner?

From behind the door, she heard floorboards creaking, and so she lifted her chin and put a pleasant smile on her face.

Then the door opened.

Her smile disappeared.

"What are you doing here?" she asked.

The travel agent from Newquay gasped. She was still wearing the pencil skirt and blouse from before, but she had taken off her heels, and was now barefoot.

"Me?" she barked out. "What are *you* doing here? Oi, are you stalking me?"

Now, Robyn gasped.

"Stalking you?" she asked. She burst into dry and disdainful chuckles. "As if!"

"I am stalk-able!" the travel agent barked.

Robyn laughed derisively.

"What the bloody hell does that even mean?" she asked. "And, I'm sorry, but don't you think I have better things to do than stalk *you?*"

"Then why are you here?" the travel agent demanded, crossing her arms.

Robyn sighed.

"I happen to have moved in next door!" she explained.

The travel agent looked to her left, at Robyn's cottage.

"*You* moved into Mrs. Burberry-Foster's?" she asked.

"I did," Robyn stated. She then sighed. "And I came over here to introduce myself." Rolling her eyes, she stuck out her hand. "Robyn Bedford."

The ginger looked at the outstretched hand, did her own eye roll, and took it in hers, shaking it.

"Tamsin Tregurrian," she said.

"Good Cornish name," Robyn said, because, quite frankly, at this point she had no idea what else to say.

"I suppose," Tamsin said. "Bloody hate having to spell it, though. Wish my mum had married a Smith. Bedford must be easier."

"I suppose," Robyn said.

The two women stood there silently for a few moments.

Finally, Robyn huffed.

"Well, it was nice meeting you, Tamsin," she said. She wasn't sure if she was lying or not, but it was the British thing to say.

Without waiting for a response—not that she expected one— Robyn turned and headed back down Tamsin's path so she could then round the hedges and return to her own cottage.

Well, she considered…unlikely she'd be borrowing a cup of sugar from this particular neighbour.

Chapter 9

After shutting the door when Robyn left, Tamsin stood in the foyer in much the same way as she had stood in Xplr earlier, following her previous encounter with Robyn: arms crossed, her weight shifted to one hip, and tapping her foot.

It bloody figures!

She loved it when the Universe pulled crap like this on other people, but not when it did to her!

Of course the BMW she had seen next door belonged to someone who ordered their business furniture from Sønderborg Interiors! It totally made sense now. People who drove BMWs were often the type who would not only purchase expensive Dutch furniture, but also instruct the deliverymen to park their enormous truck in front of a mom-and-pop (or uncle-and-niece) travel agency.

And she lived next door!

"Thanks, Universe," Tamsin muttered.

With a sigh, she left the foyer and headed to the kitchen. Normally, at this point in the evening, she'd go upstairs to take a shower before making dinner, but she rather felt that a glass of wine was in order.

In a moment, a glass of cabernet was poured, which Tamsin began drinking immediately while leaning against the counter.

"And why does she have to be cute?" Tamsin complained aloud because, the truth was, her new neighbour was cute. In fact, she was bloody beautiful, but what did that matter? They obviously had no chance of getting along. She could recognise that right away. Robyn was a toffee-nosed twat who was clearly used to getting what she wanted. However, Tamsin was not the type to put up with people like that, and she felt she had demonstrated that to good effect in the matter of the delivery truck.

She frowned, thinking back to earlier, in Newquay, at the way Robyn had shut down their conversation by pointing out that the conversation itself—initiated by her—was acting as an impediment to the deliverymen getting their job done, and the truck being able to leave sooner.

Tamsin remembered how she hadn't had a comeback for that. Instead, she had just turned around and went back into Xplr, stewing.

Which meant…

Robyn had gotten the last word then. What's more, she had ended the conversation on *her* terms, namely, that the truck would stay where it was until the furniture delivery was completed, and she didn't give a toss what Tamsin thought about it.

Taking another sip of wine, she now thought back to a few minutes ago, at how the two of them discovered they were bloody neighbours. She had wanted to scream. At the very least, she had wanted to say something snarky, maybe ask Robyn if she was now planning on parking great big delivery trucks in front of her house as well. But before the Snark Fest could commence, Robyn had very quickly seized the high ground, introducing herself properly.

It had caught Tamsin off guard, so much so that she'd had no choice but to respond in kind by introducing herself properly.

"Bugger!" Tamsin exclaimed now. "She did it to me again!"

Robyn had masterfully taken control of the situation, only this time, she also ended up looking like the nice one because, despite their obvious dislike for each other, she had still introduced herself properly.

Tamsin's eyes widened as she then realised something else.

"And she got the fucking last word in again!" she all but screeched.

Well, that just wouldn't do, would it?

She downed the rest of her wine in one gulp, placed the glass down so hard on the countertop that she worried she might have cracked the stem, and then went to her hall cupboard. Along with her wellies, she also had an old pair of trainers in here for when she needed to step out of her cottage quickly—to get something out of her car, perhaps, or to do some tidying in her garden—but she didn't want to bother going upstairs to put on nicer footwear. The trainers completely clashed with the outfit she had worn to work today, and which she still had on, but she didn't care. This wasn't a date.

Leaving her house, she marched over to Mrs. Burberry-Foster's and knocked on the yellow door, tapping her foot while waiting for her summons to be answered.

Finally…

"Oh!" Robyn said, clearly surprised when she opened the door.

Tamsin looked her right in the eyes.

"It was nice meeting you too," she declared. Then, mission accomplished, she wheeled around and began marching back to her own cottage.

***

"Seen him or her yet?" Rylea asked the next evening, Friday. She and her fiancée Darcie had just arrived at Tamsin's house for the relationship exorcism, meant to purge Kendra from Tamsin's life on a metaphorical plane.

"Who?" Tamsin asked.

"The posh car next door," Darcie answered. She was in her early thirties, with brown hair that had light-coloured highlights throughout. Taking off her jacket, she hung it on a coat peg mounted on the wall by the door.

Tamsin rolled her eyes.

"No one has seen them!" Rylea exclaimed. They all walked through the living room, and into the back garden, where Tamsin had the exorcism accoutrement waiting on her patio table, including the all-important ceremonial dagger. "Even Mrs. Arrington-Maffin hasn't laid eyes on whoever it is yet, and she could work for the bloody CIA. For all we know, lunatics could have moved in next door."

Tamsin put her finger to her lips and hurriedly shushed her friend. She took a glance at the vine-covered wall separating her garden from Robyn's.

"Would you keep it down!" she whispered. She then gestured for them all to return into the house. Once they were inside, and Tamsin had shut the French doors behind them, she said, "First of all, she's not a lunatic—at least not by the normal definition; secondly, for all I know she's sitting in her garden having a cuppa, listening to us wonder if she's a lunatic. And thirdly, yes, I've seen her."

"So…what's she like?" Rylea prodded, eagerly.

"So…what's she like?" Rylea asked again, just as eagerly.

Tamsin sighed. She wanted to launch into a tirade about Dutch furniture and enormous delivery trucks and how her new neighbour seemed to diabolically get the upper hand in every conversation. But something stopped her.

Suddenly, she realised it would be uncharitable of her to denigrate her neighbour whom, she had to admit, she didn't know very well at all.

"I only met her briefly," she told her guests. "She came over to introduce herself yesterday. Let's start the exorcism."

"Hang on!" Darcie said, blocking Tamsin's path to the French doors. "That's it? What's she like? What's she do?"

"What's her name?" Rylea added.

"Ooh, good one!" Darcie exclaimed. "What's her name?"

"Her name is Robyn Bedford," Tamsin said, actually surprised that she remembered Robyn's surname. First names she was good at; surnames usually took a while to become ingrained in her memory.

"Ooh, her name is Robyn Bedford," Darcie said, looking at Rylea, waggling her eyebrows.

"What's her middle name, Tams?" Rylea teased.

"I don't bloody know her middle name!" Tamsin said.

"Anyway, what's she do?" Darcie asked. "Hopefully not own a book shop."

Darcie owned Shelf Life Books, the only book shop in Tremont.

Tamsin shrugged.

"She apparently runs a gallery of some sort," she said. "And that's all I know! Can we *please* get on with this exorcism?"

"Young? Old?" Rylea queried.

Tamsin crossed her arms, resigned to answering the silly questions of her friends.

"About our age, I'd guess," she said, waving a finger between herself and Rylea. She then looked up at the ceiling, knowing what the next question would be. "Maybe a little older."

"Is she pretty?" Darcie asked.

"In certain cultures," Tamsin began, "she would be considered pretty, yes."

Darcie and Rylea both snorted laughter.

"Well…um, what about the culture of twenty-first century England?" Rylea asked.

"She would be considered pretty, yes," Tamsin confirmed. "Now…can we *please* get on with things?"

"Or…" Rylea said.

Tamsin frowned. Her friend was slowly walking towards the living room, in the direction of the front door.

By the time Tamsin caught on, it was too late to reach out and grab Rylea.

"Don't you dare!" she exclaimed, making a lunge for her regardless.

Laughing, Rylea sprinted to the front door.

"I'm just being neighbourly!" she called back.

"Get back here!" Tamsin demanded.

But Rylea already had the front door opened and was through it in a flash.

"Aargh!" Tamsin growled. "Why do you want to marry her?" she asked Darcie, returning to stand next to her.

Darcie put her arm around Tamsin's waist.

"I can't imagine my life without her," she replied.

"Must be nice," Tamsin muttered.

Darcie looked at her.

"It is," she said. "And you'll find that out one day. And I can't wait to meet who it is."

Now, Tamsin put her arm around Darcie's shoulders.

"Me either," she said. Then, her eyes went wide as a new thought entered her mind. "Bugger!"

She immediately pulled away from her friend.

"What's wrong?" Darcie asked.

Tamsin was already scurrying around the kitchen, her eyes having found at least a dozen items which could be deemed out of place, and her mind trying to remember the state of her living room.

If Rylea was successful in her misbegotten mission—which Tamsin would kill her for later…

"I need to bloody straighten up!" she explained.

Chapter 10

"Well, your royal highness," Robyn said to Empress, who was sitting on her lap, making her human fulfil her obligation of daily fur-stroking. "It's our first Friday in our new home. What to do? What to do?"

Robyn puffed her cheeks and blew out a breath which signified a mix of *I-have-no-idea-what-to-do* and *God-it-bugs-me-that-I-have-no-idea-what-to-do*.

Barnstaple wasn't exactly a thriving metropolis—or, a metropolis, for that matter—but at least there she had friends, favourite restaurants, a favourite pub, a favourite place to sit and have coffee. She had none of those here in Tremont.

Yet.

She knew there was a pub—quite literally *a* pub, as in singular, but that's the way these very small villages were.

She also knew there was a coffee shop on the high street with a cute name that she'd forgotten. She imagined that she could start becoming a regular there when she wanted to get out of the house and enjoy a beverage while reading.

Her Google research had similarly told her that there were also a bunch of shops and small eateries scattered throughout the village, but she figured that if she wanted a larger variety of either, she'd need to make the drive into Newquay.

Looking down at Empress, she said, "It's times like this when I wish you were a dog."

She had the notion that it might be fun to take a walk through the village and explore it a bit. Of course, she could do so perfectly fine without a dog, but she was also aware of what villages such as Tremont were like.

In places such as this, everyone knew everyone else. Literally, not figuratively. Thus, each new face stood out. If Robyn had a dog, she could take the pooch for a walk through the village, and people would see her and say, "Oh, there's that new girl who moved into Mrs. Burberry-Foster's place. What a lovely dog she has."

Sans dog, however, she suspected the chit-chat about her would be more along the lines of, "Oh, there's that new girl who moved into Mrs. Burberry-Foster's place. What's she doing lurking about by herself? Does anyone know anything about her? Could be a cat burglar for all we know!"

With a sigh, she determined to save exploratory walks around the village until after she'd met a few of the locals and somehow worked "I am not a cat burglar" into the conversation.

Still though, she wanted to get out and do *something*. Maybe she'd drive into Newquay and explore *that* town more. It wasn't exactly London, but it was much larger than Tremont, thus she wouldn't immediately be fingered as the "new girl/possible cat burglar."

Deciding that was what she would do, she gently lifted Empress.

"Sorry, your highness," she apologised, "but I need my legs back."

The white cat glared at her, in the way only a Persian can, but apparently decided to let her live for now.

Upstairs, Robyn spent some time in her wardrobe, considering what type of outfit to wear…

She wasn't meeting anybody—professionally or socially—and so she could go for strict comfort, which in her case usually meant tracksuit bottoms, trainers, and—considering it was a bit chilly this evening—a sweater and light jacket.

However…

Despite the fact that she wasn't going to be meeting anybody, there was an argument for looking cute. After all, it was Friday, which meant plenty of people would be out doing Friday night things, which meant plenty of women would be dressed in cute outfits. Did she really want to be out walking among them looking like she had forgotten to do laundry this week?

Which reminds me…I need to do laundry this week.

Fortunately, because she had pretty much stayed in this week—the exception, of course, being yesterday, when the gallery's furniture had been delivered—all she had worn were house-clothes: various iterations of pyjamas, t-shirts that were too faded (or had too many holes) to be seen in public, and joggers.

Her nicer items of clothing, meanwhile, had all been untouched and unworn.

She chose dark skinny jeans, stylish but comfortable black leather boots, and a pink cashmere sweater. She applied some makeup but didn't go overboard with it, just enough to ensure she wouldn't feel like a troglodyte should she encounter a bunch of dolled-up birds out on a hen do.

She had just decided she'd leave her brown hair down when she heard a knock on her door.

Empress, who had followed her upstairs, meowed.

"Probably the local bobby coming to check my criminal history," Robyn told her as she walked out of the en suite. "Don't you mention anything about my cat burgling days."

As she walked downstairs, she experienced a brief glimmer of hope that perhaps it was the headstrong ginger from next door.

Tamsin.

That woman may have a chip on her shoulder, but goodness was she beautiful! And a ginger! With boobs!

And okay, fine…Tamsin could learn a thing or two about making a first impression, but she was certainly striking, and Robyn determined that she could think of worse things than her gorgeous and sexy neighbour popping by unannounced.

However, when she reached the bottom of the stairs and opened her front door…

"Oh, hello!" she greeted the young woman standing on the other side.

It wasn't Tamsin, the gorgeous and sexy ginger, but this woman was also quite pretty, and Robyn had a silly thought that if attractive women were in the habit of making impromptu visits in this village, she'd enjoy living here very much.

"Hi!" her visitor said, smiling a stunning smile. "I'm Rylea Morgan."

"Robyn Bedford," Robyn told her, reaching out her hand. "Pleased to meet you."

Rylea shook her hand with a good grip which Robyn knew her dad would appreciate. He had always told his daughter that it's probably even more important for women to give good, firm handshakes. It lets the other person know they're dealing with someone who shouldn't be underestimated.

"Welcome to Tremont," Rylea said. "I understand from my bestie Tamsin that you just moved in?"

"Oh, you're mates with Tamsin?" Robyn asked. "I just met her yesterday."

She wondered how Tamsin had recalled that encounter to her friend. It couldn't have been too bad, she surmised. Rylea seemed friendly, and not like she was here to pick a fight.

"Tams and I have known each other since we were kids," Rylea told her. "Anyway…do you have plans this evening?"

"Um…no," Robyn replied. "Not as such…"

"Well," Rylea began, "my fiancée and I are over at Tamsin's, just chilling, having wine, and once Tamsin told us about her new neighbour, I thought, 'Why not invite her over to meet some locals?'"

Robyn smiled.

"That was very thoughtful," she said. She also wondered if Rylea said "fiancé" or "fiancée." If it was the former, no big deal; she could handle a bloke being among her first set of friends in Tremont.

"I would love to come over," she told Rylea. It sounded a sight better than wandering around Newquay alone. "Are you sure Tamsin doesn't mind?"

Rylea scoffed.

"It was practically her idea," she said. "Come on!"

As she was just going next door, and was already dressed, Robyn only took a moment to remove her house keys from her handbag and place them in her jeans pocket, and to grab her phone. Closing the door behind her, she fell into step beside Rylea.

"Have you ever been to California?" Rylea asked as they walked.

That was an odd question, Robyn considered. However, she figured that in a Cornish village like Tremont, she might have to get used to some occasionally eccentric behaviour from the locals. After all, she had seen *Doc Martin*.

"Twice," Robyn told her. "I love it!"

Now, there's a place she wouldn't mind Victoria Linden opening a gallery. A Linden Gallery Los Angeles, perhaps. Of course, Robyn always had plans to open her *own* art gallery someday, and "Bedford Gallery Hollywood" had a certain ring to it.

"Okay, so…maybe don't mention loving California to Tamsin," Rylea said. "It's a long story, and I promise to explain it later."

"Fair enough," Robyn said with a chuckle.

When they reached Tamsin's front door, Rylea just let herself in, and Robyn followed.

"Hey, we're back!" Rylea called out, leading Robyn through the front room, and into the kitchen.

In the kitchen was Tamsin, and Robyn made a conscious effort to keep her eyes from telegraphing just how attractive she found her.

Today, Tamsin was wearing jeans and a black sleeveless turtleneck which might as well have been a second skin for how snugly it fit, especially around her breasts.

Fuck my life, she couldn't help thinking.

With Tamsin was another woman, also a ginger—but more auburn as compared to Tamsin's *fire goddess* red. Rylea approached this woman and put an arm around her.

Ah…so it was "fiancée."

This made Robyn happy. She was making friends with at least two lesbians today, that was already quite a coup. Looking at Tamsin again, she wondered if she was about to add a third to her set.

"Good to see you again, Robyn," Tamsin said, smiling (and blushing, Robyn noted). "Um…welcome to my house. Sorry, I should have gone over to invite you myself."

Robyn waved that away.

"Not at all," she replied. "I'm sorry, I should have invited you in yesterday; you know, when you popped 'round to tell me how much you enjoyed meeting me."

She saw Tamsin's eyes flash.

"Well," the ginger said, "I'm sorry I didn't invite *you* in yesterday; you know, when you popped 'round *first* to introduce yourself."

"Great!" Rylea exclaimed. "Now that you two are done being British, Robyn meet Darcie, my fiancée."

"So pleased to meet you," Darcie said, sticking out her hand, which Robyn shook. "Sorry, I should have introduced myself as soon as you walked in."

"Delighted to meet you as well," Robyn replied. "And…sorry, I should have introduced *myself*."

"God, I hate this country sometimes," Rylea whined.

"You have a lovely home," Robyn said to Tamsin. "I would love a tour because I absolutely adore the fact that you have a lot of art hanging on the walls."

This was true. Although she had only caught a fleeting glimpse of the entryway and living room when she first walked in, her trained eye *did* notice that Tamsin's walls were hung with many framed works of art, and she wanted a chance to look at them. It could teach her quite a bit about her neighbour.

Again, Tamsin blushed.

"Absolutely," she said. "I'll show you around a bit later."

"I hope I'm not intruding on anything?" Robyn asked, looking between all three of her new friends.

Tamsin shook her head. She gestured in the direction of the French doors which led to the back garden.

"No, we were just going to have a—"

"A lovely time drinking wine!" Rylea interrupted. "Yep, that's it. Just drinking wine. You know…Friday night. Wine-drinking night. Out in the garden. As a matter of fact, why don't we all go out into the garden so we can drink wine." She paused. "Out in the garden."

"After the week I've had, I could use some wine," Robyn admitted, opting to omit the fact that she'd had plenty of wine thus far all week. Every night, in fact.

"Well, then, after you," Tamsin said, gesturing again to the French doors.

Stepping outside onto the patio, Robyn noticed that Tamsin had a very stylish set of contemporary outdoor furniture, including a glass-topped table on which several items were laid out.

One in particular caught her eye.

"What's with the dagger?" she asked.

"Bugger!" Tamsin exclaimed. "Um…that's for…um…cutting fruit to go along with our wine."

"Pretty fancy fruit-cutting implement," Robyn remarked. The dagger *was* quite fancy, with a wooden handle inlaid with what looked like jade, and a blade that was intricately decorated with filigree.

"Yeah, well…" Tamsin began, "I think it lends a nice sense of occasion to the cutting of fruit, you know."

"No doubt," Robyn said. "And the metal bowl?"

"That's for the fruit!" Tamsin said hurriedly.

"It looks scorched inside," Robyn noted.

Tamsin chuckled nervously.

"Silly me!" she said, picking up the bowl. "I brought the wrong one out." She handed the bowl to Darcie. "Darce, would you be a love and put this back inside, please? And maybe bring out some fruit—in a non-scorched bowl?"

"Of course," Darcie told her, heading back to the kitchen.

In the twilight, Robyn surveyed her surroundings.

"You have a lovely garden," she complimented her hostess.

"Thank you," Tamsin said, giving her that lovely smile again. "Bloody pain in the arse, but at least it's pleasant to look at."

Darcie popped her head back out of the French doors.

"Um…you don't have any fruit," she said, looking at Tamsin.

Robyn put her hand on Tamsin's arm, enjoying how soft the skin felt.

"I have plenty of fruit at home!" she said, also looking at Tamsin. "I did a massive shop yesterday. Please let me bring some over; it will be my contribution to our wine-drinking Friday."

"Sure," Tamsin told her. "That would be lovely, thank you."

"Be back in two ticks," Robyn said. She started heading for the French doors, but then stopped. "Wait," she said, turning back. "Any allergies I need to know of?"

That would be quite the impression in sleepy little Tremont, wouldn't it?

"Did you hear about that new girl who moved into Mrs. Burberry-Foster's place?"

"No."

"Killed off poor Darcie, Rylea and Tamsin. Didn't know they were allergic to dragon fruit, so what does she serve them?"

"Tsk, tsk, such a shame. By the way, hide your jewels…heard she might be a cat burglar too."

However, she was told that there were no allergies she needed to concern herself with.

As she hurried through Tamsin's cottage, towards the front door, she smiled.

This was much better than wandering around Newquay.

Chapter 11

"Bloody hell, Rylea!" Tamsin exclaimed, smacking her best friend's arm. "We're supposed to be doing a relationship exorcism!"

Rylea scoffed.

"*She* is your exorcism!" she stated.

"I agree," Darcie said, which didn't surprise Tamsin one bit. "And I also agree with Rylea changing up the program tonight. The last thing we need is Robyn thinking you're some kind of pathetic wanker who just got dumped."

"Hey!" Tamsin shot back.

"Right," Rylea said. "Or that you're just looking for a rebound shag."

"Or that I'm looking for a shag," Tamsin said. "Full stop."

"Oh, please," Rylea said, rolling her eyes. "Robyn is yummy!"

"Robyn may not be gay," Tamsin pointed out.

Both Darcie and Rylea burst into laughter.

"She's as gay as I am!" Rylea exclaimed, still laughing. "Actually, what am I saying? *No one* is as gay as I am! But Robyn is definitely in the club."

Tamsin crossed her arms, frustrated. She had actually suspected that Robyn was gay, but she was hoping that perhaps her friends might prove her wrong.

Just great...

It was frustrating because, if she was being honest with herself, Robyn *was* yummy, and Tamsin wanted to eat her up.

And there was something about her lips in particular. They were just so...kissable.

But for fuck's sake...

"She's a toffee-nosed twat," she stated.

She saw Darcie and Rylea share a look.

"What?" Tamsin asked.

Rylea approached her and, with the tip of her forefinger, touched the tip of Tamsin's nose. She then licked her finger and smacked her lips as if tasting something.

"Darce?" she asked, holding out her finger.

Darcie also licked Rylea's finger, and did the lip-smacking thing, her eyes turned upwards as if evaluating something.

"Do you taste it?" Rylea asked her fiancée.

Darcie nodded.

"Mm, definitely, babe," she said.

The two of them looked at Tamsin.

"Toffee," they both declared at the same time.

Tamsin gasped.

"I am *not* a toffee-nosed twat!" she said, aghast.

"Tams, I love you," Rylea said, "and I'll agree that you're not a twat." She cleared her throat. "Most of the time," she added in an undertone. Then, in her regular voice, she quickly added, "But your nose is definitely toffee-flavoured."

"But there's nothing wrong with that!" Darcie said.

Tamsin huffed. Okay fine…she enjoyed the nicer things, when she could afford them, and aspired to a life of being able to afford such things whenever she wanted them (such as a new BMW coupe like the one parked in the driveway next door), but she never believed that made her better than anyone else.

Robyn, on the other hand, just seemed…

"She's annoying!" Tamsin stated, feeling as if that was sufficient explanation.

Rylea narrowed her eyes.

"She seems absolutely lovely," she said. "So…very quickly, before she comes back, why don't you tell us why she's annoying."

Tamsin was good at this. She could encapsulate any story into a brief synopsis with ease. It was a talent of hers. She once summarised the Bible thusly…

"Despite all evidence to the contrary, God created Earth. He then fucked it up by creating man. His son made things worse and then left and hasn't been seen since, now look where we are. The end."

So, she gave a Tamsinesque recap of when she first encountered Robyn yesterday, on Bank Street, and then moved on to yesterday evening, when Robyn knocked on her door to introduce herself.

Rylea crossed her arms and cocked an eyebrow.

"Really?" she began. "This is your argument? That a delivery truck—doing its job—parked in front of your travel agency for a while?"

"Over an hour!" Tamsin reminded her. Did Rylea not get that?

"And then Robyn had the temerity," Darcie added, "to come over here and introduce herself. The bitch."

"She only did that because she didn't know *I* was the one who lived here!" Tamsin pointed out.

Rylea shook her head.

"You're crazy, Tams," she said. "Completely mad."

"You know what I think it is?" Darcie asked.

Both Rylea and Tamsin looked at her.

"You're just bothered that there is a woman in this world who is not afraid to call you out on your bullshit," Darcie said.

Tamsin rolled her eyes, chuckling.

"That's so not it, Darce," she replied. "Now, would you two mind gathering up all this exorcism stuff, please, while I go in the kitchen? I have to wash the ceremonial dagger now, since apparently I'm expected to cut fruit with it. *So* not what it's meant for, but whatever…"

***

When Robyn returned, bearing a wooden bowl with a lovely selection of fruit, the four women sat down at the patio table and began enjoying a bottle of red wine which Tamsin had bought for tonight.

The wine had originally been meant to play a role in the relationship exorcism, signifying the blood of a dead romance, but now it was just…wine.

Despite her reservations about how this evening turned out, Tamsin had to admit that it *was* nice to be hanging out with Rylea and Darcie *and* another woman. Typically, it was just the three of them on nights like this. She and Kendra had not gotten to the point yet where they did double dates with friends. This was partially because their relationship had been so new, and partially because Kendra lived in Newquay, and often worked odd hours.

And although Tamsin loved spending time with her best friend and Darcie, ever since they got together, she had been fantasising of a day when she would have her own companion with her, sitting opposite them at a restaurant table, or drinking wine here at her cottage.

The trouble was her own relationships never seemed to last long enough for that to happen.

She had begun having hopes for Kendra to be that companion but…well, it hadn't worked out that way, had it?

So, having Robyn here as a fourth to their usual threesome was nice. Tamsin was enjoying the balance it provided.

Not that *this* was going to happen very often!

Okay, fine…

Robyn was proving to be quite lovely. She was funny and smart and charming, and it was obvious that she had completely won over Rylea and Darcie. But Tamsin still wasn't convinced that she and Robyn would become great friends or anything like that. Maybe they'd be fine as neighbours, but she suspected that was as far as it would go.

In any case, they had learned that Robyn was here in Cornwall to open up an art gallery in Newquay. A Linden Gallery, in fact, which was a name Tamsin was well aware of.

Admittedly, this was an attractive line of work for Robyn to be in, in her eyes.

She herself loved art. The problem was, in this particular corner of Cornwall, there weren't very many people she could talk about art *with*. Sure, there were several old biddies in Tremont who did *crafts*—usually horrid cross-stitch creations or whimsical creatures made out of pine cones. There were fewer other old biddies who painted—horrid landscapes, mainly, straight out of the Bob Ross School of Painting Horrid Landscapes. There were even fewer other old biddies who were sculptors—most notably, Mrs. Trenance-Treforda, the Vagina Lady, who sculpted incredibly accurate renditions of female genitalia.

Tamsin had visited the many art galleries in Newquay, making sure she was kept abreast of when their exhibits changed, but she had yet to meet a woman who was into art as much as she was. This applied even to her friends. Rylea, for instance—bless her—had only a passing interest in the subject, which often manifested itself in her *passing* by any art show she came upon.

So, Robyn not only having an interest in art, but being expert enough in the field to make a career out of it was…stimulating. As was Robyn's figure…

The gallerist was her height, maybe less an inch, with a very slender figure, the kind made for elegant cocktail dresses that fit like a second skin. In addition to being captivated by Robyn's lips, Tamsin also found herself drawn to her neck. It was long, its skin flawless save for one tiny birthmark at her pulse point, and more than once Tamsin had been disturbed by unbidden images of wanting to sniff along it until she found the exact point where Robyn applied her perfume.

"That is such a cute name!" Robyn now exclaimed, the statement directed at Rylea, who had just told her that she owned Tremont's premier—well, only—coffee shop, Bean There/Done That. "I'll be by to visit it soon," Robyn added.

"The first drink is on the house," Rylea said. "A 'welcome to Tremont' gift."

"Do you serve tea as well?" Robyn asked.

Rylea looked at Tamsin and cocked her eyebrow, making Tamsin wonder what fresh silliness was about to come out of her friend's mouth.

"You two are perfect neighbours," Rylea said, returning her eyes to Robyn. "Tamsin only drinks tea too."

"Oh, I don't *only* drink tea," Robyn hurriedly explained. "Trust me, I *need* my coffee! Lots of it!" She then looked at Tamsin, who was seated next to her, and snorted a quick laugh. "What, really…?" she asked, an impudent expression on her face. "You only drink tea?"

Tamsin's brow furrowed.

"Yes," she stated. "Why?"

Again, another snort of laughter.

"It's just…" Robyn began, acting like she was at a loss for words. "You strike me as *such* a coffee drinker!"

Rylea and Darcie laughed, but Tamsin's eyes flashed.

"I beg your pardon?" she asked.

Robyn held up her hands.

"No need to get upset," she said, smiling. "It's just that you seem…well, let's just say 'feisty.' You know…driven."

Tamsin narrowed her eyes.

She wasn't sure if Robyn was having a laugh or not. Was *feisty* in this case a synonym for *bitchy?* Was *driven* being used to call her a *cow?* And how could she find out?

Unfortunately, before she could put her considerable interrogation powers to use, Rylea interrupted.

"You have no idea," Rylea said. "But it is actually a good thing. One day, she's going to own the most fabulous travelling service in all of Great Britain."

Tamsin melted.

"Aww, thank you, Rye Bread," she said, beaming at her best friend, grateful that no matter what, she'd always have Rylea's support. Mates like her were important to keep hold of.

"Excellent," Robyn said, lifting up her wine glass and swirling the contents of it. "I'll be sure to use your services the next time I want to holiday to California."

Tamsin's teeth clenched, and she gripped the stem of her own wine glass more tightly. Looking at Robyn, she thought she caught her neighbour give Rylea a wink, but she couldn't be sure.

"Like California, do you?" she asked.

"Love it!" Robyn stated, her gorgeous brown eyes looking at her, a grin on her face. "Have you ever been?"

Inside, Tamsin fumed, because she could only state the truth.

With a sigh, she said, "No, I haven't." She held up a finger. "But I currently have a grievance with California, and until I'm over it, that entire bloody state can suck it."

Robyn laughed, placing her hand on her arm as she did so. Tamsin felt a silly thrill at this physical contact, exactly like the one she felt when Robyn had touched her earlier, just before leaving to go to her cottage to get some fruit.

"I like you," Robyn told her, still chuckling. "When I first met her," she then said to Darcie and Rylea, "I was, like, 'Oh my days, let me just get this bloody woman off my back about the moving truck, and hope I never have to see her again. Did she tell you that story? I'm sure she must have."

Tamsin's mouth dropped open.

"Is that so?" she asked, evenly. "Well, at that particular moment, I certainly was not interested in inviting you out for lunch any time soon either."

"And now?" Robyn asked, quirking an eyebrow.

Tamsin blinked.

"Now what?" she asked.

"Are you interested in inviting me out for lunch any time soon?" Robyn answered.

Damn it! She did it again!

Robyn had this…*knack* for making her feel off-balance.

Tamsin wanted to groan aloud, but that would give Robyn too much satisfaction, and would also allow Darcie and Rylea to make fun of her for at least the next half century.

"I mean," Robyn went on, "I know nothing about Newquay, and I start work there next week. Knowing a great lunch place would be handy."

Tamsin could feel the eyes of Darcie and Rylea on her.

She smiled.

"Of course," she told Robyn, "what a lovely idea."

***

After about half an hour more, Darcie and Rylea stated they needed to leave. Robyn declared she should go as well.

"Before I go, however, you promised me a tour of all your artwork," she reminded her host.

"Yes, I remember you saying that," Rylea—who apparently thought she was being helpful—pointed out. "In fact, your specific words were—"

"Yes, I know what my specific words were, thank you, Rylea!" Tamsin said, cutting her off.

She and Robyn both walked the couple to the front door, where Darcie and Rylea gave Robyn hugs. Her new neighbour had completely won over those two, Tamsin knew, which meant she might as well get used to the idea of Robyn becoming part of their set.

The oddest part was when she and Robyn were standing together in the doorway of her cottage, giving their friends a few final waves goodbye. It suddenly struck Tamsin that this is what couples do! See their visiting friends off in the doorway before turning back into the house to resume their night alone together.

Having thought of that notion, she then couldn't *unthink* it, as silly—and impossible—as it was.

Still though…

She was willing to admit that she felt a flash of enjoyment at being part of this faux domestic tableau, and actually wished that she and Robyn could simply kick off their shoes—those really stylish boots Robyn was wearing, and her own well-worn ballet flats—and commence with the clearing up of the wine glasses, before settling on the sofa to watch some telly.

She shook her head. She needed to stop that train of thought.

"I see you like Bouguereau," Robyn said, walking back into the house from the entryway.

Tamsin smiled. She was also impressed. Robyn had a good eye.

Bouguereau was one of Tamsin's favourite artists, a Frenchman who had worked in the late-nineteenth and early-twentieth centuries. She had a lot of prints and reproductions of his works in her home, including her absolute favourite, "The Young Shepherdess," which she had a giclée-on-canvas print of, dominating a wall which faced the entryway, so that it was one of the first things visitors to her cottage saw upon entering.

"I love his women," Tamsin said, approaching not the Shepherdess, but another giclée print—framed, behind glass—titled "Young Girl Defending Herself Against Eros." It was another of her favourites. It depicted a nude young woman, sitting on a block of stone, gently holding the winged Eros and his arrow of love out, at bay.

Tamsin loved this painting because even though it is clear that the young woman in the painting will eventually succumb to love, it also shows that she has a choice in the matter, a hand in determining when she is ready for that to happen for her.

"His women project so much strength," Tamsin went on, "especially his peasants. Plus, I just love his skill at painting, and as you can see, I'm heavy into figurative realism."

This was true. She enjoyed artists who were masters at capturing the human form—Bouguereau, Sargent, Ingres, and others—and she had plenty of reproductions of their works on display. She also had several original works, done by local artists, which she had purchased at various art fairs or from galleries.

"Oh, this is lovely!" Robyn said. She walked halfway up the staircase leading to the bedrooms. On the wall, Tamsin had an original painting of a young woman mounted. The subject of the picture was wearing a short dress, and she was leaning against the parapet of the Old Bridge, which crossed Lewisham Creek here in Tremont.

"Wait…" Robyn said, looking more closely at the painting. "I've seen this bridge, haven't I? As I drive through town? That's here in Tremont, right?"

Tamsin, who had remained at the foot of the stairs, nodded.

"Yeah, we call it the Old Bridge," she answered. "Been here forever. Anyway, let me show you this other piece downstairs. I don't want you thinking I'm only into figurative works."

There were several abstract artists she liked as well, though not many.

Robyn started heading back down the half a flight she had climbed.

"But who painted the one with the bridge?" she asked.

Tamsin, her back turned to Robyn as she started heading to the room off the kitchen which she used as her office, rolled her eyes.

"No one," she said. "I mean, it's just a local artist. She died a few years ago. Anyway…"

"Well, this is another of hers, isn't it?" Robyn said.

Tamsin wanted to groan. Instead, she turned and smiled.

Robyn was now looking at another full-length portrait of a different young woman. This time, the subject—Anne—was laughing while looking right at the viewer and standing in the doorway leading to a bedroom.

"Yep," she confirmed. She then made a vague gesture, meant to indicate the entire cottage. "You'll see several of hers throughout the place."

"I can understand why," Robyn said. "Her work is fabulous. There's such an immediacy to it, and the photorealistic effect she creates are amazing. It's too bad she's dead."

Tamsin shrugged.

"Yeah, well…people die," she said, flippantly. "Now, come on, let me show you what I have in my office."

Chapter 12

A short while later, Robyn left Tamsin's cottage.

She was feeling…buzzy, she considered as she let herself into her own home.

Part of it was the wine, no doubt—which had been good; Tamsin definitely had taste.

Part of it was knowing she had made some new friends in Darcie and Rylea, who were charming, funny, and cute as fuck as a couple. She looked forward to getting to know them better. And apparently, they had a little girl!

However, part of her buzzy feeling—a big part, she knew—was the extra time she had spent with Tamsin.

She still wasn't quite sure about her neighbour. The ginger seemed a bit headstrong, but then again, weren't most gingers? Tamsin also seemed to have this…persecution complex, as though she was certain that any little thing which was an inconvenience or a mild annoyance, had been done personally to her.

Case in point, the delivery truck yesterday.

No doubt other shops on Bank Street had been a tad inconvenienced by the enormous truck unloading furniture for the gallery. No doubt a few pedestrians and drivers had been as well. But only Tamsin had come out from her travel agency to say anything, acting as if Robyn had plotted the whole scheme just to irk her.

It also seemed as if Tamsin's default setting was "shields up," to borrow a phrase from *Star Trek*. One could almost *see* the wall the woman immediately erected around herself. Granted, Robyn had only encountered her yesterday and today, but still…the wall had been there.

Maybe it was something to do with new people, she considered, which made sense.

The good news was that, as the night wore on, Tamsin *did* seem to warm up to her quite a bit, to the extent that, by the time she left her neighbour's cottage, Robyn was entertaining the possibility that Tamsin had started to *like* her.

Well, only time would tell if they became friends.

In her bedroom upstairs, Robyn sat down on the edge of the bed to remove her boots, smiling to herself.

Her little trick to get Tamsin to have lunch with her next week in Newquay had worked. They hadn't settled on a day yet, but Robyn would make sure it happened. She had purposely avoided telling Tamsin that she had discovered the sandwich shop across the street from the gallery, and that she had seen Tamsin in there. She had done this because she just knew that if she had mentioned it, Tamsin would have said something like, "Well, you don't need *me* to show you any lunch places, do you?"

And Robyn really wanted Tamsin to show her some lunch places…and maybe some other things.

With her boots off, she sat there, thinking.

She rolled her eyes.

Actually, *thinking* wasn't quite right, and she knew it. What's more, Empress, also on the bed and staring at her, obviously knew it also. What she was really doing was waiting for herself to admit that she was attracted to Tamsin and would be willing to employ a few more "tricks" to get her to sit down with her for a meal or a drink.

"Okay, fine," she huffed. Standing, she carried her boots to the wardrobe. After putting them down, she turned to Empress. "You know I have a thing for gingers, so don't judge me!"

She lifted off her cashmere sweater, placing it in the rattan basket she employed to keep things to bring to the dry cleaners. Which reminded her…

Still need to find a dry cleaners.

A moment later, she had her bra off, which she tossed in the laundry bin.

"And she is like the *ultimate* ginger!" she told Empress, standing in the doorway of the wardrobe, with her hands on her hips. "Seriously, wait until you meet her!"

Back in the wardrobe, she shimmied out of her skinny jeans, pulling her knickers down with them, tossing both in the laundry bin as well. Completely nude now, she returned her attention to Empress.

"Okay, fine," she began, "I'm still obsessed with that writer who lives in California. She's ginger too! But we both know *that's* not going to happen!"

She walked to her dresser. In a few moments, she had clean knickers, pyjama shorts and a faded Stevie Wonder tee on. In the en suite, she started the work of scrubbing her face clean of makeup. As she did this, she thought about Tamsin.

The woman was *gorgeous*. But that…attitude of hers!

Hang on…hang on…

Sure, Tamsin might not make the greatest first impression, but all of her impressions afterwards had been spot-on.

Okay…maybe not *all*, but a good many of them. Once she had loosened up a bit, Tamsin had proven to be funny, charming, and a good storyteller.

"Oh!" Robyn called out to Empress, her eyes shut because her face was still sudsy with L'Oréal Cleansing Milk. "And she likes art too!"

As she rinsed off her face, she thought about those paintings in Tamsin's cottage, the ones by that artist Tamsin had told her had died.

It seemed there was more to that story, but her instincts had told her that she shouldn't press that topic because it could possibly be a sore one.

Robyn wondered now, had Tamsin been close to the artist?

Were they related? A sister? A cousin? Was it her mum?

If it was someone outside her family, had they been lovers?

Best to avoid mentioning that artist again, she decided, until Tamsin started opening up to her more.

She stopped in the midst of patting her face dry with a towel, as a very salacious thought came to mind…

She could start by opening her legs.

"Stop it, Robyn!" she chastised herself.

She peed after cleansing her face, and then decided to watch some telly downstairs. Empress decided to follow her, possibly to learn more about her human's new ginger friend.

A few minutes later, Robyn had an action movie playing on Netflix, her feet resting on the coffee table, while Empress lay curled up on her lap, purring as her fur was stroked.

"Let me take a few days and think on it," Robyn said. She was referring to whether she wanted to perhaps throw a bit of flirting Tamsin's way and see if it led to anything.

Because if so…

She would definitely not say "no" to the concept of her and Tamsin being more than neighbours. If that meant dating, great; but if it meant just being friends-with-benefits, also great. She wasn't averse to casual flings, especially with gingers who looked like that.

"Oh my days, what is it about me and gingers?" she muttered, while on the telly Tom Cruise blew something up.

And *if* something happened between her and Tamsin, she also wasn't worried about the fact that they were neighbours. If *whatever* happened between them didn't work out, well…they were adults and as such, Robyn would hope that they would be able to continue living next door to one another without it becoming an awkward *thing*.

Scratching Empress's favourite spot under her chin, Robyn sighed.

"This is probably just a stupid infatuation," she told the cat. "I'll let you in on a little secret, young lady…it *has* been a while since I've gotten laid."

Empress turned her head and looked at her, as if informing the human that she was very much aware of how long it's been since she'd gotten laid.

"Hey!" Robyn complained.

Chapter 13

At that moment, in the cottage next door, Tamsin was unknowingly watching the same Tom Cruise movie as Robyn.

She was wearing harem pants and a tank top, her red hair pulled back into a ponytail, and a small smile was on her lips.

She still wasn't quite sure about her new neighbour. Robyn seemed the type who enjoyed pushing someone's buttons. She was snarky and impishly sarcastic, and it seemed as if she had made it her personal mission to always have the dominant hand in a conversation.

During the *getting-to-know-one-another* phase of tonight's little party with Darcie and Rylea, Tamsin had learned that Robyn was twenty-nine. So why then did she seem to act so much older?

Case in point, the Sønderborg Interiors Delivery Truck Incident yesterday (as Tamsin now referred to it internally).

Robyn had acted as if she was a…a forty-five-year-old schoolmarm trying to reason with a recalcitrant child.

"And I wasn't being recalcitrant," Tamsin muttered, as Tom Cruise blew something up.

Quickly, however, the small smile returned to her lips.

Okay, maybe Robyn was a bit of a pill, but Tamsin knew the fact was that she had enjoyed the back-and-forth they seemed to naturally fall into, especially tonight. There was something stimulating about it, which was totally new to her. She was British, after all, culturally raised to be polite and accommodating. Yet it had been fun—well, *stimulating*—to interact with Robyn on a level that involved a bit more attitude.

Biting her lip, a thought came to her.

It was as if I could be more myself with her.

That was interesting! Of course, she was very much herself with people like Rylea and Darcie—friends she'd known for a long time. But when it came to new women she met, she usually put on something of a façade. That perfectly polite British façade, turning herself into a slightly different version of herself.

Wait!

That wasn't entirely true either, she realised!

That metamorphosis didn't happen with *all* women.

It only happened with the women she was attracted to.

"Oh, fuck my life," she groaned. However, she immediately sighed afterwards, deciding to cut herself some slack. "She's fucking hot," she said, as Tom Cruise blew up something else.

Those lips, that neck…and her eyes! What Tamsin would give to have those eyes staring at her with the warm affection of someone crazy about her. And what Tamsin would give to have those same eyes staring at her with unbridled lust.

And goodness…she was into art!

Not just into art, but actually *in* the industry!

How hot would it be having a girlfriend who runs an art gallery?

She gave her head a quick shake, dispelling any thoughts that could be associated with the word "girlfriend."

Besides, it was kind of putting the cart before the horse, wasn't it?

Right now, it was enough to wonder if they would make good neighbours, or if they would actually become friends.

It was possible, Tamsin supposed.

When she wasn't being a pill, Robyn had shown herself to be delightful, enough so that Tamsin had realised at several points throughout the night that she had let her guard down a bit, that she had put down the walls she normally put up whenever she encountered new people.

Which probably was a good thing, she now figured.

After all, she had apparently shown enough of her fabulous true self to make Robyn wrangle a lunch date out of her.

Okay…maybe not a date! More like an…appointment.

Tamsin gave a little chuckle.

There was something about the way Robyn had done that, though…She had tried to sell it as, "I'm a new girl in town and I need help finding my way," but Tamsin was pretty sure there had been more to it than that.

"Ooh," she told Tom Cruise. "That could be fun."

Of course, she probably shouldn't be thinking about *any* woman right now, let alone the new neighbour. She and Kendra had just broken up, after all.

"Bugger!"

She *still* hadn't exorcised Kendra, thanks to Rylea!

"Hey, Siri," she called out, "remind me to yell at Rylea tomorrow at ten a.m.!"

"Okay," the HomePod she had on the end table spoke. "Your reminder is set for tomorrow at ten a.m."

Relationship exorcisms were important, and Tamsin had no intention of skipping this one.

In any case, it was probably a moot point regarding her and Robyn vis-à-vis she and Kendra.

If…

"And it's a big fucking *if!*" she said aloud.

If she and Robyn somehow got involved as more than just neighbours, it certainly wasn't going to happen soon. That kind of shit only happens in romcoms and bad fiction. Therefore, she'd be well over Kendra by then.

She smiled as she remembered something.

"She's your exorcism!"

Rylea had said that. The funny thing was, Tamsin realised now, looking back on the time they all spent in the garden, she hadn't thought of Kendra once. Then later, when she was showing Robyn some of the art in her house, she hadn't had a single thought along the lines of, *I wonder if Kendra might text me tonight,* or, *Maybe if I send Kendra a selfie wearing that black bra she likes, I might entice her to come over.*

Instead, she had simply enjoyed Robyn's presence, accompanied by the odd thought here and there that she enjoyed having Robyn in her home. It had given her quite a buzz, a buzz she was still feeling.

Again, she gave her head a quick shake.

Wine also gives me quite the buzz.

As true as that was, Tamsin knew she was lying to herself. Wine buzzes felt different. They were all contained in the head, leading to that spirit of goofiness and of feeling slightly off-balance.

Women buzzes, however, were full-body affairs. They made her feel wide awake and energised, as if she had just taken a B_{12} shot. They also made what felt like a mild electric current radiate through her body, a current seemingly generated from a place in her chest, near her heart.

This was the buzz she was feeling now, and she might as well acknowledge it.

"Eh, so what?" she told Tom, who happened to be in a scene wherein he was looking straight at the camera. "Robyn was good company tonight, although I suspect she's still something of a toffee-nosed twat. I guess time will tell, Tom."

She rolled her eyes. She was actually talking to Tom Cruise about the buzz she was still feeling from being with her new neighbour. If that wasn't a sign of impending madness…

"Bloody hell," she muttered, "I need to get a cat."

Chapter 14

Despite having made a handful of friends, Robyn decided to stay in for the weekend, her last before she started the work of prepping Linden Gallery Cornwall for its eventual opening.

To that end, she gave herself permission to be lazy on Saturday and Sunday. She spent those two days reading, watching telly and taking naps. She had bought enough groceries to withstand a siege by the Achaeans, and so she didn't even need to go out for any sustenance, although she felt a little guilty about not visiting Rylea's coffee shop, but she resolved to stop by there on Monday on her way out of town.

Sunday proved the most interesting day of the two.

On that day, she had started feeling the stress of the work week that was going to start the next day, and because of that, she had ended up masturbating *a lot*. It truly had been an all-day thing, starting in the morning, when she woke up with her mind already thinking of the thousand-and-one tasks which needed to be done to get the gallery ready for Sasha's exhibit.

It had continued later that morning, after the caffeine from her tea kicked in, glomming onto her anxiety about the coming week, and heightening it. So, right there in the kitchen, she had propped her feet up on the edge of the breakfast table and gotten herself off once more.

When that orgasm subsided, leaving her huffing out ragged breaths, she had thought, *Okay, fine…that should hold me for a bit.*

A bit turned out to be just before lunch, when she had a strong yearning to feel the suction vibe on her clit because, well…suction vibe on her clit. Oh, and because she was still feeling stressed.

And so it went…

By the time she went to bed for the night, she'd had quite the day below her waist, and it had helped, so much so that when she laid down, she fell asleep almost instantly.

On Monday, she baked extra time into her commute to stop at Bean There/Done That, wanting a strong espresso drink to help jumpstart her morning.

The Bean—as Rylea had told her it was known as—was a charming shop, with exposed brick walls and hardwood floors. Even as early as when she walked in—just past seven a.m.—she saw a few tables already occupied by pensioners, either alone or in small groups. She figured they were regulars, and she was willing to bet they all queued up outside before Rylea even opened the place.

As soon as she stepped inside, they all stopped their conversations, looked up from their teas or coffees, and stared at her.

Robyn smirked.

Well, at least I'm looking good.

Even though her day at the gallery would involve a lot of cleaning and moving furniture around, she had made an effort to be sure to still look stylishly professional and capable. After all, this would also be the day when she would meet—for the first time in person—her two assistants. So, she was wearing stretch jeans which looked expensive but were not, and which she also didn't mind getting dusty, and a burnt sienna-coloured mock turtleneck top, with short sleeves. Both items fit her well, flattering her figure, but were also comfortable for doing physical work in.

"Hooray, you made it!" Rylea greeted her from behind the counter.

Robyn shrugged.

"Well, I've been driving around looking for a Starbucks, but I can't seem to find one in this teeny-tiny hamlet, so I figured I'd stop in here."

Rylea laughed.

"Very funny," she said. "Hey, meet Bridget, she helps me here."

Rylea indicated the other woman, who looked to be in her forties, working behind the counter.

"Bridge, this is Robyn," Rylea said.

"The new lass," Bridget said, turning away from a coffee grinder to face Robyn. "Moved into Mrs. Burberry-Foster's. You're the one with the posh car, right?"

Robyn chuckled as she shook Bridget's hand. She was willing to bet that the true locals—the ones who have been here for generations—probably knew her bra size by now.

"Guilty," she said. "Although, it's really not that posh. Anyway, this is a lovely village."

She figured the quickest way to earn at least a smidgen of favour with this lot was to compliment Tremont. It wasn't a lie, though. Tremont was a lovely village.

Bridget smiled and nodded approvingly.

"That it is," she said. "Even more so now that there's a posh car in it."

She returned to her grinder.

Robyn gave Rylea a look.

"Surely mine isn't the poshest car in town," she whispered. If the realm of BMWs were equivalent to the hierarchy of British servants, her model would rank somewhere slightly above scullery maid. She had only been able to purchase it following a period of rather stringent saving in order to make the down payment.

"Afraid so," Rylea told her. "In fact, sometime in the 1960s, a bloke arrived in Tremont driving a Rolls-Royce and stopped off for lunch at the restaurant that used to be where Mrs. Trellis-Cocklin now has her bakery. People still talk about it. Anyway, what'll you have?"

"Americano, please," Robyn told her. "To go."

"Americano, Bridge, and give it legs," Rylea said.

"Got it," Bridget replied.

Robyn laughed.

"That's a cute way to state my order," she said.

Rylea shrugged.

"I've been trying to become more creative," she replied. She leaned forward, resting her arms beside the till on the counter. "So…" she began.

Robyn knew what was coming. There is a certain tone of voice all women use when they're about to probe for gossip-level information, but without wanting to seem like they're probing for gossip-level information.

"Yes?" Robyn asked innocently.

"How did you and Tamsin get on after Darce and I left last night?" Rylea asked.

Robyn made a show of looking behind her, as if checking for eavesdroppers. Then she leaned forward. Rylea did the same, an expectant gleam in her eyes.

"Can I tell you something in confidence?" Robyn whispered.

"Of course!" Rylea insisted.

Robyn paused, letting the expectation build.

"I think I'm bloody in love with her," she said.

"What?" Rylea asked, her mouth dropping open, her eyes going wide.

Robyn nodded.

"She is just the sweetest thing!" Robyn went on.

"Sweet?" Rylea asked. "*Tamsin?*"

"Yes!" Robyn insisted. "She just…" She breathed a *heroine-in-a-Jane-Austen-movie* type of sigh. "She just captivated me! I…I don't want to be without her."

Now, Rylea was looking at her as if she was some kind of nutter.

Robyn quirked an eyebrow, a smirk on her lips.

It took a moment, but the penny finally dropped.

Blushing, Rylea looked up at the ceiling.

"Oh my days, I can't believe I fell for that," she muttered.

Robyn laughed.

"The new lass has got jokes!" she said.

Rylea was laughing as well.

"You're going to fit in just fine here," she said. "So…did Tamsin show you her paintings?"

Robyn blinked.

"Wait…when you say, '*her paintings…?*'" she prodded.

"The ones *she* painted," Rylea clarified.

Tamsin paints?

"Um…no, she didn't show me those," she told Rylea.

Now, Rylea looked perplexed.

"Buuuuuut…she gave you a tour of the art in her house after Darcie and I left, right?"

"Yes," Robyn said.

"Well then, you must have seen her paintings," Rylea said, with a chuckle. "The one along the staircase? Um…let's see…there's another one on the way to the living room. Another one in the *actual* living room. Two more in the upstairs hall…"

"We didn't go upstairs," Robyn said softly, thoughtfully.

With the exception of those two, Robyn knew exactly the paintings Rylea was talking about.

Tamsin painted those?

"One Americano," Bridget said, placing a to-go cup on the counter.

"No charge," Rylea said.

Robyn snapped herself out of her reverie about this new intel she had received about Tamsin.

"Oh, right!" she said. "Thank you so much! Well, I need to run; first day at the office, so to speak."

"Good luck," Rylea told her.

Robyn and her Americano-with-legs started walking towards the exit.

Again, the pensioners all stopped and looked at her, but this time they were trying not to be as obvious about it.

Smirking, Robyn remembered her theory that the locals might be worried she was a cat burglar. With this in mind, her smirk got wider.

"Meow," she whispered to herself as she pulled open the shop's door.

***

"Oh my god! You're *beautiful!*"

This came from Lucien, a tall, reed-thin bloke, sporting a goatee. He was in his late-thirties, Robyn knew, and had striking eyes that kind of bulged from his skull. Dressed entirely in black, he looked as if he could star in an advert on the telly entitled, "So You Want to Work in an Art Gallery."

Lucien had just arrived at Linden Gallery Cornwall, to begin his first day of work. Like Tina—the other person Robyn had hired—Lucien's job would be to greet visitors and talk to them about the art on display, help with organising exhibitions and writing promotional materials for them, and basically just help the gallery run smoothly.

As the resident bloke, however, Robyn also expected him to be in charge of handling any tasks which required decent upper body strength, and to be in charge of killing spiders.

She didn't feel threatened by Lucien's effusiveness regarding her beauty. She had known he was gay three minutes into their Zoom interview a few weeks ago. This was primarily because he had stated—three minutes into their Zoom interview—"I'm gay! I just wanted to put that out there in case this is going to be a problem for you."

In response to his compliment, Robyn said, "Thank you! You're beautiful as well."

"So lovely to meet you in person," Lucien said. "And I'm so excited about this gallery. I can't believe Sasha Hoffman is our first show! I love her!"

Lucien's comment made Robyn feel immensely proud. It was no small thing to have scored Sasha as this gallery's first show. Even the great Victoria Linden had been impressed, which augured well for Robyn's career.

She thought back to the phone conversation she had with Sasha just the other day. It had been a checking-in type of call, making sure that the artist hadn't run away to Peru or some such place. As well-regarded as Sasha was already, this was going to be her first public showing, and she often needed Robyn to soothe her nerves with calming words of encouragement.

"Hiya!"

This came from a young woman who now entered the gallery.

She looked like a teenager, though Robyn knew she was twenty-four. Still, though…seeing her in the flesh did make her want to ask to see her ID.

She was very pretty, with jet-black hair cut in a graduated bob style. Robyn was pleased to see that she had also dressed for the day in comfortable clothes, suitable for doing the harder, more physical work most people who visit galleries don't see being done.

Robyn was especially excited about Tina being on staff. She was a graphic designer, and Robyn expected to utilise her skills in creating the marketing materials for the gallery. She was also a self-described social media guru, which Robyn also considered herself to be. Working together, she figured, they would be able to really put Linden Gallery Cornwall on the cyberspace map.

"I'm Tina," the newcomer said. "Lovely to meet you!"

Introductions all around were made, and then Robyn put her hands on her hips, looking at both Lucien and Tina.

This was her team, and this was her gallery.

"Right," she said. "Let me go over what we need to do today. First…the windows. I have some rolls in my car. Lucien, if you can help me…"

Chapter 15

Tamsin had to wonder…

Like, really wonder.

In fact, she had even gone into the loo at Xplr at one point to look at her reflection in the mirror, just to make sure, but saw nothing there. For example, a sign on her face or clothing which read, "Talk to me about booking your next holiday to California!"

Three separate sets of couples had come in today asking for help planning their California holidays. Two of them were cishet married couples, one with three small children. That couple wanted to do the basic Disneyland-Universal-Hollywood-and-beaches itinerary. The other cishet couple were about her age and wanted to do the whole bars-beaches-bars-beaches-more bars-more beaches-*Do you know where we can score good weed in California?* itinerary. They didn't really need a travel agent's help. They could have booked their trip completely online without any expert advice, but Tamsin had mentally shrugged that off. A paying client was a paying client.

The third couple she knew. They lived down the bloody street from her in Tremont. Ellen and Maria, who—traitorously—wanted to do the Carlsbad-L.A.-San Francisco itinerary, with Maria showing Tamsin photos on her phone of a Carlsbad beach, saying, "When it's wet, cold and miserable here in November, that's where we'll be luv."

Tamsin had smiled, her jaw feeling tight.

Paying clients. Paying clients.

"Well," she had said pleasantly, "be sure to say hello to all the giant lesbians there."

"Oh, we will!" Ellen had replied enthusiastically. "We're hoping they'll find our British accents quite attractive."

Tamsin hadn't known how to reply to that. In fact, she was beginning to suspect that Ellen and Maria were planning on…*opening* their relationship a bit while in bloody California.

What the hell is up with that place? she had wondered.

When those two left, her Uncle Richard had approached.

"Goodness," he began, "that state is a goldmine for us. Perhaps we ought to promote it more, yeah? You can do all of your social media magic, maybe do one of those cute, little videos you do.

You know…'California! Your escape from the British climate!' Something like that. I'll leave it to you. You're the expert."

Tamsin had bristled at hearing her videos referred to as "cute" and "little," but her uncle—she reluctantly admitted—had a good point. Booking holidays in California for sun-starved Brits (gay, straight, or otherwise) could truly be an earnings bonanza for Xplr, and at the end of the day, it was all about bringing in money.

Now, he was back in his office at the rear of the agency, and Tamsin was left to herself.

It was almost two p.m. She had been so busy today that she'd had lunch delivered for her and Uncle Richard from The Sarnie Shoppe, rather than going to pick it up herself, which she enjoyed doing as it got her out of the agency for a bit.

While eating her ham and mustard sarnie, she had thought of Robyn, and their vague plans to have lunch at some point soon. It would be a good opportunity to get to know her better, she supposed.

Obviously, it wasn't going to happen today. Even if Robyn had suggested it, Tamsin knew she would have had to beg off, given how busy her morning had been.

She wondered now how Robyn's day had been going thus far. She was tempted to low-key walk past the gallery, look through the window as she passed, maybe catch a glimpse of what "setting up an art gallery" was all about.

Maybe catch a glimpse of Robyn as well.

Just out of curiosity, of course! Just to see what her new…friend looked like in her natural habitat.

Besides, a walk now—between appointments—would be a good idea. Curtis, the owner of The Sarnie Shoppe, had really packed on the meat in her sandwich today, and so it had been a bit heavier than usual.

"Uncle Richard," she called out, standing from her desk. "I'm going for a stroll. Won't be gone long."

"Enjoy, luv!" he called back. "I'll hold down the fort."

She gathered up her handbag and set off.

The new Linden Gallery was to her left as she exited Xplr, several shopfronts down Bank Street, and so she headed in that direction.

It was a fair day, a little chilly—surprise, surprise—and there were plenty of people about, going in and out of the various shops.

She felt herself getting nervous as she drew closer to the gallery and hated herself for it. She had nothing to be nervous about! All she was going to do was walk past the place, sneak a look through the windows, and see if she could get a sense of what was going on inside, and how the space was being developed by Robyn and her staff.

She *wasn't* hoping that Robyn would spot her and wave her in.

Nope. She wasn't hoping for that, at all.

But…well, if Robyn *did* do that, then she'd be obliged to accept that invitation and spend a few minutes talking with her, wouldn't she?

A bloke in torn jeans and a denim jacket, walking in the opposite direction, smiled and said, "Nice tits."

"Bog off, you nutter," Tamsin shot back, not breaking stride.

Really, what did straight women find appealing about men?

When she was about ten yards away from the gallery, Tamsin's brow furrowed as she noticed something.

Huh!

Stepping up to the gallery now, she stopped and examined the windows.

They were completely covered with what looked to be large sheets of kraft paper, and the job was so well done that there wasn't even a sliver of an opening between the sheets for someone curious—like herself, for example—to peek inside.

Additionally, taped on the inside half of the door's window was a sign…

Coming Soon!
The Linden Gallery Cornwall
Fine Art at Its Finest
Opening Exhibition: The Works of Cornwall Artist Sasha Hoffman

A date was included, which was only about three weeks from today.

Sasha Hoffman.

Tamsin knew of her. She was a Cornish abstract artist, of the Colour-Blocking school, and whose works had a very Mondrianesque style to them. Her paintings could be striking, and Tamsin even liked a few of them, but she had always been less impressed by contemporary abstract artists.

The pioneers of the various styles—Mondrian, Pollack, Rothko, Basquiat, et cetera—she had a great deal of respect for, as she did for anyone who forced the art world to look outside the box. But the fact of the matter was, in her opinion, that nowadays *anyone* could create abstract art; it was a discipline which required little talent, and most of the current abstract artists were simply poor imitators of the greats who had come before them.

Sasha Hoffman was better than most, however, and Tamsin was excited to see this opening show. Moreover, it was clever of Robyn to have called out that Sasha was from Cornwall. People in this county *loved* having one of their own featured prominently in something.

Anything.

If it was advertised that a Cornwall man would be taking a shit live on telly, *all* of Cornwall would tune in to watch it.

Therefore, for a Cornish artist to be featured in something as posh as a showing at a gallery, well…that would go over quite well here in Newquay.

In any case, with the kraft paper blocking the view of the inside, there was nothing for Tamsin to see here, so she decided to continue her walk and use it to get some exercise before heading back to Xplr.

***

Tamsin needed to do a bit of a shop at Tesco in Newquay before heading home that evening. In addition, she needed to stop at her favourite petrol station between Newquay and Tremont. These stops meant she got home considerably later than she normally would. However, as she pulled into her driveway, she noticed that Robyn's BMW was not there.

Looking at the clock on the car's dash, she saw that it was nearing half past six.

She didn't know fuck all about getting an art gallery up and running from scratch, but she could imagine that it was a lot of work (which apparently had to be done behind impenetrable Kraft paper).

She imagined Robyn was working late tonight, then, putting in extra time to make this—her first day at the gallery—even more productive.

She turned off the Clio's engine and sat there for a few moments, not moving, simply looking to her right at Robyn's empty driveway.

Her brow furrowed.

For some reason, hypothesising this about Robyn—specifically that she was working late because of her dedication to getting the gallery up and running—was making her even more attractive in Tamsin's eyes. It spoke—strongly—to that part of herself which was also committed to doing what was needed in order to succeed professionally.

"Mm," she murmured, thoughtfully, combining this theorised aspect of Robyn with all of the other attributes which made her neighbour…appealing.

Her brow furrowed even more deeply, and she rolled her eyes before turning them upwards. Granted, they were now looking at the ceiling of her car's cabin, but in her mind and heart they were pointed at the heavens above.

"Why are you doing this to me?" she asked the unseen goddesses she believed to be up there.

Before the goddesses provided an answer, however, the sound of another car's engine caught her attention.

It was Robyn's BMW pulling into the driveway next door.

Tamsin briskly shook her head to clear her mind and focus on the task at hand: getting her groceries out of her own car and into her cottage.

She and Robyn stepped out of their cars at the exact same moment.

"Hiya!" Robyn greeted her from over the roof of the coupe.

Tamsin smiled.

"I almost didn't recognise you without your delivery truck," she quipped.

"Cute," Robyn said. She then furrowed her brow as she looked Tamsin up and down. "Huh!"

Tamsin frowned. She looked down at herself, wondering if there was a stain on her skirt or blouse. A child had inadvertently bumped into her at Tesco earlier, and children were like living, breathing oil spills.

"What?" she asked, not seeing anything untoward on her.

Robyn shrugged.

"Oh, nothing…" she began. "It just seems your posture is a little slouchy today. I'm guessing you left the stick that's normally up your arse back at the office?"

Tamsin gasped, her eyes wide with shock. But then she burst out laughing. That *had* been funny. She decided to call this one a draw.

"So," she began, smiling. "How was work?"

"I'm knackered," Robyn answered, with a tired sigh. "Such a long day! But *so* productive!"

Tamsin wanted to scream in frustration. The way Robyn had said '*so* productive' was sexy, which was a stupid thing to find sexy.

"How about your day?" Robyn asked.

"Not as long," Tamsin replied with a shrug. "But we did a lot of business today, so that's always good."

"You're getting home later than normal, though," Robyn noted.

Tamsin worked hard at keeping a straight face.

So…Robyn was aware of when she usually reached home following work?

She felt an exciting little thrill course through her veins. That is, until she remembered that Robyn literally lived next door to her, and that she had spent most of last week in her cottage, settling in. Therefore, it wasn't beyond the pale that Robyn would have noticed her routine.

Quickly, however, an unsettling notion followed on the heels of that thought.

If Robyn had made note of when she usually got home from work, that could also mean…

Did she ever see Kendra come over?

"Grocery shopping," Tamsin told her, realising she was taking too long to respond to Robyn's statement.

"Need help carrying it all in?" Robyn asked.

"Thank you, but you're knackered," Tamsin told her. "Besides, it's not much."

Because I'm single, she wanted to add, just in case Robyn *had* noticed when Kendra had come over.

"You go in and treat yourself to a nice bath, maybe with some wine," she told her neighbour.

"That sounds perfect, actually," Robyn said with a smile. "Well, have a good night."

"You too," Tamsin said, opening the boot of her car to extract the groceries.

"Hey!"

Tamsin looked back over at Robyn.

"Lunch tomorrow?" Robyn asked. "You promised you'd show me a good spot."

Tamsin made a face.

"*'Promised'* seems a little strong," she said. "I remember it more like you conning me into agreeing to do that."

Robyn smiled.

"You say 'potato,' I say 'potahto,'" she said. "Anyway, what do you say? I'll buy."

Tamsin's heart beat a little faster, not because Robyn was offering a free lunch, but because *she* was going to be having lunch with Robyn. And…

Well, it seemed that Robyn's eyes had a somewhat hopeful look to them, as if she was really wanting Tamsin to say yes.

"Yes," Tamsin answered. "That sounds lovely."

As lovely as your eyes.

Chapter 16

In her cottage, following her little chat with Tamsin, Robyn leaned against the closed front door.

She was inordinately excited about having lunch plans with Tamsin tomorrow. In fact, she felt as if she had just boarded a train that was leaving a station, destination unknown. She was just along for the ride.

Which was silly! It was lunch! With a new friend! Her neighbour, in fact.

She wondered what happened to the blonde. She hadn't seen the Puma next door for nearly a week. That in itself meant nothing, as did the fact that the blonde had spent nights at Tamsin's meant nothing. For all she knew, the blonde was Tamsin's cousin from Sweden, which is where the world kept most of its blondes.

Her fishing expedition—mentioning to Tamsin that she had gotten home later than normal—had yielded the intel that her neighbour had gone grocery shopping, rather than having been out on a date, or out with a "friend" (said in that special way one uses when it is more than a friend). This meant she was still in the dark about the status of the blonde.

Oh well, all will be revealed in time.

She started walking upstairs.

In her bedroom, she began stripping off her clothes, and considered her day.

It had been a good one! Lucien and Tina had proven to be capable assistants, and Lucien seemed to have no issues whatsoever taking instructions from a younger woman, which was always an unusual trait to find in a man. Both of them had a love for art and were quickly able to envision her overall concept for what she wanted the gallery to look and feel like.

Unsurprisingly, both Lucien and Tina were artists themselves. People often assumed that about her as well, that she painted or sculpted or did…something, but no. Instead of creative talent, she had been given a talent for analysing and critiquing art, as well as being quick to spot trends and discover new, unknown artists who could ride the waves of those trends (while they lasted).

To that end, Tina's art showed promise, Robyn believed, after looking through pictures of it on the young woman's phone.

She was a painter who created large-scale works that featured Waterhouse-like women in very H.R. Giger-like settings. The results were striking, the kind of paintings which invited the viewer to come up with a narrative for why each woman was where she was. Quietly, out of earshot of Lucien, Robyn told Tina that she'd like to see some more one day. She wouldn't make any promises, but she could imagine giving over *some* space in the gallery to Tina's work during a multi-artist showcase in the near future.

On the other hand, Lucien's paintings would never grace a gallery that Robyn was in charge of. To begin with, his style and brushwork was a direct rip-off of Frank Auerbach's, but without the vitality. Secondly, he only painted in Day-Glo colours which, even when recreated on his phone's screen, were hard on the eyes.

In any case, together, the three of them had managed to arrange the prematurely-delivered furniture to Robyn's liking, even though it had taken several attempts to get the pieces placed exactly so—that is, matching the vision in her head. They had also given the space a good cleaning and painted one wall a beautiful indigo that Robyn had purchased at B&Q in St. Austell, driving there over her lunch hour. She believed that two of Sasha's paintings in particular would look spectacular on such a backdrop.

All of this work was done after they had covered the windows with paper. She didn't want bystanders to see the *In Progress* phase of the gallery's birth, she only wanted them to see what she called the *Reveal* phase, and that would happen only when they had Sasha's artwork hung.

All in all, it had been a fantastic day, professionally. And now…

As appealing as Tamsin's idea of a bath sounded, Robyn was too knackered to bother with all that preparation. The way she figured it, there wasn't a woman on Earth whose bath prep involved less than eleven steps, and right now, that was ten steps too many. She'd indulge in a bath on Friday night; it would give her something to look forward to. Between now and then, showers would suffice. After cleaning herself, she would make a quick dinner. Following that, cuddles with Empress on the sofa while watching telly, and then off to bed.

Starting the water running in the shower, she smiled to herself.

She wondered if Tamsin enjoyed cuddles on the sofa. Not the *let's-start-shagging* kind of cuddles, but the *I'm-so-glad-we're-sharing-this-moment-in-time-together* kind of cuddles.

"Though I wouldn't mind the *let's-start-shagging* kind," she told Empress, who had just wandered in, apparently to get an update on how things were developing with the human next door.

*****

"Care to join us for lunch, boss?" Tina asked the next day.

She and Robyn were in the office of the gallery. This was Technology Day, as Robyn had termed it on her Google calendar. All of the gallery's high-tech gear had been delivered and installed this morning. Laptops with external monitors, a colour laser printer, Wi-Fi gear, and, most importantly—as far as she was concerned—the security system. Once those blokes left, she felt as if she was in the most secure facility on Bank Street. With the system they had, a mouse couldn't fart in here without triggering an alarm *and* causing a crack unit of security company stormtroopers, armed with Kalashnikovs, to appear in minutes.

Okay, maybe not Kalashnikovs, she conceded, due to Britain's strict gun laws, but the stormtroopers would arrive with quite stern faces, at the very least.

"Ta," she responded to Tina, "but I have other plans for lunch today." After a moment, however, she added, "But let's all have lunch tomorrow, what do you say? Celebrate our first half-week working together?"

She didn't want Tina and Lucien thinking she was the type of boss who wouldn't hang out with her staff, and normally she would have accepted Tina's offer today. But she was a lesbian who was starting to become friendly with the hot neighbour, and she and that hot neighbour were set to have a meal together in a short while.

In other words, lunches with her staff could wait.

Of course, it was possible nothing would come of this lunch with Tamsin other than a deepening of their friendship and neighbourly relations. If that was the case, Robyn knew she'd be fine with it. She figured she would use occasions like lunches or perhaps the odd drink or two with Tamsin to discover not only if they were compatible as a couple, but also if she herself was drawn to Tamsin for reasons other than her beauty and incredible figure.

Tina told Robyn that lunch tomorrow sounded like a terrific idea. With that settled, Robyn excused herself to go to the loo. She didn't need to pee—she had just done that not too long ago—but she simply wanted to give her face and hair a look before she left to meet Tamsin at Xplr.

Knowing that her eyes were one of her best features, she had done them up today with an alluringly smoky eyeshadow which she normally wouldn't have used on a day like this. After all, the gallery was still closed to the public, and all she and her staff were doing was a lot of grunge work. But she had wanted to put in a little extra effort for this lunch.

To that end, although the outfit she had chosen today was functional in a *suitable-for-moving-some-boxes-and-also-hanging-some-shelves* way, it was also flattering. Her jeans fit perfectly, and the bra and top she had chosen definitely drew one's eyes to her breasts, which were much smaller than Tamsin's but not so small that the top drawer of her dresser was stocked with push-up bras.

Her brow furrowed.

The bra and top were all well and good, but maybe Tamsin wasn't a breast girl.

She shrugged.

Oh well.

The point was, she looked very nice, and if Tamsin was even the slightest bit interested, her appearance today wouldn't hinder things.

Exiting the loo, she found Lucien had joined Tina in the office.

"I'm off," she told them. "I'll be back by one."

She knew her next words would be important. She also knew that the next time she left the gallery in their hands, she'd have to counteract them by changing who she said the exact same thing to. She didn't want her small staff developing any notions of hierarchy among themselves—at least not yet.

But because Lucien was the elder of the two…

"If you both go out for lunch, Lucien, be a love and make sure the gallery is locked up good," she instructed.

"Will do," he replied.

Next time, she'd ask the same of Tina, that way Lucien wouldn't start thinking he's in charge every time she left the gallery. Blokes…give them an inch and they take a mile.

A few moments later, she was out on Bank Street, walking in the direction of Xplr. Unlike yesterday, she had chosen stylish flats to wear rather than trainers. She'd had an idea to bring high heels with her in a bag and change into them before leaving the gallery, but she knew if she had done that, it would have been noted by Lucien and Tina, and started them gossiping amongst themselves.

Just as she was approaching the door to the travel agency, it opened, and out stepped Tamsin.

Robyn's nipples hardened.

Her friend was wearing a short skirt, her beautiful legs on display, made even more mouth-watering by the open-toed high heels she had on.

Up top…

Robyn wanted to gasp in lesbian.

Up top, Tamsin had on a fitted yellow blouse, her large breasts pressing against the fabric, the top few buttons undone, showing off her cleavage. Not that those buttons could have been fastened anyway.

"Hey," Tamsin said.

"Hiya," Robyn managed to reply. "I was just about to walk in."

"Yeah, I saw you coming," Tamsin said. "Thought I'd meet you out here and spare you my uncle."

Robyn cocked an eyebrow.

"Is he horrid?" she asked.

"No," Tamsin began. "He's actually one of the sweetest and most generous people you'll ever meet. It's just that, if you came in and he learned you were a mate of mine, not just a client, he would put you to sleep with stories about God knows what. He gets chatty like that."

"Ah," Robyn said, trying her hardest to keep her eyes above Tamsin's neck.

Although…

Now that Tamsin had finished explaining about her uncle, *her* eyes fell down to Robyn's chest and lingered.

And my nipples are hard, Robyn thought, a little self-consciously. With the bra she was wearing, there was no hiding that fact. She probably looked like Jennifer Aniston on any episode of *Friends*.

Well, since her top and bra were doing what she had intended them to do, she felt at liberty to enjoy a bit of an ogle at Tamsin's chest.

She swallowed.

Whatever Tamsin's girls were harnessed in, was also not hiding the fact that her nipples were also erect.

"We should go!" she suddenly said, wrenching her eyes from the sight as soon as she felt her centre responding.

"Yes!" Tamsin agreed, looking back up at her face. "We're just two doors down. Is Italian okay?"

"Italian sounds yummy," Robyn assured her.

Not as yummy as you, I'm sure, but it will do.

***

"So…" Robyn began.

They were in a noisy fast-serve Italian place, and were seated with their food, which Robyn had to admit was quite good.

"Hm?" Tamsin prodded.

"I heard a rumour," Robyn said.

She almost burst into laughter at the way Tamsin's eyes widened with fear. It made her wonder what kind of rumours were out there about her…and how many of them were true.

"What rumour?" Tamsin demanded.

"An interesting one," Robyn said, looking down at her plate of food and spearing some of her baked ziti with her plastic fork. She placed the bite in her mouth and chewed it slowly. Across the table from her, Tamsin's eyes narrowed. It was sexy as fuck.

After swallowing her food, Robyn went on.

"The rumour I heard is that *you* are the one who painted those pictures I loved in your cottage," she stated.

She wasn't upset about being lied to regarding this. If there was one thing her career as a gallerist had taught her, it was that artists are an eccentric lot, and there were quite a lot of them who *did not* like talking about their works, or even having people know that they created them.

A look of relief came into Tamsin's eyes, but it was quickly followed by one of irritation.

"Urgh!" she groaned. "Who told you? Was it bloody Rylea?"

"Yes, it was Rylea, and I'm glad she told me!" Robyn replied, defending the coffee shop owner. "Why did you tell me the artist died?"

Tamsin rolled her eyes and let out a frustrated sigh.

"Star Wars," she stated, as if that explained everything.

Robyn's mouth dropped open.

"Wow!" she exclaimed. "I feel like I need that Enigma coding machine the Germans used in World War II to even attempt to decipher that answer."

Tamsin sat back in her seat and crossed her arms.

"So…my dad is a big fan of Star Wars, yeah?" she said.

"Okaaaay…"

"So, I watched a lot of it growing up, yeah?" Tamsin went on. "And you know how Ben Kenobi tells Luke Skywalker that his father died, when in fact he was very much alive, just as Darth Vader?"

Robyn nodded. The whole *Star Wars* thing was something she had never gotten into, but even she knew the basic lore.

Sort of...

"So, wait…" she began. "Are you Luke Skywalker in this scenario?"

Tamsin scoffed.

"No, I'm Darth Vader!" she stated.

"Um…" Robyn had to admit defeat on this one. She had *no* idea how this related to Tamsin's paintings.

Tamsin rolled her eyes again.

"Ben told Luke his father died because the good man that had been Anakin Skywalker was effectively dead, replaced by the evil Darth Vader. I told you the artist who painted those pictures died because she's effectively been replaced by the woman I am now."

"You're evil?" Robyn asked.

"No!" Tamsin exclaimed. "But I'm no longer the woman who painted those pictures! I have a business that's about to be passed on to me, and I'm focused on making sure it succeeds! I don't have time to be an artist anymore. I have more important things to do."

Now the penny dropped.

Robyn turned down the corners of her mouth.

"Oh, but that's sad," she stated. "Your paintings are fucking brilliant!"

"Thank you," Tamsin said. "For forty-five thousand quid, one of them could be yours. That gives me a bit of a raise from my current salary, but of course I would need that extra money to buy art supplies, wouldn't I? And then next year, you can buy another painting, with a bit of a cost-of-living upcharge, though."

Robyn laughed. She made a show of looking in her handbag, which was hanging off the back of her chair.

"Sorry," she said, "I seem to have left Beyonce's chequebook at home."

"Then you're out of luck," Tamsin replied, "I can't help you."

"Tamsin, being an artist is a spectacular thing!" Robyn pointed out.

"I agree," Tamsin said. "But you know what else is spectacular? Paying my bills. Eating. Buying cute clothes. I am not made to be a starving artist."

Robyn wanted to argue—and she knew she'd come back to this topic with Tamsin one day soon because this conversation was *so* not over—but she also wanted to flirt. She was a Capricorn, after all.

"Well, you do have cute clothes," she said with a smile. "Really. You always look…fabulous."

Tamsin's face coloured a red almost as deep as her hair. She uncrossed her arms and tucked a stray lock behind her right ear. Under the table, Robyn was aware that she also crossed her legs.

"Thanks," Tamsin said, smiling shyly.

Robyn decided to leave it at that for now. She could tell that she had hit her mark, and that Tamsin had enjoyed it. That told her what she needed to know.

The woman sitting across from her liked being flirted with.

The woman sitting across from her liked that it was *she* who was flirting with her.

Which meant…

Yes, the woman sitting across from her was attracted to her as well.

Her breasts started doing that Rachel-on-*Friends* thing again…

Chapter 17

Tamsin felt a little foolish.

She had reacted to Robyn's obvious flirtation like a lovestruck teenager, neither of which she was. That is, lovestruck, or a teenager. She would willingly admit to anyone that she was very attracted to Robyn, but lovestruck was quite a way off.

Well, maybe she wouldn't admit that to *anyone*.

Certainly to Rylea, because they were practically sisters. And probably Darcie because Darcie was part of the whole Rylea package now. But everyone else could bog off and mind their own bloody business.

Mentally, she quickly regrouped. She sensed that Robyn was feeling somewhat pleased with herself, and she refused to yield too much ground to her.

She took a sip of water from the bottle she had purchased with her meal.

"I'm pleased you noticed my wardrobe," she said. "Anything in particular you've enjoyed seeing me in?"

Bingo!

Robyn turned beet red and looked away, chuckling.

While her companion's eyes were thus diverted, Tamsin took advantage and stared at Robyn's chest.

Jesus! Her tits in that top!

Robyn's breasts, smaller than her own, were nonetheless full, pert and round—qualities emphasised by whatever bra was under the clingy, chocolate-brown top she was wearing, a bra which did *nothing* to hide how hard her nipples were.

It's like I'm on the set of bloody Friends.

She returned her eyes to Robyn's face just as Robyn looked back at her.

"Well," Robyn said, staring at her evenly, "I do like you in yellow."

Tamsin couldn't help grinning. She had chosen today's top with an eye towards this lunch, hoping that Robyn would like it, though still not understanding *why* she wanted such a thing to happen.

Fine, she was wildly attracted to her neighbour, but she was also just six days gone from being dumped by Kendra. Granted, theirs hadn't been the romance of the century. When she thought about it rationally, their five weeks together was hardly a significant portion of her life—or even the *year*—but surely she needed a buffer between the End of Kendra and the Start of…Whoever. Didn't she?

Yet, the Start of Robyn was *right there*, Tamsin felt. It was so bloody obvious that Robyn was just as attracted to her, and under normal circumstances, she would invite the gallerist out for drinks later, making it clear in the manner of asking that it should be considered a date.

However, before she could contemplate that train of thought more, Robyn suddenly changed the subject. Tamsin actually felt grateful.

"So…your paintings," Robyn said. "They're amazing!"

Tamsin wanted to roll her eyes but didn't.

As appreciative as she was about the compliment, she also knew Robyn—like Rylea, like her parents, like anyone else close to her—was about to pester her about why she didn't paint any longer. With this in mind, she decided on a pre-emptive strike.

"Look, I love to paint, Robyn," she said, "but I've also chosen a career that is competitive and eternally threatened by the likes of Booking.com and Expedia. This means I spend a lot of time at home thinking of ways to drive more business to Xplr. Usually, by the time I'm done with that, I'm ready to switch off the creative centre of my brain and do anything other than paint."

She was quite proud of her talent, and the works she had produced. She hoped to one day reach a point—professionally *and* financially—where she could feel empowered to enjoy creating art once again, but she didn't know when that day would come. All she knew was that right now, she didn't have the space for it in her heart, not when she, like virtually everyone else, had to remain focused on just surviving.

Robyn smiled.

"I get that," she said. Then, a wicked smile formed on her lips. "But…" She stopped.

Tamsin's brow furrowed.

"What?" she prodded.

"We're not done discussing this," Robyn stated. "I think you're a phenomenal talent and I hate to see talent not recognised."

"Are you just saying this because you feel guilty about the whole delivery truck episode last week?" Tamsin asked, wanting to deflect the conversation away from her art. Really…there was nothing to talk about on that score.

Robyn quirked an eyebrow.

"Erm…no!" she stated. "The *delivery truck episode*, as you term it, doesn't even factor into my consciousness. And it was only made into an *episode* by you being all…ginger about it."

Tamsin gasped.

"And what does that mean?" she asked.

Robyn scoffed.

"Everyone knows gingers are inherently evil," she said, teasingly. But she then rolled her eyes.

Tamsin licked her lips. Even the way Robyn rolled her eyes was alluring.

"Guess I ought to stop dating them, then, huh?" Robyn went on.

Tamsin laughed.

Very interesting…

"Got a thing for gingers, do you?" she asked, smirking.

"Don't look so smug about it," Robyn said, narrowing her eyes in a playful manner. "I may have a thing for gingers, but I'm also single, so what does that tell you?"

"Well," Tamsin began, "I'm spitballing here, but maybe you don't know anything about dating gingers?"

Robyn made the face of one who has just heard an idiotic statement.

"No, that can't be right," she said. "I mean, what's to know? You lot are sassy, you can get sunburned in a dark room, and you steal peoples' souls."

Tamsin couldn't help it. She burst out laughing, attracting the attention of some nearby diners.

When she was finished, she looked at Robyn.

"What's frightening is how accurate that is," she said.

What was also frightening, she realised, was how badly she wanted Robyn right now.

***

"What do you mean you can't?" Tamsin asked that evening as she drove home to Tremont.

On the phone, via her car's Bluetooth connection, was Rylea.

"I mean, I can't," Rylea answered, chuckling. "Darcie and I are taking Cleo out to celebrate getting high marks on her English Lit paper."

Tamsin nearly choked on her disdain. She adored little Cleo, and was happy she was doing well in school, but...

"*She's English!*" she pointed out, negotiating a curve on the A39. "Not just English-speaking. *English!* Of course she should bloody do well in that class! Take her out to celebrate when she *bollockses* up an English Lit paper, because *that* takes effort!"

"Okay, so, if you ever decide to have children...maybe don't," Rylea told her. "Anyway, we can do it tomorrow."

Tamsin scoffed.

"Tomorrow I will have bloody well slept with her!" she pointed out.

Rylea laughed.

"I've seen Robyn, remember," she began. "I do *not* see the problem with what you are saying."

After her lunch with Robyn, Tamsin knew she was in trouble. There was such an obvious attraction between them that it truly seemed as if it was inevitable *something* would happen between them. Whether it would be dating or just casual shagging, she had no idea. Moreover, during lunch, there had been an undeniable sexual undercurrent in the air, surrounding them both like a private bubble. It had been so bad, that once Tamsin returned to Xplr, she'd had trouble concentrating because of how energised her centre felt. She'd even considered masturbating quietly in the loo but there was no way she was going to do *that* with her uncle in the next room.

In any case, when she had left work, she had immediately called Rylea, demanding they conduct the relationship exorcism that had been aborted this past Friday night. She really needed that catharsis their ritual brought. She needed to feel that Kendra was well and truly gone, because if—*if*—things did happen with Robyn, she wanted to know that she was going into it with a clear head and heart.

"Tams," Rylea now said. "Why can't you just admit that I was right?"

Tamsin rolled her eyes.

"Right about what?" she asked.

"Stop being so thick!" Rylea exclaimed. "Right about how Robyn is just like an exorcism for you. It's obvious that *she* is helping you get over Kendra really fast!"

"But Kendra and I just broke up a week ago!" Tamsin whined. "Shouldn't I take some time to, you know, *grieve* a bit?"

She heard Rylea groan.

"Sod that," Rylea said. "Grieve between Robyn's legs. Besides, you and Kendra…" She trailed off.

"What?" Tamsin prodded.

Rylea hesitated. Tamsin started tapping her steering wheel with impatience but didn't say anything.

"I don't know…" Rylea eventually said. "You two didn't *go* together, if that makes sense."

"It doesn't," Tamsin informed her. "How didn't we *go* together?"

"I don't know…" Rylea repeated. "She wasn't your girlfriend?"

Tamsin briefly took her hands off the steering wheel to make a *what the fuck* gesture.

"But she *was* my girlfriend!" she pointed out.

Rylea sighed.

"No, I mean, she wasn't *your* girlfriend!" Rylea said. "Like, the one for *you*. I mean, I've known you all your life, Tams. I think I'm a good judge of when a woman is right for you. Kendra wasn't it."

It was tempting for Tamsin to argue, to say that what Rylea was suggesting was just a bunch of silly, romcom nonsense, except it worked both ways.

She had known Rylea all *her* life and had seen her bestie with plenty of girlfriends.

Darcie, without a doubt, was the right one for Rylea.

Still though…

"Don't tell me," she began, "that you can tell Robyn is the right woman for me already."

"No, I'm not saying that!" Rylea insisted. "I'd need to know her more and see the two of you together—if that ever happens. But…"

“But what?” Tamsin pressed.

“But I *am* saying that if you really feel you need to grieve over the breakup with Kendra, you should definitely grieve between Robyn’s legs.”

“Oh my god, you are so stupid!” Tamsin exclaimed.

Chapter 18

Three days went by, and they did so in a blur for Robyn.

She and her staff at Linden Gallery Cornwall had worked hard getting the space ready for the eventual delivery of Sasha's art, and now Robyn could plan for that milestone, as well as start making the final preparations needed for the vernissage—which was only 13 days away now—*and* the public opening, the day after.

But she'd tackle the logistics of all that on Monday. Right now, it was Friday, and she was ready for that bath she promised herself earlier in the week.

And wine. She was ready for wine, maybe even enough to feel on the edge of being drunk.

Of course, she needed to figure out her dinner plans for the evening also, but then determined that wouldn't be so hard. She was too knackered to consider cooking, which meant she would make do with one of the frozen meals she kept a supply of for such contingencies. It was pretty lame for a Friday night, especially being a young and attractive woman, but until she made some more friends here in Cornwall and developed a social life, it would have to do.

Turning onto Penhallow Lane, she also decided it would behove her to find out where all the gay women in this region of Britain were. Developing a dating life would reduce the number of *home-alone-with-a-frozen-meal* Friday nights in her future.

Right now, she personally knew a grand total of three gay women in all of Cornwall, and two of them were engaged to each other.

As her BMW approached her cottage, she saw the third.

Tamsin must have also just arrived home because the ginger was getting out of her car, dressed stylishly as Robyn knew was her wont.

She didn't know if anything would ever develop between her and Tamsin, but if it didn't, she needed to figure out how to meet other lesbians and possibly find herself a girlfriend.

She gave two short, friendly honks of the BMW's horn as she drove past Tamsin's driveway.

She and Tamsin hadn't seen each other since lunch on Tuesday. She'd had lunch with Lucien and Tina on Wednesday, and then the past two evenings, she had gotten home well past six o'clock, after Tamsin's Clio was already parked in her driveway.

"Hiya," she said, when she had gotten out of her car.

"Hey," Tamsin greeted. "Stalking me?"

"Yep," Robyn answered. "Even rented the cottage next to yours."

"That's next level," Tamsin retorted. "Anyway, you're home early this evening."

Robyn cocked an eyebrow. For some reason, it gave her a bit of a thrill to know Tamsin had noticed.

"Now who's stalking who?" she asked playfully.

Tamsin shrugged.

"Your posh car has a loud engine," she said. "It always disturbs my quiet time."

"Quiet time when you could be painting," Robyn pointed out.

Rolling her eyes, Tamsin said, "Oh my days, don't start that again!"

Robyn held up her hands.

"Relax, I won't," she promised. "Yet," she added, waggling her eyebrows. "Anyway, big plans tonight?"

Blonde plans?

"No, I'm boring," Tamsin said. "Staying in, cooking some fish I have for dinner, and watching telly. You?"

"I'm even more boring," Robyn said. "I'm not even cooking. I'll be microwaving a Sainsbury's lasagne."

Tamsin stared at her for a few seconds before looking down at her high-heeled feet.

"Sainsbury's lasagne is better than Tesco's at least," she said.

"Fair point…so I've got that going for me," Robyn conceded.

"But not better than my fish," Tamsin added, looking back up at her. She shrugged. "I've got plenty, so…"

Robyn swallowed.

"I couldn't impose like that," she said, in proper British form.

"Who's imposing?" Tamsin asked. "Neither of us have plans anyway, so why not?" She then smirked. "Besides, I've already had lunch with you the other day and so I know you're not a horrible person to have a meal with."

Robyn laughed.

"Such a sweet talker," she said snidely. "Anyway, will you let me bring the wine?"

"I *insist* you bring the wine," Tamsin replied. "But I hope you're not about to faint with hunger. I want to take a shower before I start cooking."

"Me too!" Robyn replied, having decided right there to change her bath plans into shower plans so as not to keep Tamsin waiting. Or herself. Suddenly, her night was looking up, and she didn't want to delay her enjoyment of it.

Robyn narrowed her eyes playfully.

"Let me guess…" she began, "…like all gingers you probably take, what, forty-five minutes in the shower?"

Tamsin's face took on a look of humorous indignation as she chuckled.

"Who are these fucked-up gingers you used to know?" she asked. She crossed her arms under her breasts. "I'll have you know that in an emergency, I can be in and out of the shower in less than ten minutes. This, however, does not constitute an emergency, so you need to give me twice that."

Robyn crossed her arms as well.

"Well, I need that much time too," she said. "So…I'll come over in…?"

"Come over in an hour," Tamsin told her.

Robyn thought that made sense.

The actual shower itself might only take fifteen or twenty minutes, and if they were men, that would be the end of the story.

But they were women, which meant the shower was merely one part of a ritual which would also include finding the right playlist to have playing during the shower; shaving; at least rinsing the hair—though Robyn intended on washing hers; drying the hair; putting on lotion; finding another playlist to have playing while carefully determining what to wear and while dressing; and putting some makeup back on their freshly cleaned faces.

If they were older and closer friends—just friends—half of those steps could be eliminated, particularly the makeup and the careful choosing of what to wear. But they were women who were brand-new friends, and as such, even an innocuous dinner such as what was planned, required more finesse in order for each of them to ensure that the other woman wouldn't feel she has the upper hand.

Add to this calculus that they were both lesbians, and a whole other dynamic was introduced.

"An hour it is," Robyn told her, smiling.

***

An hour later, Robyn, wearing a casual but flattering maxi dress with an ombré colour pattern to it, knocked on Tamsin's door. In her right hand, she was carrying a chilled bottle of white wine, the same bottle she had planned to knock back single-handedly when she thought her night would be a bath followed by a Sainsbury's lasagne.

When Tamsin opened the door, they both started laughing.

"Great minds," Tamsin said.

She was also wearing a maxi dress, and it took Robyn's breath away. It had a high waist sash which tied just under her breasts, making them seem even more prominent, and it was patterned in a playful tie-dye style, with colours that complemented her hair.

"You look really wonderful," Robyn told her, not caring if her voice was telegraphing the fact that her statement was more than just a friendly compliment; that it was, in fact, one gay woman telling another gay woman just how attractive she found her tonight.

"Thank you," Tamsin said. "So do you."

Robyn's clit began pulsing. Tamsin was looking her up and down, and it was as if Robyn could feel her eyes on the skin under her dress as they moved along her form.

Finally, Tamsin blinked rapidly and shook her head.

"So sorry!" she said. "Where are my manners? Please come in!" And she stood aside to let Robyn pass through the doorway.

Robyn, perhaps feeling a little emboldened by Tamsin's visual survey of her, said, "It's okay, I temporarily lost the power of speech when I saw you in that dress."

"That's the nicest thing anybody has said to me all week," Tamsin said, walking past Robyn and gesturing for her to follow. They were heading in the direction of the kitchen.

"Certainly not!" Robyn prodded.

In the kitchen, Tamsin picked up a wine glass from the counter.

"I started without you," she said, and then drained what remained of the white wine in the glass. She then took the bottle Robyn had brought, produced a corkscrew and another wine glass, and in moments had two full glasses poured.

"I'm exaggerating," Tamsin went on. "People have said nice things to me all week, but…"

"Only because they've had to, right?" Robyn guessed. "Like, just normal pleasantries."

"Exactly!" Tamsin said. "Cheers."

They touched glasses, the rims making a musical *tink*.

"Of course," Tamsin continued after taking a sip of the wine, "I'm not including the three blokes who told me how great my tits looked in various tops I wore this week."

Robyn raised her glass.

"Men…" she said. "Arguably the second best reason for women to be gay."

Tamsin laughed.

"And the first?" she asked.

Robyn put a pondering look on her face.

"Erm…doubling your wardrobe?" she offered.

Tamsin quirked an eyebrow.

"If that's a euphemism for oral sex, then I completely agree," she said.

They both laughed.

Robyn felt completely at ease here, doing this with Tamsin. At times—very briefly—she was able to ignore how beautiful the woman was and instead focus on how safe she felt with her, and how much she was enjoying getting to know her better.

"And on that note," Tamsin said, putting her wine glass down on the countertop, "I promised you dinner. I marinated the fillets overnight, so all they have to do is bake in the oven for twenty minutes, and while they're doing that, I can make the rice and green beans."

"And I will help," Robyn declared. The combination of the shower and Tamsin's company had revived her. She certainly felt energetic enough to do more than microwave a Sainsbury's lasagne. "Just tell me what you want me to do."

Tamsin sniggered. When she did so, Robyn realised that what she had just said could be taken in a way that had nothing to do with cooking.

Blushing, she added, "Cooking-wise, that is."

***

Tamsin proved to be an excellent dinner companion. She also, as it turned out, proved to be quite a good cook, which ticked off another box in her favour in Robyn's mind. She couldn't wait to get back home and tell Empress that.

During their meal, Tamsin gave her the rundown on life in sleepy little Tremont…

"Nothing much to bloody do except trivia night at the pub," she said. "So, if you're looking for excitement, you'll have to go to Newquay."

Robyn shook her head.

"I wouldn't say I'm looking for excitement," she said. "Although, I do love a good trivia night at the local. Do you go?"

Tamsin shrugged.

"Every now and then," she said. "Rylea and Darcie are on a team with some geezers; sometimes I join them. Apparently Mr. Trelawney—one of the geezers—thinks I'm smart enough to merit the occasional guest spot."

Robyn laughed.

"Anyway," she said, "I wouldn't mind having a social life, but I don't need to hit a rave every weekend. It's kind of why I picked Tremont to live in instead of Newquay. I wanted a nice, chill location for my home base."

"Oh, I assumed you picked Tremont because of all the lesbians," Tamsin said before taking a bite of her fish.

Robyn blinked.

"I'm sorry…?" she prodded.

Tamsin put an amused look on her face.

"You mean, you didn't know?" she asked.

"Know what?" Robyn pressed.

Tamsin laughed and rolled her eyes.

"Bloody lesbian central around here nowadays," she answered. "My friends Liz and Jemma even sell t-shirts in their shop that say that." She drew her hand across her chest. "'Lesbian Central' it says, right on the front."

"I had no idea," Robyn said, still processing this information. "And here I was wondering if perhaps I had met the only three other gay women in town."

"Hardly," Tamsin told her. "And I'm sure by now word has gotten out about the cute new gay girl in town, which means you can expect the buzzards to be circling."

Robyn looked to the heavens, as if on the lookout for the buzzards.

"I'm not sure I want that," she said. "I mean, a girlfriend would be lovely. But I could do without a ridiculous amount of unsolicited attention."

Tamsin started chuckling as she speared a couple of green beans with her fork.

"What?" Robyn asked.

Putting her fork down, Tamsin looked at her.

"Well, chances are you won't have to worry much about that after tonight," she answered. "But don't worry! That can all be fixed."

Arching an eyebrow, Robyn said, "I'm afraid I require a bit more clarification, please."

"So, this is a small town, yeah?" Tamsin began. "And chances are, at least one person on this street saw you come over here to mine tonight, dressed nicely. Which means, by tomorrow, the word around bloody Tremont will be that you and I are not only dating but also planning a honeymoon in Ibiza."

Robyn broke into laughter.

"Wow!" she exclaimed. "I think this is the least amount of work I've had to do to get a girlfriend. I mean, I've walked, what, ten yards from my front door to yours?"

Tamsin grinned.

"Usually I'm much more difficult to obtain," she said.

Robyn wanted this repartee to continue, because it seemed as if the path was only leading in one direction. As much as that excited her, and as much as she wanted that destination to be reached, she needed to know something first…

"So…" Robyn began, "can I ask you something?"

"Erm…sure," Tamsin replied in that guarded manner Robyn noticed she used whenever challenged with a question out of the blue.

Robyn took a sip of her wine, and then swirled the remaining contents around in her glass.

"I don't want to seem like I was being nosy—because I wasn't—but I live just next door, so it was kind of hard *not* to notice certain things. Anyway…whatever happened to that blonde?"

Tamsin coloured and reached for *her* wine glass. She took a long sip before answering.

"Kendra," she said.

Pretty name, Robyn considered, feeling an absurd flash of jealousy over this intel.

"She and I were seeing each other," Tamsin continued. "But now we're not."

"Was it serious?" Robyn asked.

Slowly, Tamsin shook her head.

"It had only been five weeks," she said.

Being a woman, Robyn took Tamsin's answer with a grain of salt. Women may, in fact, be the superior sex, she considered, but she also knew that they were prone to falling deeply in love very quickly. She'd done so herself—well before the five-weeks mark—and she'd also had girlfriends who swore they'd be with her for eternity after only a handful of dates.

But she decided to trust Tamsin when she said that, for her, five weeks with Kendra didn't constitute "serious."

"Good," she said, smiling. "Buuuuuut, I have another question."

Tamsin rolled her eyes.

"Bloody Sun reporter, you are," she said.

"Hey!" Robyn exclaimed, pointing her fork at her. "If I worked for a newspaper, you'd better believe it would be for the *Times!*"

"Sorry," Tamsin said with a smirk. "Ask your question."

Robyn took another sip of her wine. It wasn't for Dutch courage, it was to notice again the way Tamsin's eyes locked onto her lips whenever she did this. Tamsin had been doing that all night.

"Want to consider this our first date?" she asked, after swallowing her sip of wine.

She asked it breezily, ready to laugh it off just in case she had read the room wrong.

Tamsin stared at her.

"No, I don't think so," she eventually said.

Chapter 19

Tamsin wanted to laugh at Robyn's reaction. It was pure gold. A mixture of surprise, confusion and embarrassment, it affected her in the most delicious way because it made Robyn look even more beautiful.

What am I doing?

This still felt…weird. She and Kendra were history, sure, but recent history. She typically didn't jump right into a new romance with another woman so quickly, but then again, no one like Robyn had ever breezed into Tremont before and set up house right next door.

Add to that the fact that Robyn…

Well, Robyn got to her, exciting her on a level that went beyond her looks—which were considerable.

"Let's call this our second date," Tamsin said.

She did laugh this time when Robyn breathed out a sigh of relief and then followed that up by downing the rest of the wine in her glass. She silently held out her glass for a refill, which Tamsin happily provided.

"Oh my days," Robyn said, nodding her thanks when her glass was full again, "I thought I'd made a right arse of myself."

"Sorry," Tamsin said. "I probably should have led with that."

"You think?" Robyn retorted. "So…I take it our lunch together the other day was our first?"

Tamsin nodded.

Why not?

Ever since Robyn arrived at her cottage this evening, she had been unable to focus on much else other than how…*buzzy* she'd been feeling. It was as if there was an invisible current flowing between them in both directions.

It was a little frightening if she was honest with herself. Something in her spirit was telling her that she liked Robyn significantly more than any of the women she had been involved with recently, including Kendra.

What is it about her?

The sassiness had something to do with it, she knew. And that snarky sense of humour was another thing which turned Tamsin on. Like, a lot.

Robyn was also very clearly driven, professionally, and Tamsin found that next-level-hot. For Robyn, her job wasn't just a way to earn a paycheque. Being a gallerist helped define her because she had a passion for the world of art. Moreover, on that first night she was over here, the night of the cancelled exorcism, she had confessed to wanting to open her very own gallery one day.

So, she was a woman who, like herself, worked very hard at making sure she succeeded in her current situation, but who also had goals for bigger and better things—things she'd have to bust her arse to achieve.

Like me…

Her eyes widened.

Good lord, I want to date myself.

"Tamsin…is something wrong?" she heard Robyn asked. "Your eyes just did this thing…like you'd seen a ghost."

Tamsin blinked and then gave her guest a reassuring smile.

"No, nothing," she hurriedly said. "Everything is fine. I was just thinking…We're very much alike, and maybe that's why I want to get to know you better. You know, despite the fact that you park delivery trucks wherever the hell you'd like and potentially ruin other peoples' businesses."

Robyn rolled her eyes.

"Okay, first of all, *I* did not park the truck, those blokes did. Secondly, I just *love* how you make it seem as if the truck was parked right up against the door, preventing pensioners from getting in and booking holidays to bloody Majorca. Anyway, forget how silly you were being that day…"

"Silly?" Tamsin interrupted.

"Yes, silly," Robyn told her. "Let's forget about that for the time being…"

Robyn leaned forward, with her elbows on the dining table. Tamsin felt that invisible current between them growing stronger, making her pulse quicken and her nipples harden. It didn't help that Robyn had a predatory look in her lovely eyes, a look which Tamsin's centre took notice of, because stirrings of anticipatory pleasure began swirling beneath her mound.

"How *much* better do you want to get to know me?" Robyn purred.

Fuck, this is moving fast!

Tamsin did a quick self-diagnostic, assessing how she felt about that.

Almost instantly, the report came back…

More than fine with this!

Without giving her brain a chance to overthink, she also leaned forward, put her left hand on the back of Robyn's neck and pressed her lips against hers.

There was no tentative phase to this kiss, the way there usually was when a first kiss begins. As soon as their lips touched, she and Robyn cranked the intensity up to *Full*, their lips sliding and moving hungrily against one another's, their tongues already entwining.

This was *not* how Tamsin envisioned her night going.

She had intended on cooking dinner for herself and then spending a good portion of the night on her laptop, plugging Xplr on social media. She especially wanted to put together a video montage of—as it turns out—bloody Majorca, because she had booked a young couple on a three-week holiday there for their honeymoon.

But this was better…

Robyn moaned as Tamsin kissed her, which only made Tamsin wetter and her clit pulse even faster. She only hoped…

Reluctantly breaking the kiss, she kept her lips close to Robyn's and said, "Bloody hell…you need to tell me now if this is as far as it's going tonight. Please."

"Fuck you, it's going way further than this," Robyn murmured before recapturing Tamsin's lips for another passionate kiss.

Tamsin cut this one short, however. Kissing over a tabletop probably looked fabulous on an episode of *Normal People,* but it was awkward as fuck, and it didn't let her feel any of Robyn's body against hers.

She stood up as soon as their lips separated, Robyn doing the same. Coming around the small table, Tamsin pressed her guest against the wall, her mouth finding Robyn's again.

This time, the kiss was accompanied by Robyn entangling her fingers in Tamsin's hair, and Tamsin grabbing the fabric of her dress at the waist and gripping it tightly, pulling their pelvises together.

"I said," Robyn breathed out when they broke for air, "that I want this to go *much* further than this."

That did it.

Tamsin's pussy *clenched*, and she grunted as she felt thick arousal flow out from between her folds, making her knickers even more soaked.

In the next instant, she brought her right hand to Robyn's pelvis and began pushing the soft fabric of her maxi dress between her legs, holding the woman's eyes with her own.

"Fuck!" Robyn muttered.

Tamsin felt her spread her thighs a bit, and so she pushed the dress fabric even more until she was able to rub Robyn's centre over it and the underwear she felt on the other side.

"Oh god…fuck, Tamsin," Robyn gasped, not breaking eye contact. But that didn't last long.

Though there were layers of fabric between Tamsin's fingers and Robyn's sex, they were thin layers and Tamsin easily located the hard button that was her clit. She pressed against it firmly, causing Robyn's eyes to flutter shut, and her to mewl and pull Tamsin closer.

Ghosting Robyn's ear, Tamsin asked (though she already knew the answer), "Far enough for tonight?"

"No!" Robyn grunted. "Oh fuck…I'm already so close!"

Tamsin was sorely tempted to take Robyn all the way to the finish line. There was something so incredibly sexy about making a woman come when she was still fully clothed, about the skill required to make her overcome being dressed and bringing her to release.

But she quickly decided that what was even sexier was *tasting* a woman when she came—especially in this case, when it would be the first time making Robyn come.

She pulled away and immediately took Robyn's hand.

"Come here!" she demanded breathlessly. She was so excited with anticipation, her mouth was starting to go dry, and so she licked her lips and swallowed as she led Robyn to the stairs.

They hurried up them. In the bedroom, Tamsin helped Robyn lift her dress over her head.

What was revealed was stunning.

Robyn's lithe and toned form was that of a woman who took care of herself, a body of power and femininity. Her full breasts were harnessed in a cute lilac-coloured lace bralette, and her sex was covered by rather plain blue cotton knickers which were displaying a prominent wet spot between her thighs.

"Bloody hell, you're sexy!" Tamsin uttered, needing to lick her lips again.

She pulled aside one cup of Robyn's bralette, freeing a dark nipple whose areola was as big around as a 50p coin. The nipple was already rock hard. She'd been fantasising about these ever since lunch on Tuesday, when she'd seen them poking against the fabric of Robyn's top. She lowered her head and sucked it into her mouth, circling her tongue over the elongated and rigid tip. Robyn moaned as she did this, her breath ragged.

After a few moments, Tamsin freed the other breast, repeating her oral attentions on that one, savouring it, sucking on the nipple even harder than the first one, noting how the pace of Robyn's breathing increased.

She released it with a pop and then pulled the bralette off her lover, over her head.

"You now," Robyn said, her voice practically pleading.

Tamsin grinned devilishly.

She knew what Robyn wanted. Any woman she ended up in a bedroom with wanted the same thing.

That moment.

That moment when her own breasts were revealed.

However, over the years, Tamsin had learned that it was often quite fun to keep *that moment* away from her playmates, and she planned on doing so with Robyn now.

Besides, she could smell Robyn's arousal. She *needed* to taste her…

"Patience, beautiful," she whispered, already guiding her to the bed. At the foot of it, she kissed Robyn again, but this time, she took hold of her knickers and started pulling them down. Robyn looped her arms around her neck as she did this, and then Tamsin became aware of her dutifully stepping out of the underwear once they had fallen to the floor.

"It's time," Tamsin whispered when the kiss ended. "Lay down."

With her arms still looped around Tamsin's neck, Robyn smirked.

"So bossy," she said.

Tamsin cocked an eyebrow.

"Shall I say 'please?'" she asked.

"Absolutely not," Robyn told her.

She pulled away from Tamsin and got on the mattress. She seemed to be able to read her host's mind because when she laid down, she did so with her legs open and her feet flat on the sheets, near the foot of the bed, unabashedly revealing herself.

Tamsin let out a breath at seeing Robyn's pussy exposed, waiting for her. Unlike herself, her neighbour was completely shaved, and her nether lips were parted and glistening with arousal which caught the lights in the room, letting Tamsin know just how wet she was.

In her knickers, Tamsin's clit was a jackhammer.

"I think that deserves a bit of a reward," she said. She undid her dress's sash and then crossed her arms, grabbing the fabric on either side of her and lifting the dress off.

"Oh my fucking god!" Robyn said, her eyes wide, staring at Tamsin.

There was nothing spectacular about the underwear Tamsin had chosen to put on after her shower earlier because she'd had no idea that what was happening now, would happen. But—and this was one thing she was uber-cocky about—it didn't matter. With her body, any underwear looked jaw-droppingly amazing on her, even the workaday plain white bra she had on now, accompanied by nude-coloured cotton boyshorts.

If she wasn't already, Robyn was definitely under her spell now.

Now to keep her there...

Tamsin dropped to her knees at the foot of the bed, took hold of Robyn's narrow hips and brought her face close to the warmth between her thighs.

She ran her nose along the length of Robyn's pussy, inhaling deeply, letting the woman's scent fill her skull, her own pussy practically streaming now.

When she had inhaled all she could, she then let out a slow exhale, making sure the current of air from her nostrils flowed over Robyn's swollen clit.

"Oh fucking Jesus!" Robyn moaned.

Tamsin watched her clit jump and quiver, as if the tiny button was doing all it could to get her attention.

Well, it worked.

Tamsin couldn't wait any longer.

Starting at the dripping opening, she licked her way slowly up Robyn's pussy, between the folds, her eyes rolling back in her head at how delicious the woman was, and how completely her essence coated her tongue. When she reached the clit, she circled it with the tip of her tongue, drawing out moans and squeals from Robyn who now had a hand in Tamsin's hair.

"*Fuuuuuuuck!*" Robyn cried out. "*Pleeeeeease! Fuuuuuuuck!*"

Still circling the clit, Tamsin quirked her eyebrow.

Well, since she said 'please…'

Wrapping her arms around Robyn's waist as a pre-emptive strategy to keep her under control, Tamsin swiped the flat of the underside of her tongue over Robyn's clit rhythmically, firmly, and rapidly.

Robyn's orgasm struck almost immediately.

"*NNNNNNNNNGGGGHHHH!*" she grunted a moment before she screamed, "*YESSSSSSSSSSS!*"

Her hips started bucking with the release, but Tamsin's arms minimised the disruption to what she was doing that this might have otherwise caused, allowing her to bring her tongue back to Robyn's opening in order to lick all the sweetness that was now streaming out of her.

Chapter 20

Robyn knew that had been a fast one, but she didn't care. She was certain Tamsin wouldn't think any less of her. Besides, it was her fault for being so damn sexy.

Honestly, she had almost made her come downstairs, in the dining room, with all of her bloody clothes on!

Now, on the downslope of her climax, Robyn was looking at that fiery red hair between her legs as Tamsin's skilled mouth helped ease her down from this release, licking up her come and moaning delightedly as she did it.

She wanted Tamsin to stay down there all night. She wanted to beg, demand, cajole, whatever…anything to get her to remain where she was, getting her off over and over again. And she'd watch every second of it—at least whenever the pleasures didn't force her eyes shut. She'd watch that red hair, and the gorgeous face under it, eating her out until she couldn't take it anymore and either passed out or pleaded for it to end.

But she was also desperate to fuck Tamsin…

By this point, also, she *needed* to see her nude.

Gingers had always been her weakness, yes. For other women, it was blondes. For her friend Cheryl, it was women who coloured their hair blue, for some reason.

For her…red was the colour.

But she had also always had a weakness for large breasts.

It wasn't a requirement by any means. In fact, most of her past girlfriends had breasts smaller than her own large-C cups, but it was still a weakness for her.

Which meant Tamsin was practically a goddess.

A goddess who had tantalised her by removing her dress and displaying her underwear-clad form just before eating her out, and when Robyn had orgasmed, the vision of that white bra straining to hold Tamsin's breasts in check flashed through her mind and made the pulsing of her clit during the climax so much stronger.

"Get up here!" she now ordered breathlessly, her pussy starting to experience the aftershocks of her climax.

Tamsin poked her tongue inside her opening one last time, making Robyn gasp, but then she obeyed, crawling up from between her legs until she was topping her, Robyn feeling the mass of Tamsin's bra-clad breasts pressing down onto her chest.

Robyn kissed her, tasting herself, revelling in it, the walls in her passage responding by fluttering, wanting more stimulation. While they kissed, her hands found the back clasp of Tamsin's bra and began unhooking it. When it was undone, Tamsin sat herself up astride Robyn's waist. With a self-assured smirk, she then pulled the straps off her shoulders and down her arms, freeing her girls and then tossing the bra to the floor.

Robyn began shivering with excitement.

"Oh my god, I'm going to fucking lose my mind!" she muttered.

Tamsin chuckled.

"You are so silly," she said.

Her breasts were stunning, like the rest of her. Full and teardrop shaped, they were capped-off with large nipples of an almost-not-there pale pink, darker at the tips, which were pointing proudly outwards.

Reaching up with both hands, Robyn cupped the bottoms of them, letting their weight settle into her hands. She gave a little grunt of pleasure as her pussy—reacting to this—trembled and pushed out a stream of come from her still-flooded passage.

"I'm sorry," she muttered softly, suddenly feeling guilty.

"For…?" Tamsin asked, looking down at her.

Robyn was able to wrench her eyes away from the perfection of Tamsin's breasts to meet her eyes.

"For making such a big deal about your boobs," she said. "I'm sorry. You're more than spectacular boobs, I know that, it's just…bloody hell."

Tamsin took hold of Robyn's wrists and removed her hands from her breasts. She then leaned forward. Robyn licked her lips as now, Tamsin's right nipple was over her mouth.

"Hush," Tamsin cooed. "And show me how much you love my boobs."

With that, Robyn took the hard nipple into her mouth, using her left hand to squeeze the breast as she sucked on it.

She pulled hard on it with her mouth, eliciting pleasurable groans from Tamsin above her. She was conscious of how small her hand felt in comparison to the mass it was fondling, and it made her suck more rapidly because of how much that fact turned her on.

Experimentally, she gave the diamond-hard nipple a soft bite. The sound of delight which Tamsin gave in response to this told Robyn all she needed to know and so she bit harder.

"Fuck, yes…!" Tamsin purred, and so Robyn repeated it. She then released the nipple from her mouth and bit down on the pillowy softness of the flesh just below it, not caring if she left a mark. She wanted to leave a mark, in fact. She didn't know yet what this thing with her and Tamsin was yet, but if Tamsin had plans to fuck another woman in the next couple of days, at least that woman would see evidence that someone else had gotten to her first.

With the right breast taken care of—for now—Robyn lavished the same attentions to the left one, and by the time she had suckled and bit that nipple, and then sunk her teeth into softness of that breast, leaving another mark, her pussy was quivering strongly again and her clit pounding.

She needed to go down on Tamsin.

Now.

Utilising all her upper body strength, she pushed against Tamsin and rolled her over onto her back. Topping her now, she kissed her deeply and while she did so, Tamsin brought one of her thighs up between Robyn's legs, pressing it against her centre.

"Mmmmmmmph!" Robyn grunted at the contact. She immediately began rocking her pelvis against the surface Tamsin was providing, almost helpless not to. Selfishly, she wanted to come again, to release so hard and so liquidly that Tamsin's thigh would be covered with her essence. But she managed to pull herself back from such greedy thoughts, wanting instead to provide pleasure to the woman she was with.

She pulled her wet and hyper-excited pussy away from Tamsin's leg and, before she could change her mind, immediately repositioned herself so her head was between her lover's legs.

There was the small matter of the boyshorts which needed removing first, knickers that were showing a large damp spot which was making the thin cotton cling more closely to Tamsin's sex.

Robyn licked this wet area, getting her first taste of Tamsin. With her lips, she grabbed the cotton and sucked on it, extracting more of the trapped liquid.

"Unnnh!....Unnnh!...Unnnh!" Tamsin moaned, the sound of a woman anticipating the pleasure yet to come.

And Robyn was anxious to get to those pleasures. Having tasted Tamsin's arousal filtered through her underwear, she now wanted to drink directly from the source.

Taking hold of the waistband of the knickers, she started pulling them off. She didn't get far before she gasped, her clit *thrumming* now.

"Oh my god, I fucking love this!" Robyn mewled. "Even your mound is ginger!"

This was true. Tamsin had a neatly manicured triangle of reddish hairs, pointing towards her sex. Robyn hurriedly pulled the boyshorts the remainder of the way off, her eyes never leaving the hairs at the apex of Tamsin's thighs. When the underwear was thus dispatched, Tamsin opened herself entirely to Robyn, her legs spread wide, and Robyn placed her head back where it belonged.

She began by kissing Tamsin's pubes, noticing how soft those ginger hairs felt against her lips. She then started licking them, making them wet with her saliva, feeling this odd need to show her appreciation for this visual treat.

Tamsin being a ginger was sexy enough.

Tamsin also having large breasts upped her level of sexiness to a stratospheric level.

But Tamsin also having a sexy little ginger bush rocketed her sexiness straight to the Moon.

Beneath Tamsin's mound, all was shaved smooth, and Robyn finally started tasting her, running her tongue along all that smoothness, sucking on her dark-pink folds, teasing her clit with a few swipes before poking her tongue into her warm opening, loving how it was instantly covered with sticky arousal which she then swallowed happily.

All the while, Tamsin gave voice to her delight…oftentimes swearing, sometimes squealing Robyn's name, other times giving low, drawn-out moans.

Robyn wanted to take her time—Tamsin tasted that good—but she also wanted to make her come, and then lick up the results afterwards.

She clamped her lips onto Tamsin's swollen clit, loving how the hairs on her mound brushed against her nose in this position. She then showed no mercy, swiping her tongue firmly and rapidly over the excited nub.

"OH FUCK!" Tamsin shouted, fisting her fingers in Robyn's hair.

Robyn swiped even faster.

"*Robyn!...Bloody fucking hell!...Don't stop!...Keep going!...Don't stop!...*"

Robyn had no intention of stopping. She was going to make Tamsin come hard and then make her come hard again.

Without ceasing the actions of her tongue, her fingers found Tamsin's pubic hairs and began pulling gently on them—not enough to hurt, just enough to add a little spice to everything else she was doing.

Plus, she just fucking loved that hair!

"*Holy FUCK!*" Tamsin shouted. "*Aaaaaaaaaaaaah...I'm COMIIIIIING! NNNNNNNNNNNGHOhhhhhfuuuuuuuuuuuuuuuck!*"

"Mmmmm," Robyn murmured, feeling Tamsin's vulva come alive against her chin, throbbing as her pussy came undone.

With the orgasm firmly in control of Tamsin, Robyn released her clit, placed her hands under her ass, and pushed upwards slightly, giving her mouth a better angle with which to cover her winking opening and drink what was streaming out of it.

Chapter 21

It didn't even occur to Tamsin to stop what was happening.

As soon as her orgasm crested, her mind once more became lucid enough to realise that Robyn already had her well on the way to another one.

This time, fingers were inside her, curling upwards, stroking her g-spot as her inner walls—still fluttering from the climax she had just experienced—clutched at them.

Simultaneously, her clit was being edged and then sucked…edged and then sucked…and then finally just sucked.

She grabbed her breasts, twisting her nipples, and then let out a guttural cry as she came a second time, the remnants of the first one feeding this new one, making it potent.

"*Oh my fucking GAAAAAAAAAHD!*" she shouted, mashing her boobs together and pulling on both nipples as waves of pleasure consumed her.

It was a particularly wet one, this orgasm. She could feel how flooded her passage was and how the contractions of the climax were forcing her come out onto Robyn's waiting face.

Robyn certainly didn't complain, however. Throughout the wild ride of coming this second time, her neighbour…

Now lover?

Now girlfriend?

…never took her mouth away, licking up whatever her body was producing.

Finally, though, it ended.

Giving her trimmed bush a kiss, Robyn then came up to lay beside her.

They lay on the bed side by side, on their backs, both of them breathing audibly, Tamsin, of course, breathing a bit harder.

"That was fun," she managed to say once she felt she was able to speak steadily.

"Mm-hm," Robyn agreed.

Tamsin turned her head to the left to look at her.

The woman really was spectacular, a true beauty and absurdly sexy. There was nothing about her that Tamsin wished was different, bigger, or smaller. From the standpoint of looks, Robyn was a dreamgirl.

But all of them had been, hadn't they?

Tamsin was used to having spectacular-looking girlfriends because she was a spectacular-looking woman. Such women were who she pulled, even without trying. Yet all of them were now in the past. All because of the *Sex Thing*.

Robyn turned to look at her.

"Penny for your thoughts," she murmured.

Tamsin was tempted. But she decided that *When will you leave me?* was too heavy a thought to share with Robyn on this, their first night together.

However…

She resolved to do something different this time with Robyn. Call it an experiment of sorts. Just not tonight.

Maybe tomorrow…

"I was genuinely thinking of how bloody beautiful you are," Tamsin said, settling for telling Robyn half of the truth.

She also realised that, despite two great orgasms, she was *now* thinking of…

Tamsin rolled on top of Robyn, making the other woman gasp.

"Open," she instructed, flicking her eyes downward quickly to indicate what she meant.

Robyn spread her legs and then Tamsin snaked her arm and hand between their bodies, found the other woman's pussy and entered it with two fingers. It was easy. Robyn was soaked.

Robyn's eyes clouded over with desire at this penetration, Tamsin felt hers clouding over as well, at feeling how utterly liquid Robyn's vagina was.

With an adjustment to her hand's position, she was able to press the crook of her thumb against Robyn's clit and rock it side to side, causing Robyn to make adorable little mewls of pleasure.

"I want to sleep with you, Robyn," Tamsin purred, ghosting her lips with her own. "Please stay the night."

She wanted that. It wasn't that she missed having Kendra beside her in bed. In fact, she was discovering that she wasn't missing Kendra at all. It also wasn't that she was missing having *any* woman beside her in bed.

It was that she really wanted *Robyn* beside her in bed.

The tip of Robyn's tongue traced Tamsin's bottom lip.

"Convince me," she growled.

Tamsin's clit went *bam-bam-bam!*

"Yeah?" she challenged.

"*Nnngh*…that's right," Robyn told her through clenched teeth. "Fucking convince me!"

"Yes, ma'am," Tamsin replied.

She withdrew the two fingers she had inside Robyn's tight vagina and instantly replaced them with three, Robyn drawing in a hissed breath as her opening stretched to accommodate the added digit.

Tamsin began fucking her, not gently, but hard, thrusting the fingers in deep, pulling them almost all of the way out, and then slamming them back in, making sure the crook of her thumb pounded against her clit each time.

She felt Robyn's arousal spraying out as she fucked her, heard the wet, squelching sounds of her pussy caused by the motion of her hand, felt how hard and swollen her clit was every time her hand touched it.

Robyn put both hands on the sides of Tamsin's face and kissed her forcefully, grunting into the kiss as Tamsin continued thrusting into her with her fingers.

No more than a moment later…

Robyn squealed without breaking their kiss, and Tamsin knew she was tipping over the edge. Sure enough, Robyn began bucking beneath her and Tamsin felt her fingers being squeezed rhythmically by her vagina at the same time a gush of come spurted out.

"*Oh CHRIIIIIIIIIIIIST!*" Robyn shouted, so loudly that it forced Tamsin to spare a thought on whether or not her bedroom window was shut, and if anyone happened to be walking by. "*Fucking hell…Yes, I'll stay with you tonight! Oh fuck, YES, I'LL FUCKING STAY WITH YOU!....NNNGH!*"

***

When the spasming of Robyn's vagina lessened, Tamsin withdrew her fingers from the warm tightness of her passage and then lay down beside her.

She looked at her fingers. They were covered with Robyn's juices, and as she held them up, a couple of slow drips rolled down the back of her hand.

"Goodness, that was a big one," Robyn muttered.

"Indeed," Tamsin said. "Hey…"

When she noticed Robyn turn her head towards her, she used her fingers to paint her right nipple with the woman's come, until it was glistening and streaky with it.

Robyn gasped.

"Oh fuck," she whispered. "That is so fucking hot! Yes, please!"

She rolled over, topping Tamsin and immediately began sucking her come off the nipple, sending tingling thrills through Tamsin's breast and making her moan. She placed those same fingers in her mouth and while Robyn cleaned her nipple, she cleaned the fingers thoroughly, wanting all of what Robyn left behind on her hand, in her mouth.

She felt a sharp smack on her hip and even though this was hers and Robyn's first time together like this, she instantly knew what Robyn wanted and so she spread her legs.

Sure enough, she was penetrated by fingers.

"*Unnnnngh!*" she groaned at how good it felt, and she now grabbed Robyn's ass with both hands, digging her short nails into the soft flesh, to which her lover responded by biting and pulling on her nipple.

"Take me, take me, take me," she whispered, and when Robyn complied, Tamsin knew she wouldn't last long.

A minute later, as she was coming, letting herself yell out her pleasure, she wondered why this orgasm was hitting so much harder, making her feel as if her very bones would shatter.

When it was all over, she and Robyn once more lay side by side on the mattress, looking up at the ceiling. When she had recovered enough to speak, she said, "I'm so glad you moved in next door."

Robyn giggled.

"So am I," she said. "I mean, you are *slightly* annoying with your demands that *no one* park on the kerb in front of your travel agency, but I do like you nonetheless."

Tamsin smirked.

"Well, despite being a toffee-nosed twat who drives a posh car and buys expensive Dutch furniture, I like you also."

Robyn sighed.

"My car is not posh!" she stated. "Anyway, speaking of next door, I should go and get some things for tonight, since someone asked me to stay—"

"And then convinced you to do so," Tamsin interrupted.

"Sooooo…" Robyn began but left it hanging.

Tamsin turned her head to look at her.

"So what?" she asked.

"Well, I know it's dark out already," Robyn answered, "but…I mean…should I be extra stealthy when I return? Bad enough me coming over just for dinner has us planning a honeymoon in Ibiza; can you imagine what the gossip mongers will come up with seeing me come *back* over, but this time wearing pyjamas and fuzzy slippers?"

Tamsin howled laughter.

"I will *pay* you actual money to walk over here dressed like that!" she exclaimed. "It'll show those bloody busybodies that I don't give a shite what they think."

"Mm, I like that about you," Robyn said.

That simple declaration warmed Tamsin's soul, but before she could respond appropriately, Robyn rolled to her left, kissed her quickly and got out of the bed.

"I'll take a shower before I come back over," she said as she headed towards the en suite, "but I'm just going to tidy up a bit down there before I leave, if you don't mind."

"Take your time," Tamsin told her, watching her walk and admiring the perfection of her bum.

When Robyn was behind the closed loo door, she couldn't help chuckling softly.

Wow! That actually happened!

She ran the tip of her left index finger over her still-hard right nipple, circling it slowly, remembering every detail about Robyn, especially her pussy and how it tasted, and everything they had just done together. But then she stopped, surprised at how quickly and powerfully her centre was responding. Despite three orgasms, it was still feeling revved up and tingly, ready for more action, and she could feel her inner walls swelling again.

She blinked.

Three orgasms…

Robyn had gotten her off three times.

For fuck's sake, when was the last time that happened?

The answer, of course, was *never.*

Usually, if—*if!*—she had a second orgasm during sex, she would indicate that she was done for the time being, ready to do *anything* else. This was why she always tried to make any sexual activity front-heavy with pleasing her *partner* multiple times so that once she tapped out after her first climax, they'd have little cause to complain.

Well…except they *did* complain, she realised. They complained by breaking up with her.

Yet, Robyn had given her two quick orgasms with her mouth, and she *still* wanted things to continue, which was how she ended up fucking Robyn with her fingers and then…

She had enticed Robyn into fucking her also, by doing that thing with Robyn's come and her nipple—which was a cool trick, she decided, and one she needed to remember—leading to her third climax.

"And what else did I want to do tonight?" she asked herself so softly that it wouldn't carry into the loo.

Some kind of vid about…something. Right? Was it about Spain?

She heard the toilet flush and then the sink running. Moments later, Robyn emerged from the en suite in all her spectacular nudity. Tamsin's clit took notice and began beating in time with her heart.

Calm down, little girl, calm down, she chided it.

Robyn dressed quickly and then came over to the bed, knelt beside it, and gave Tamsin a lingering kiss. Almost immediately, Tamsin wanted to take it *well* beyond kissing.

What is going on with me?

"Shall I just head over when I'm ready?" Robyn asked her.

Tamsin nodded.

"Please," she answered. "Interested in watching some telly with me before bed?"

"Sounds great," Robyn said, standing up. "Be back soon."

Tamsin got out of bed to clean herself up as well, and when she was done, she put on her pyjamas—a dark-green silk set with black piping. She went braless beneath the button-up top, feeling that it was safe to say *that* bridge had been crossed with Robyn. Besides, she wanted her girls to breathe. Having a chest like hers meant hardly ever going braless except in the privacy of her own home. She envied women who had small enough breasts to be able to step out in public without a bra, and still not break any local decency laws.

Tea would be nice…

She wondered if Robyn would like some too. If so, she'd wait until she returned before putting the kettle on.

Downstairs, she found her phone in the kitchen, where she had left it, and was about to send Robyn a text, asking about her desire for tea when she stopped and gasped in disbelief.

I don't have her bloody number!

She had actually just had sex with a woman whose mobile number she didn't have! That was a new one! And it made her laugh out loud as she felt herself blushing scarlet.

Chapter 22

Entering her cottage a few moments after leaving Tamsin's, Robyn spied Empress curled up on the sofa in the living room. The cat raised its head to see who it was entering her domain, and the narrow-eyed glare she gave Robyn seemed to suggest that she had believed—as she perhaps believed daily—that she had seen the last of humans.

"Guess whaaaaaa-uuuuut!" Robyn said in a singsong voice, hurrying over to the sofa and scooping up Empress before the cat had a chance to get away. "Me and the giiiin-*ger*!"

She buried her face in Empress soft fur.

"Whose name is Tamsin, by the way," Robyn informed her pet. "Have I told you that? I can't remember."

Empress started sniffing Robyn's hand very intently, as if picking up the scent of a stranger.

Robyn smiled down at the white furball. She had washed her hands in Tamsin's en suite, but it wasn't as if she had been scrubbing for surgery. No doubt, to a cat's sensitive nose, traces of Tamsin still remained.

The most intimate traces.

At that thought, Robyn, blushing, put the cat down and stood up.

"That's not for you!" she chided the animal. "Anyway, I'm invited next door for an adult sleepover," she added as she walked towards the stairs. The cat meowed and followed her, evidently still intrigued by the new scents her human was bearing. "No cats allowed."

In her bedroom, she stepped into her wardrobe and placed her hands on her hips, trying to decide what to bring next door.

It would be Saturday tomorrow, but she didn't know how much time she would have with Tamsin after they both woke up. For all she knew, the ginger had plans. For that matter, *she* had plans...of sorts. She had a notion of going to a local garden centre to buy some houseplants now that she was properly settled in the cottage, but those were loose plans, susceptible to change should she and Tamsin come up with other ideas.

"I shouldn't get too ahead of myself, however," Robyn said, scrutinising her casualwear. She didn't know exactly *what* she and

Tamsin were yet, and she shouldn't take Tamsin's request for her to spend the night as a signal that they were now a couple. Like, officially. As in, Darcie and Rylea making lunch plans one day, and one of them saying, "Shall we invite Robyn and Tamsin?"

Okay, so she'd play it cool with regards to tomorrow. To that end, she chose clothes—jeans, a long-sleeved fitted tee, and a sweater to wear over the tee in case it was a bit chilly—that would be perfect for either the garden centre or hanging out with Tamsin.

"Now, before you start thinking I'm some kind of slut," Robyn said to Empress as she took the selected items, tossed them on the bed, and started undressing for her shower, "can I just say that what happened was pretty much inevitable. I mean, there has just been this…*pull* between us since we met."

Out of her dress now, she stopped and considered what she had just told the cat.

"Okay, maybe not *since* we met," she amended, taking off her bra. It could be worn again tomorrow, and so she added it to the items she was going to pack. "I mean, when I first met her, I thought she was a meddlesome cow. A *cute* meddlesome cow, but a cow nonetheless."

She shucked off her knickers and walked them to the hamper.

After arranging her hair into a tight ballet bun, she showered quickly. While doing so, as she washed her vulva, she couldn't help feeling a bit of regret that she was scrubbing away Tamsin's touches.

But she smiled when she considered that, with any luck, Tamsin's fingerprints would be all over her sex again quite soon.

***

"Don't judge!" Robyn scolded Empress, who was looking at her and definitely judging. "Besides, she said she'd pay me. Be a good girl while I'm gone."

With that, Robyn opened the front door and stepped out into the night.

Typical for Cornwall (or anywhere in England, for that matter), now that the sun was several hours gone, it was quite nippy, despite it being summertime, but she didn't have far to go.

Penhallow Lane was quiet. It was getting on to nine p.m., and so she figured that for the most part, sleepy little Tremont was shut down for the night. Perhaps that pub she'd heard about, the Ladle and…Something, was still open, but she was willing to wager that most everyone else in town was buttoned up in their homes, not to be seen again until tomorrow.

Of course, she was also willing to wager there was a good chance a nosy neighbour or two, hearing her door shut and then her scraping footsteps, would peek between their blinds to see who on earth was out and about at this hour. It made her smile thinking it would reinforce the cat burglar hypothesis.

Moreover, considering what she was wearing, it would probably reinforce the honeymoon-in-Ibiza hypothesis as well.

When Tamsin opened her door a few moments later, she burst into laughter.

"Oh my days," she said, "I love that you did this!"

Robyn smiled and turned around, giving Tamsin the full 360.

She was wearing her pyjamas and fuzzy slippers, just as they had discussed earlier.

"I figure doing this is worth about two quid," she said.

"I'll buy you a cuppa at The Bean tomorrow," Tamsin told her.

"Excellent," Robyn said. "Now, let me in, it's bloody cold out here!"

"I was about to make some tea," her host said.

"Oh, you're a star," Robyn replied, placing her tote bag containing tonight's overnight essentials (including an extra pair of knickers just in case the ones she was wearing now ending up becoming…unwearable) and tomorrow's clothes on the floor. "Love your pjs, by the way."

Green was such a lovely colour on Tamsin, as it was on all gingers. What's more, Robyn's trained eyes told her that Tamsin's breasts were braless under the button-up pyjama shirt she had on. Reflexively, she licked her lips, but decided against pushing Tamsin up against the nearest wall and ravishing her right now.

They'd had amazing sex earlier, true, but perhaps Tamsin was ready for some quiet time now, which Robyn was fine with. After all, they had kind of put the cart before the horse, hadn't they? Sex and now a sleepover, all without really understanding what it was they were each seeking from the other.

Whether that would happen tonight, she had no idea, but the point was, at this stage she didn't want Tamsin thinking she was some kind of sex-crazed lunatic who only wanted her for her body.

Sure, she was somewhat sex-crazed—she *really* enjoyed fucking. YOLO and all that.

Lunatic was up for debate, although her younger brother would probably say the book has been closed on that discussion, and not in her favour.

And Tamsin's body was…well, *Jesus-fucking-Christ*-level hot, but Robyn really was drawn to her for more than that and really *did* want to get to know her better.

Still in the entryway, Tamsin leaned closer to Robyn and inhaled deeply.

"You smell great," she said.

Robyn felt her nipples harden.

"Thanks," she said. "New bodywash."

Tamsin's eyes became afire with what Robyn interpreted as lust, but just as quickly they reverted back to normal.

"Erm…how about that tea?" Tamsin asked quickly.

Bugger!

Robyn guessed that Tamsin probably had performed the same mental gymnastics she had just done a few moments ago. All that stuff related to not appearing like a sex-crazed lunatic who only want her for her body.

Robyn wanted to tell her, however, that sex-crazed lunatics were exactly what she was into, and as far as being wanted only for her body…well, who was she kidding? *All* women yearned to be wanted for their bodies to at least *some* degree. It was why the entire fashion industry existed, and why women bought what they were selling. In any case, if Tamsin declared right now that she only wanted her for her body, would she pout?

No.

They walked to the kitchen together. In there, Tamsin flicked on a glass electric kettle which had blue LED lights that came on, illuminating the water.

"What kind of tea would you like?" Tamsin asked.

"What do you have?" Robyn prodded.

Tamsin cocked an eyebrow and smirked. She opened a cabinet near the kettle.

Robyn gasped.

The cabinet contained what looked to be every single tea available for sale in the United Kingdom.

"Well!" she exclaimed, approaching the cabinet so she could better see the selections. "When the zombie apocalypse happens and normal society shuts down, I'll know where I can still get a cuppa. Anyway, considering the hour, I think this one will do nicely."

This one was a decaf vanilla-chai. She loved vanilla anything and had never tried this particular tea before.

"Excellent choice," Tamsin said, taking the box from Robyn and then proceeding to take two mugs off a mug rack. She then chuckled. "This reminds me," she went on, "I don't have your number." Turning to face Robyn, she then added, "I mean, unless you don't want me to have it."

Robyn blinked.

"Why wouldn't I want you to have my number?" she asked. "I expect my girlfriend to have my number."

Bugger!

Blushing, she tried to come up with a way of walking back that last statement, but she knew it was useless to even try.

"Sorry!" she said. "My mouth sometimes speaks before my brain has given it clearance to do so. Anyway, sorry if the *girlfriend* label isn't appropriate in our case. And if it's not, I'm totally fine with that!"

Tamsin crossed her arms and leaned against the counter.

She shrugged.

"I mean, why not?" she asked. "I *do* like you and would find myself in a jealous rage if I found out you were bloody seeing someone else."

Robyn laughed, but her clit also pulsed. Something about Tamsin confessing to being jealous if she messed about with another woman was sexy as fuck.

Grabbing hold of Tamsin by the hips, she pulled the ginger close to her, their pelvises touching.

"Ooh, I like that you're jealous," she purred.

Tamsin quirked an eyebrow.

"Is that right?" she asked, smirking.

"Mm-hm," Robyn confirmed. "I am too, by the way. Which means I'd better not be seeing a Puma driven by a blonde in your driveway anytime soon."

"Speaking of…" Tamsin began, putting her arms around Robyn's waist. "You're really not bothered by the fact that last week, I technically still had a girlfriend? A blonde. Who drives a bloody Puma?"

"Nope!" Robyn assured her. She really wasn't. She had a sense for these things, and she could tell that Tamsin wasn't using her as a rebound romance. There was an undeniable attraction between the two of them, and a chemistry they had together helping to support that attraction. In short, Tamsin was into her.

"Besides…" she went on, "I think it's interesting that you and she broke up the very week I moved in. Just saying."

"Ohhhhh," Tamsin said. "Inevitable, was it?"

"Kinda," Robyn confirmed. "I mean, women tend to break up with their girlfriends whenever I move to town."

Tamsin laughed.

"So I was doomed to be standing here in my kitchen with you like this?" she asked.

Robyn narrowed her eyes playfully.

"More like blessed," she answered.

***

They decided to watch some telly and found *Big Trouble in Little China* on Amazon Prime Video and put that on because, as Tamsin said, "Anything with a young Kim Cattrall is worth watching."

However, *watching* turned out to be a bit of a stretch.

At least for Robyn.

On the leather sofa in the living room, Tamsin settled herself in the notch made by one of the sofa's arms and the back. She then stretched out her legs, resting her feet on a sienna-coloured ottoman. Robyn, seeing the perfect opportunity to cuddle with her new girlfriend, then settled *herself* by leaning her back against Tamsin's chest and stretching her legs along the sofa's seat cushions.

Things were normal for about the first fifteen minutes of the film. They were just two women enjoying a quiet Friday night, cuddling together on the sofa, enjoying some mindless entertainment.

Then…

Tamsin, who had her right arm wrapped around Robyn, started stroking the underside of her left breast, over her pyjama top. The touch was feather-soft, but it had instantly turned Robyn's nipples to stone and caused her respiration rate to increase.

Soon after, her nipple was being pinched through the fabric of her top, and she had started groaning, her eyes closed as her entire breast began tingling and her core came alive by lubricating her passage and swelling her inner walls.

"I thought we were going to watch this film," she had said.

"We are," Tamsin had told her.

Suddenly, her left arm snaked around Robyn's upper chest, just below her clavicle, her hand grabbing hold of the pyjama top at Robyn's right shoulder.

Robyn felt captured, and she had started breathing audibly with excitement as her clit began throbbing harder.

What followed next was the best movie-watching experience Robyn ever had.

Tamsin's hand had found its way into her pyjama bottoms and knickers, and as *Big Trouble in Little China* played, Robyn's folds and clit were played with in a teasing manner, Robyn whimpering in pleasure as her level of arousal kept rising.

Eventually, when she was absolutely soaked between her legs, Tamsin used that lubrication to really start rubbing her clit hard and fast, making her come quickly in her underwear.

Her quaking pussy was then palmed by Tamsin as the orgasm rode its course through her body.

After that first one, Robyn had thought perhaps they'd either go upstairs or strip off their clothes and fuck right there on the sofa. But Tamsin kept her captured with her left arm, and when she evidently sensed that Robyn's pussy had settled down, began stroking it again with her fingers…softly, almost as if she was doing it absentmindedly. Sure enough, after some time, her clit had once again started being firmly swiped by Tamsin's fingers and she came again, straining against Tamsin's hold on her as the climax burst from her mound, causing white light to flash behind her closed eyelids.

Robyn had considered protesting, wanting to turn this into a proper shagging session of give-and-take, because at the height of that orgasm, she wanted to ravish Tamsin, to have her tongue as far into the ginger's pussy as it could go while the intense pleasures Tamsin had given her were still roiling through her centre. But when the climax had started subsiding, she had needed time to recover from it, her body twitching because of the aftershocks, as if live wires were being touched to her skin.

In any case, at that point, whatever protest she had considered making died in situ once Tamsin started caressing her pussy gently again, building up such an erotic sense of anticipation that Robyn had felt helpless to say or do anything.

And so it went…

Throughout the film, Tamsin continued this pattern of gentle, almost loving strokes of her sex, followed by furious, rapid and firm attacks on her clit that pulled ever more stronger orgasms out from Robyn's core, until…

Now, *Big Trouble in Little China* was nearing its end, and Robyn was screaming.

Sweat was running down the sides of her face, her lips felt dry, and her pussy was detonating with the incredible potency of this latest orgasm, one that seemed to take all of the leftover pleasures from the previous climaxes and add them to its power.

Against Tamsin's hold on her, she bucked and writhed as she came undone, shouting out her delight.

When it was over, she fell still against Tamsin, breathing heavily, completely spent. Combined with the two climaxes she'd had earlier tonight, before she had gone home to shower and get her overnight things, the orgasm she just had counted as number six. It wasn't a record for her, but it had been a while since another woman had taken her that far.

Her face felt numb, and her muscles felt like jelly. She didn't even want to attempt to stand or walk now. Between her legs, she was as wet as she'd ever been, her underwear *and* her pyjama bottoms soaked with the arousal that had been streaming out of her vagina almost since the film had begun, and which had sprayed out of her each time Tamsin made her come.

Regarding the bottoms, there was no way she was going to be able to sleep in them tonight, and she sure as shit was happy she had thought to bring spare knickers.

"Movie's over," she heard Tamsin softly say.

Was it?

The pleasure Robyn was feeling now had robbed her of the perception to determine if that was true or not.

"Ready for bed?" Tamsin then asked.

Robyn licked her lips, needing to do so in order to speak.

"Can't walk yet," she murmured. Honestly, it didn't feel like she had legs so much as two hollow cardboard tubes that would have zero chance of supporting her weight.

Tamsin laughed and Robyn wanted to tell her to sod off for making fun of her plight—especially since it was *her* doing—but she didn't even have the strength to do that.

It only took a few more minutes, after which Robyn—with a groan—sat herself up on the sofa and then—with another groan—stood up.

Her eyes widened.

"Christ!" she exclaimed, chuckling as a reservoir of come that had been trapped in her passage started obeying gravity and leaking out of her. She definitely needed to clean herself up before getting into bed with Tamsin, who she assumed was done with her now, meaning it was time for her to return the pleasure.

However, upstairs no more than fifteen minutes later, when she was cleaned up, she felt her head swimming with fatigue as soon as she got into Tamsin's bed.

"Goodness!" she uttered, yawning. "I feel like I'm going to pass right out!"

"So pass right out," Tamsin told her, chuckling.

"But…I was planning on doing all sorts of devious and possibly illegal things to you now," Robyn mumbled, struggling to keep her eyes open.

She felt a kiss land on her cheek.

"I'm good," she heard Tamsin say just before she gave up the fight and let herself fall asleep.

Chapter 23

Tamsin awoke before Robyn the next morning. Before she got out of bed, however, she spent a few moments looking at the woman asleep next to her, and she smiled.

Quite the turn of events, she considered.

Just ten days ago, it would have been Kendra she was staring at now. Now it was Robyn. Not that she was complaining.

Fine, things had moved *fast* with her and Robyn, but it was a good kind of fast. Even better, it didn't feel as if she was using Robyn as a means to get over Kendra. Instead, it felt as if Robyn was making her forget there ever was a Kendra.

Just like Rylea had predicted.

She carefully got out of bed, not wanting to disturb her guest, who looked like she was quite lost in slumberland.

In the en suite, she peed, brushed her teeth and rinsed with mouthwash. After applying deodorant, she fixed her ponytail, which had come undone a bit while sleeping.

Back in the bedroom proper, Robyn was still lights-out, so Tamsin quietly changed out of her pyjamas and the underwear she had slept in, and into clean knickers, lounging pants and a black ribbed tank. She also took a bath towel and two flannels down from the top shelf of her wardrobe and placed them on the foot of the bed where Robyn would find them.

Downstairs in the kitchen, she put the kettle on and then checked her fridge.

She had plenty of food to offer Robyn for breakfast, though she had no idea what Robyn enjoyed, or if she even *ate* breakfast. Speaking for herself, Tamsin felt like having a big meal to start today with. Not a full English—she still had a figure to maintain—but at least eggs and bacon. She'd appease the goddess of waistlines by adding some diced fruit, but it would be a token gesture.

Creaking noises above her head told her that Robyn was up and moving about the ancient floorboards of the bedroom. By listening carefully, Tamsin was able to follow the woman's progress from the bed (over the refrigerator) and into the en suite (which was actually beyond the kitchen, over the downstairs loo).

The electric kettle clicked off, meaning the water was ready, and she prepared herself a mug of Earl Grey. She heard the shower running upstairs and decided to wait for Robyn in the living room.

As she sipped her tea on the sofa, she remembered last night, needing to cross her legs as she recalled the specifics of how often she had gotten Robyn off, and the ever-increasing volume of her cries each time she had come.

And what it felt like touching her…

Tamsin let out a breath remembering that.

By the end, the apex between Robyn's thighs had been soaked, slippery and warm, her knickers drenched, and her own hand covered with her neighbour's arousal.

She'd been quite turned on by the time they went upstairs to bed, ready to fuck well into the night, despite the three orgasms Robyn had given her earlier, which was…unusual for her.

In fact…

The whole thing on the sofa while watching *Big Trouble in Little China* had been unusual for her. The very fact that she had come up with the notion to masturbate Robyn to silliness after having had sex with her not terribly long before was…

Unusual.

In the Cora days, or the days of Angie or Micah…even in the Kendra days, that wouldn't have happened.

Would it?

No, she realised. It would not have.

In the days of *those* women, she and whichever one of them she happened to be with would have sat down on the sofa and watched *Big Trouble in Little China*—which actually was a pretty cool movie, Tamsin had determined—and she would have been content just to have the companionship of a girlfriend.

Especially after having had three orgasms earlier, which still blew her mind.

Sipping her tea, she mentally shrugged.

New woman.

That had to be it.

She remembered what she had originally planned to get done last night for her business, all of that social media posting as well as putting together a video about Majorca. That Mediterranean island was a top destination for British travellers looking to escape the dreariness of typical UK weather, and if she could flog more travel packages to there, it would do nothing but help Xplr.

She'd work on that today.

Although…

She had no idea what expectations Robyn had for them spending time together today, and Robyn—unlike Kendra—had not yet been indoctrinated into how she would often spend time at home, even on weekends, working on marketing gimmicks for the travel agency.

She sighed, the idea of having to train yet another girlfriend making her feel slightly overwhelmed.

She was just about done with her tea when Robyn made her appearance, coming down the stairs wearing skinny jeans and a long-sleeved top which fit her very nicely.

"Hey, you," she said, coming to the sofa and sitting next to Tamsin. She smelled so nice and looked so pretty—even without any makeup on—that Tamsin immediately leaned over to give her a kiss good morning, wanting to have some kind of intimate contact with her right away.

"Tea?" Tamsin offered. Robyn, however, made a face.

"In the mornings, I'm a coffee gal," she said.

"Well, you're in luck," Tamsin began. "I happen to keep some on hand for non-patriotic Brits like you."

Robyn laughed.

"I will have you know," she said, quirking an eyebrow, "I read somewhere that we're the second-largest consumer of coffee after the States."

Tamsin rolled her eyes.

"Bloody America can suck it," she said, standing up and then reaching for Robyn's hand. "Come on…I'm starving and would like to cook you breakfast. Unless you're one of those women who don't eat breakfast?"

Robyn took her hand and stood also.

"I will have you know," she said, repeating her phrase from just a few moments ago, "that not only do I eat breakfast, I also eat lunch and dinner. It's a strange habit I picked up when I was very young, and it's how I stay alive."

Holding hands, they walked to the kitchen.

"Well, excuse me," Tamsin said. "Given that you've been to California so many times, I thought maybe you picked up their eating habits. From the pictures I've seen, the women there look like they eat one almond and two pieces of kale and call that dinner."

"Oh my days!" Robyn exclaimed. "That's rich coming from you!"

In the kitchen now, Tamsin turned to face her.

"Meaning?" she asked.

"Meaning that you look *exactly* like an L.A. waitress-slash-actress with fake boobs, waiting for her big break in Hollywood."

Tamsin gasped indignantly.

"*I do not!*" she barked, though her quick and analytical mind instantly made her realise the futility of her argument. The fact was, if she was somehow transported to downtown Los Angeles, using that device in *Star Trek*, she would fit right in—appearance-wise. So would Robyn for that matter, who also had that *obsessed-with-my-figure* look California women seemed to have, at least in the photos Tamsin had seen.

However, she suspected their pale British skin would give them away as denizens of a land where a sunny day was front page news in the tabloids.

"Anyway…" Tamsin said resignedly, "my boobs aren't fake!"

"I know that, sweetie," Robyn told her, "and I am so very happy that's the case."

She leaned forward and gave Tamsin a quick kiss.

"So, what's for breakfast, Cornwall Barbie?" she then asked. "One almond and some kale? If so, I'd like my almond scrambled, with a bit of cheese."

***

I have work to do…I have work to do…I have work to do…

"That sounds like fun!" Tamsin told Robyn.

They were at the breakfast table, enjoying a meal of eggs, bacon and toast, not almonds and kale. Tamsin had another cup of tea in front of her, while Robyn was sipping coffee from a *Bean There/Done That* mug.

Robyn had just told Tamsin her idea of going to a garden centre to look for houseplants.

It sounded delightful, Tamsin considered, especially since she knew the best garden centre was in St Columb Major, a town between Tremont and Newquay, whose high street had several adorable shops and boutiques.

But of course, as delightful as it sounded, Tamsin had remembered all the marketing work she wanted to do for Xplr, work she could have gotten done last night—if she and Robyn hadn't been too busy making one another come.

However, the urge to spend more time with Robyn today made the idea of staying home and working unpalatable, and so she told her new girlfriend that she'd love to accompany her plant shopping.

Nonetheless, she decided she'd better appease the goddess of earning money…

"Although," she began, "when we return to Tremont, I need to do some agency work."

Robyn waved her hand in a *no big deal* gesture.

"Totes understand," she said. "In fact, I should also probably use part of my Saturday to do some work of my own. Sasha Hoffman's show opens to the public two weeks from today and— eek!—the vernissage is only thirteen days away now!"

Tamsin blinked.

"The what?" she asked, not familiar with that word.

"The vernissage," Robyn repeated. "It's like a preview before the show opens to the public. Totally invite-only. I'm hoping you'll be able to come?"

"Definitely," Tamsin told her, smiling. "That will be our date night for that week."

"Love it!" Robyn said. "I want to invite Darcie and Rylea as well. They seem amazing, and if I get them tipsy with enough free Champagne that night, maybe they'll tell me all your secrets."

Even though Tamsin knew Robyn was being facetious, she suddenly got very worried that, yes, with enough alcohol in her system—whether in two weeks at that vernissage thing, or this evening at the Ladle & Spoon—Rylea *would* start having loose lips. Normally, she trusted her best friend implicitly, but Robyn was a charmer, Tamsin realised.

This made her think about the "experiment" she had thought of last night, the one she had considered trying out today.

"Sooooo…" Robyn began, interrupting Tamsin's thoughts. "About last night. Sorry, I really meant to be more…*reciprocating* after we went upstairs, but damn! You depleted me!"

That settled it in Tamsin's mind.

"No worries," she said. "And about that…"

"Yes?" Robyn prodded, before taking another bite of her eggs.

Tamsin took a fortifying sip of her tea.

"The thing about me is," she said, "that I *don't* need to have orgasm after orgasm each time we have sex. I mean, I like sex! I *love* it, in fact!" She shrugged. "I don't know…I just find myself ready to move on after I get off."

"Oh, I see…" Robyn replied.

"Don't get me wrong!" Tamsin hurriedly added. "I loved everything that you did to me last night! I had *such* a good time! I'm just letting you know that my…I guess, *threshold* for having sex all night long is pretty low."

Robyn nodded slowly.

"You act like this is something I may want to fix," she said.

"Well, won't you?" Tamsin asked, snidely, the frustrations from an endless series of failed relationships sneaking into her tone of voice. She then closed her eyes and internally chided herself. "Sorry," she went on. "It's just that this has been an issue with all my exes. In fact, that's why they're exes."

Robyn nodded again and swallowed the piece of bacon she had just popped into her mouth.

"Bloody cows," she then stated.

Tamsin couldn't tell if Robyn was winding her up or being serious.

"Erm…well, I mean…"

"I'm serious!" Robyn declared. "It's not like you're an axe murderer or an animal abuser—wait, you like animals, don't you? Because I have a cat."

"I love animals!" Tamsin insisted. "I mean, I don't have any myself, but that's only because I never felt a pressing need to have a pet, that's all."

Robyn smiled.

"You'll love Empress," she said. "Anyway, back to what we were talking about…" Her brow furrowed. "Wait a minute…"

"What?" Tamsin asked.

"Last night, I got you off three times," Robyn replied. "I know because I keep track in a little notebook. Was that okay?"

"Yes!" Tamsin assured her. This was what she was afraid of, that Robyn would think that she didn't get any enjoyment from the pleasures of sex. "It was surprising, but totally okay!"

"Surprising how?" Robyn pressed.

"Just…I mean, I don't usually…have that many," Tamsin admitted.

Robyn smirked. She then huffed a couple of breaths on her fingernails and then rubbed the nails against her top—the universal gesture of *I'm pretty damn satisfied with myself.*

Tamsin, chuckling, rolled her eyes.

"God, I've created a monster, haven't I?" she said.

"Welllll, you know," Robyn began, "it's always nice to hear you're *that* good."

"You're going to be impossible to deal with now, aren't you?" Tamsin said.

"Maybe," Robyn replied with a laugh. "Anyway…about this sex thing. Everyone's sex drive is different, and as much as I may have the capacity to…well, go all night long, I'd also like the opportunity to get to know you better. Outside the bedroom, I mean. That is, if this has the potential to turn into…something."

Tamsin didn't know how to respond. What Robyn had just told her seemed…so understanding. She wondered if, this time, she would be able to drop her guard a bit.

"I'll do you a deal," Robyn then said.

Tamsin's brow furrowed. She wondered what was coming.

"What kind of deal?" she asked warily. Instantly—and she didn't know where this came from—her mind imagined that Robyn was going to suggest they have an "open" relationship. One in which they would "technically" still be girlfriends, but with the codicil that Robyn be allowed to fuck other women who had the sexual drive to make an afternoon shag last until dawn the following day.

Robyn cocked an eyebrow.

"You can have as *few* orgasms as *you'd* like," she said, "as long as I get to have as *many* orgasms as *I'd* like."

Tamsin looked to the side, an automatic gesture when she was contemplating something knotty. She was trying to find the catch in Robyn's offer.

What her past lovers hadn't understood—despite how many times she had told them this—was that she *loved* pleasuring women. She could spend quite a bit of time on it, in fact, just as she had last night while watching that movie. It's just that, once she herself had been given an orgasm, or maybe two, she was ready to do other things.

Although, Kendra had a valid point, she considered now. That point about how she denied her lovers the pleasure of…well, of pleasuring her. She didn't know what to do about that yet, nor how it might one day affect her relationship with Robyn, whom she was realising that she *really* liked.

She sat back and crossed her arms under her breasts. She smugly noted how Robyn's eyes dropped down to look at her chest.

"And you're not going to get upset," Tamsin began, "if I say, 'That's enough,' even though you may still want to…do things to me?"

Robyn leaned forward, a leering look in her eyes.

"Sweetie," she said, reaching forward and tucking a strand of hair behind Tamsin's ear, "make me come so much that I forget my name, and I'll gladly leave you alone."

Tamsin gasped out a short breath as her clit felt like it was inflating to twice its normal size.

"Deal," she purred.

And now she knew what she wanted to do after breakfast…

Chapter 24

About ninety minutes later, Robyn, her hair dishevelled and her shirt on inside out, stepped into her cottage on legs that were still quivering.

"Goodness, Empress!" she said to her cat, who was in her favourite spot on the sofa, looking at her. "She's…oh my days!"

She and Tamsin had sex right after breakfast, which had led Robyn to make a stupid joke about them waiting at least twenty minutes after eating lest they get cramps, but Tamsin showed no interest in delaying things. It had struck Robyn that for a woman who professed to lose interest in continuing to have sex once she'd had an orgasm, Tamsin was nonetheless *very* generous with her time and carnal talents. Yet again, Robyn had found herself on the receiving end of things—this time with a vibrating strap-on that Tamsin had produced from a box in her wardrobe.

Robyn had insisted that she be fucked with it while on her back, rather than from behind, because she wanted to feel Tamsin's enormous breasts rubbing against her own while she was being taken care of. It also allowed her to kiss her lover and to wrap her legs around her, which helped Tamsin plunge the toy deeper into her.

When she came, it was so violent that the bucking of her body flipped them over on the mattress. Then with herself on top and Tamsin beneath her, Robyn had finished that orgasm and then started riding that dildo, wanting another one. It didn't take her long to reach it, either. Once she became aware of her clit rubbing against Tamsin's ginger pubic hair—that she absolutely thought was the hottest thing on Earth—the sensations in her pussy skyrocketed and her second climax burst open right on the heels of the first one.

Robyn, who had already been cupping her breasts, pinched both her nipples at the moment it hit, adding that much-desired pain to the exploding pleasures in her pussy.

When it was over, she was left shattered, collapsing onto Tamsin's chest, breathing in deep lungfuls of air as she whimpered, Tamsin holding her tightly and kissing her left shoulder and pulse point.

Once recovered, she had un-impaled herself from the still vibrating toy and immediately went down on Tamsin, using her left hand to hold the pink dildo that was covered in her come away from her head as she started licking Tamsin's sex, which was primed and dripping. After making sure she had the ginger's full and undivided attention, Robyn had then quickly unfastened the dildo from the harness Tamsin was wearing and guided it into her vagina, pushing it in all the way, her own clit pulsing at seeing how Tamsin's folds wrapped around the shaft.

Tamsin had climaxed within seconds at that point, and Robyn had waited until she knew the orgasm had subsided before sliding the dildo out, finding the switch to turn it off, tossing it on the mattress and then licking Tamsin's opening to coat her tongue in her juices.

Afterwards, they lay holding each other as they both came down from their highs.

While doing so, Robyn had been curious.

She had just gotten Tamsin off…did that mean Tamsin was done—sexually—for the *day?* According to the clock in the bedroom, it was only going on half ten. The day was still young. It almost seemed against the Lesbian Code of Behaviour to be *done* having sex so early on a weekend.

But she certainly wasn't going to ask Tamsin about that. For starters, it seemed her new girlfriend was sensitive about that particular topic, and she didn't know Tamsin well enough yet to *not* be certain that making such an inquiry wouldn't live in her head for hours or days, whispering to her and telling her that she was bound to leave her as well.

For another thing, the way Robyn figured it, she had no cause for complaint. Fine, personally, she had felt as if she could continue having sex right now, sod the garden centre and anything else today. And she knew her libido well enough to know that later today she'd want to have sex. But, really…Tamsin had just taken care of her *very* well. On top of that, she had gotten to reciprocate. If that was it for today, then that was it for today. It would be more important learning about this new and special person in her life and enjoying all of the other things which she found so attractive about her.

Which was why Robyn was now back in her cottage, talking to Empress, while still feeling a little quivery from the orgasms Tamsin had given her.

She and Tamsin had decided they still wanted to go to St Columb Major for shopping, only Robyn had to come back here to get into clean knickers once again—oh, and to fix her shirt, which she knew she had put back on the wrong way around.

"Get yourself cleaned up," she told Empress as she headed for the stairs, removing her shirt as she did so. "The ginger will be here shortly, so you finally get to meet her."

In her en suite, she spent the requisite time cleaning her sex, amazed at how wet she still was. With that in mind, she chose one of the least sexy pair of knickers she owned.

Last year, she had jumped on board the period underwear craze and now owned a few of the rather dull-looking and purely functional briefs. As a sexually active woman, however, she had also learned that the underwear came in handy for times like these: when she was so aroused that her vagina's lubricating glands didn't seem to have an Off switch.

If she was going to be spending part of the day with the incredibly sexy woman who had made her come strongly twice this morning, she suspected that the Off switch would be malfunctioning again, at least for a while.

She heard Tamsin knocking on her door just as she finished applying some makeup and kinda/sorta styling her hair.

"Oh my days, you didn't tell me she was a Persian!" Tamsin squealed when she entered the cottage and caught sight of Empress on the sofa.

Empress, her eyes wide, stared at this new human, but before she had a chance to flee from the unknown, she was captured by the stranger, finding herself cradled in its arms.

Robyn smiled, but she watched Tamsin closely. She could spot a fake a mile away, someone who was only *pretending* to like cats just to keep her on a string and in their bed. Tamsin, however, was genuine in her adoration of Empress, even though the subject of that adoration evidently wished she was anywhere else.

"This fur must drive you *crazy!*" Tamsin exclaimed before smooshing her face into it.

"You have no idea!" Robyn said, and then explained the effort needed to keep Empress's coat smooth and free of knots. "Which reminds me," she said when she had finished doing that. "I need to find a good groomer in this part of Cornwall."

"Daylor," Tamsin said. "She has a mobile service, *and* she lives in Tremont. She goes to trivia at the pub every Saturday. I suppose I can introduce you to her there one night."

"Do you want to play tonight?" Robyn asked.

Tamsin looked at her.

"Can we put that off until next week?" she offered. "I'd rather have another movie night while holding onto this beautiful cat all night long!"

Empress looked at Robyn and meowed.

Help me!

***

Once they were in St Columb Major—which Robyn thought was a charming town—they browsed some clothing shops on the high street. Robyn reined in her impulses to buy every cute outfit she saw, however. She may drive a BMW, but she wasn't rich and still needed to budget. There was a series of lesbian fiction romances she enjoyed, wherein the characters were able to walk into any boutique and buy whatever they wanted, but she wasn't at that point in her financial life yet.

Nonetheless, in one shop, she did purchase an adorable sweater that she just couldn't walk away from, and in another shop she just had to have a boho-style dress which simply screamed *stylish lesbian*. And since she was apparently living in the lesbian central of Cornwall, she figured the dress would help her fit right in. Well, that and the fact that she enjoyed licking vaginas.

The decision was made to have lunch before heading to the garden centre, and they found a shop which, according to reviews on Google, served terrific pasties, near the end of the high street. Interestingly enough, though she'd eaten plenty of Cornish pasties in her life, Robyn realised that she had never eaten one *in* Cornwall, and so she was looking forward to this experience.

They found an empty table inside the establishment, but rather than sit across from each other, they sat side by side, the way new girlfriends often do.

Robyn was glad for it.

As predicted, there were only a few handful of times since leaving Tremont when her core *hadn't* been aware of Tamsin's proximity. It was as if, on its own—without any help from her eyes or brain—it knew the woman who had given it so much pleasure since last night was nearby. Her excitement was aided, several times, by Tamsin pulling her in for a kiss as they moved along the high street, or by that moment in the shop where she had bought the boho dress, when Tamsin, walking past her, ran her hand along her bum.

After their server took their drinks order, Robyn leaned close to Tamsin and whispered in her ear, "I want to pull you into the loo and shag your brains out."

Tamsin groaned.

"Love the shagging my brains out idea," she said, "but not in the loo. Not after the last time."

Robyn pulled away, a smile on her face.

"Ooh, this I have to hear!" she said.

Tamsin rolled her eyes and sighed.

"Bloody *L Word!*" she exclaimed. "Makes it seem as if women can have sex anywhere! Anyway, this happened…three—no four—girlfriends ago."

"Okaaaay…" Robyn prodded.

"Now, I'm not going to name names," Tamsin said, "but let's just say that we were at a restaurant serving authentic dishes from a nation whose food is known for…shall we say, moving things along?"

Robyn laughed. She understood clearly. It was why she only ever ate Mexican food when she was alone.

"Was it Mexican?" she asked.

"I'm not saying!" Tamsin chided her. "Because the next thing I know, you'll tell me you're bloody one-quarter Mexican and then think I'm anti-Mexican!"

"I will not!" Robyn exclaimed.

"Hush!" Tamsin ordered. She then continued.

"So, we're in the toilet…getting started as it were, and we hear another woman rush into the loo. Seriously…the door to the loo *banged* open and we could hear her footsteps hurrying, like she was rushing to catch a plane."

"Oh my days, was there only one stall?" Robyn asked. "The one you were in?"

"I wish," Tamsin said. "Instead, there were *two* stalls, so of course, the woman rushes into the empty one right next to us."

She was interrupted when the server returned with their drinks. They then told her they needed another few minutes to look over the menu, which Robyn totally had no intention of doing because she was engrossed in Tamsin's tale.

"So, there I was," Tamsin went on after the server left, "with my girlfriend's hand up my skirt, and *my* hand up hers, when all of a sudden an arse *explodes* in the next stall!"

"No!" Robyn exclaimed, eyes wide.

Tamsin seemed to have trouble finding the proper words to continue her story.

"Did you see that film *Dumb and Dumber?*" she eventually asked.

Robyn nodded.

"It was like that scene where either Dumb or Dumber—I forget their names—was on the toilet at Lauren Holly's house—"

"Oh my god, she's so bloody gorgeous!" Robyn just had to interject.

"*So* fucking gorgeous!" Tamsin agreed. "Anyway, it was like *that* scene in the film. It was as if everything the poor woman had ever eaten *burst* out of her arse all at once!"

Robyn was laughing, imagining the setting.

"So, naturally," Tamsin said, "the…erm…sound effects, combined with the odour, completely turned us off continuing what we had been working on, and even now the idea of having sex in a public loo makes me shudder."

Robyn, still laughing, said, "I love that story. Also, duly noted…I won't try to seduce you in a toilet."

"Thank you," Tamsin said.

"Was it an Indian place?" Robyn then asked.

Tamsin looked at her.

"And have you tell me that despite your British-pale skin your father is from Bangalore?" she asked. "Nope, not answering that question."

Chapter 25

Upon returning to Tremont late that afternoon, Tamsin helped Robyn into her cottage with the new houseplants she had bought. They agreed that Tamsin would return later that night to watch movies and stay over. She then returned to her home in order to get some Xplr work done.

She'd had such a fun time with Robyn in St Columb Major today. She supposed it was a good test. After all, if they were really going to explore having a relationship, it had to work outside of the bedroom also, and today she had truly enjoyed Robyn's company.

She went upstairs in order to change into one of her *Tamsin from Xplr* outfits she used when she recorded vids of herself talking about the "amazing travel deals you can get from Xplr." The outfits—there were six of them—had been strategically chosen by her so that she looked capable, smart, and professional. Yet they also highlighted her…assets so that she would keep the attention of any blokes watching but did so in such a way so as to not alienate any potential female clients—particularly if those potential female clients happened to be watching with one of those blokes.

After changing, she would go into the spare room that was also upstairs, that she used as a video studio. She had quite the set-up: a mirrorless Panasonic Lumix digital camera which also shot 4K video, a button mic, like what's used on all those BBC talk shows and which attached to her clothing, and two softbox studio lights which made her look just as good on camera as bloody Nigella Lawson.

She had just removed the short-sleeved Henley she had worn today when she heard her phone ringing.

Picking it up from her bed, she frowned.

Why was Rylea *calling?* Theirs was a friendship of texting, Snapchatting and Instagramming. If they needed to speak, they texted arrangements to meet up somewhere.

"Why are you calling?" Tamsin answered.

"Oh, just wondering if you were going to join us for trivia tonight?" Rylea replied.

"You mean, the same bloody question you usually bloody ask me via text?" Tamsin shot back.

"Just thought I'd call this time," Rylea declared. "I missed the sound of your voice."

Tamsin rolled her eyes.

"Alright, what's going on?" she demanded.

"Funny you should ask," Rylea said. "So…word around town is that my best friend is dating the new girl with the posh car. It was practically the sole topic of conversation at The Bean today."

Groaning, Tamsin said, "Of course. What a shocker. No surprise, really. I'm sure half the village knows when I have to pee before I do."

"Hey, you want privacy…" Rylea began.

"I know, I know, move to London," Tamsin finished.

"And what's this about a honeymoon…?" Rylea then prodded.

"*There is no honeymoon!*" Tamsin exclaimed.

"Even so, that didn't take long," Rylea said, and Tamsin could hear the smugness in her friend's voice.

Tamsin bit her lower lip, thinking.

"You don't think it was *too* fast, do you?" she asked. "I mean, after Kendra?"

Rylea scoffed.

"Sod Kendra," she stated. "And sod Cora and Angie and whoever the hell else, Tams. You can't keep thinking about past relationships, not if you have something good in the present." She paused. "Wait, Robyn is *good*, right? I don't mean in bed—though we *will* discuss that later…*at length*—I mean, good to you?"

"Well, it's only been twenty-four hours, Rye Bread," Tamsin pointed out, "but, yes, so far she's not a bitch to me. In fact…"

"In fact?" Rylea prompted.

Tamsin sat down on the edge of the bed.

"I did something different this time," she began. "This morning, I told Robyn about…you know, how I'm typically a one-and-done kind of gal."

"Oh shit!" Rylea exclaimed. "How did that go?"

Tamsin smiled, remembering.

"I'm paraphrasing," she said, "but essentially she told me that this wasn't a problem and that I didn't need to be fixed."

"Marry her," Rylea said flatly.

Tamsin laughed.

"No, I'm serious!" her best friend insisted. "Get on a plane, fly to Las Vegas and have Elvis pronounce you wife and wife."

"A bit too fast for me," Tamsin said, standing again and heading to her wardrobe to choose a *Tamsin from Xplr* outfit. "Let's see if we stay together long enough to celebrate a major holiday together first."

***

A few hours later, at a little past eight p.m., Tamsin was over at Robyn's cottage, sitting on the sofa, with Empress in her lap. The cat no longer had that wild-eyed, *I'm-being-held-hostage* look on its face, nor could Tamsin any longer feel that coiled tension in the muscles beneath her silky fur, telling her that Empress would spring away from her the very moment she could.

Whether it was resignation to her fate, or because Tamsin had seduced her, Empress was now chill and relaxed on her lap, purring and slowly blinking her eyes.

"You two are getting along, I see," Robyn said, emerging from the kitchen with two glasses of white wine. She handed one to Tamsin, who took it with her left hand, while with her right she continued scratching the spot beneath Empress's chin, which was making the animal purr even louder.

"Pussies can't resist me," Tamsin quipped.

"Ah…" Robyn said, sitting down next to her. "Well, mine sure couldn't." She paused for a few beats. "Obviously, you just have a way with pussies."

Tamsin nodded.

"It's a gift," she sighed, as though she were a superhero burdened by her special powers. "Pussies just…adore me."

Now Robyn nodded. She reached over and scratched behind Empress's ear.

"Must be something in the way you handle them," she said. "You know, with your fingers."

"Mm, I think you're right," Tamsin said. "See, the thing with pussies is, you need to start off with a gentle touch…"

"Is that so?" Robyn asked.

"Quite," Tamsin stated. "Then, you can start stroking them more firmly."

"My goodness!" Robyn exclaimed. "Here I am, the one with the cat but you seem like quite the pussy expert!"

Tamsin shrugged.

"Well, I believe others would concur with that statement," she said, looking down at Empress.

"Perhaps I should call some of these *others* and find out what they say," Robyn offered.

Tamsin laughed.

"Don't you dare!" she ordered. "In fact, just shut up and kiss me."

Robyn did as she was bidden. Tamsin was delighted at how she immediately felt Robyn's tongue enter her mouth as soon as their lips touched. She enjoyed that kind of aggressiveness.

When they separated, she said, "By the way, remind me to wash my hands before I start fingering you later." She then looked down at the cat in her lap to make her point.

"Ooh, so I can expect fingering later?" Robyn asked.

"Should I have said 'spoiler alert' before I told you that?" Tamsin asked, chuckling.

"Not at all," Robyn assured her. "Just delighted to have something like that to look forward to."

"And what do *I* have to look forward to?" Tamsin asked.

She was horny…very much so. Enough time had passed between her orgasm this morning and now for her libido to have recharged itself. She also knew that because she had gotten that work for Xplr done earlier back at her place, her mind was now unencumbered enough to think about sex.

Plus, Robyn was…yummy.

"Well…" Robyn said, "…you're not the only with toys, you know."

Tamsin's clit started beating hard.

"Well," she said, "let's watch a movie and finish our wine. Besides, I'm kind of still busy with this other pussy on my lap."

Robyn laughed.

"I just love that she likes you," she said. She then picked up the remote for her television. "If you have no objections," she went on, "why don't we keep with our young-Kim-Cattrall theme? I noticed that *Police Academy* is on Netflix."

"Oh my god, I love that movie!" Tamsin said. "It's *so* stupid, it's actually hilarious."

Robyn set about using the remote to pull up the film on the telly, and then they sat back and watched it, sipping their wine, Tamsin continuing to stroke one pussy on her lap, while also looking ahead to eventually stroking another upstairs in the bedroom.

***

Three hours later it was well into the night, and Tamsin was in heaven…or hell. She couldn't decide which.

She was lying on her back on Robyn's mattress. Her hands had been washed even before they had come upstairs, but by now both sets of her fingers were sticky with Robyn's arousal, and she currently had two from her left hand in her mouth, sucking them clean of the results of her girlfriend's most recent orgasm.

Meanwhile, between her legs, Robyn was eating her out, but masterfully and wickedly keeping her from bursting into climax. Thus, on the one hand she was in a type of heaven wherein her entire body was being kept in a state of heightened sexual charge, whereas on the other hand, she was in the hell of having a massive orgasm prevented from being unleashed.

"*Mmmph!*" she grunted now as she felt herself penetrated again by the glass dildo Robyn owned. It easily slipped all the way inside her vagina, her walls clutching at its unyielding hardness as she also felt Robyn's tongue edging her throbbing clit.

Suddenly, however, Robyn's mouth pulled away.

"I want to come again," Robyn stated.

Tamsin gasped, looking down at her girlfriend wide-eyed.

"Fuck! Now?" she asked. "I'm so fucking close!"

Holding her eyes with what could only be described as a glare, Robyn slid herself along Tamsin's body until she was properly topping her and staring down at her. In her pussy, the glass dildo continued filling her flooded passage.

"*I'm* not done yet!" Robyn hissed, cocking an eyebrow.

Tamsin, her clit feeling even more energised now, grabbed Robyn's arse with both hands and squeezed it hard.

"Oh, is that how it is, huh?" she growled.

"That's how it is," Robyn confirmed. Then, before Tamsin could reply, she quickly repositioned herself, straddling Tamsin's face, with her bum resting on her chest, just above her large breasts.

Her pussy was swollen and dripping, the result of the three previous orgasms she'd had.

Tamsin took hold of Robyn's hips and immediately jammed her tongue as far into her pussy as it could go, feeling trapped arousal start to leak out onto her chin, her eyes closing in pleasure at the taste.

But then her eyes popped open again and she squealed in surprise against Robyn's sex when she felt Robyn, evidently reaching behind herself, grab hold of the base of the glass dildo that was still inside her and start deep-pumping her with it, in rhythm with the gentle rocking of her hips as she rode Tamsin's face.

"Mm, I know what you want, baby," Robyn cooed. "Make me come again, and then I'll take care of you."

Tamsin decided not to waste any more time. She had never been kept waiting like this. Most women were only too eager to make her come. Yet Robyn had decided not only to deny her but had also managed to keep what was a titanic orgasm at bay, trapped beneath her mound, expertly preventing it from breaking free.

Tightening her grip on Robyn's hips, she captured her girlfriend's engorged clit with her lips and started sucking on it.

"Oh FUUUUUUUUCK!" Robyn shouted as Tamsin felt her vulva immediately begin convulsing against her mouth a second before a spurt of warm arousal from deep inside the woman began dribbling over her chin. She was glad she had a tight grip on her hips because Robyn was shaking rather violently above her. Despite this, however, what she also did was press her fingers firmly against Tamsin's clit and start rubbing fast.

Tamsin didn't care if Robyn's pussy still needed her mouth on it. She didn't care if pulling it away prematurely would interrupt her release and water down its potency. She *needed* to pull her mouth away as soon as she started coming.

Though she arched her head back and opened her mouth as if about to give voice to an epic scream, this orgasm was so strong it stole her voice.

Her vagina became an epicentre of delight when the climax burst its banks and came free. She lost awareness of everything else as she came harder than she ever had before, her pussy still grasping that rigid dildo but starting to push it out with the strength of her contractions.

Finally, her scream became unlocked.

"AAAAAAAAAAHHHHHHHHHHHFUUUUUCKFUCKFUCK FUUUUUUUUUUCK!"

When the dildo was pushed out, she gasped, first at the sudden emptiness of her passage, and then at how she squirted once the toy was completely out.

Quick as a flash, Robyn lifted herself off Tamsin's chest, only to turn herself around and sixty-nine her.

In the throes of her massive orgasm, Tamsin felt her clit being licked and heard Robyn's moans of delight. Everything Robyn was doing now was preventing her current climax from subsiding. Instead, it was keeping it going, building on it, in fact, until another tipping point was reached, and she started coming again…

I can't believe this is happening!

As the explosions of pleasure kept detonating in her core, and as she screamed bloody murder with delight at it all, Tamsin was aware of one thought and one thought only.

She wanted to keep feeling like this all night long.

***

Bloody hell, what has gotten into me?

She was Tamsin Tregurrian, and she was having sex all night long.

What's more, she was doing it with a woman she'd only met last week, and whom she'd only been involved with for twenty-four hours.

She was well past her usual point of having lost interest and stopping things. Her mind was *not* thinking of what else she could be doing with her time now, nor was her mind calculating all the work she could have gotten done between her first orgasm and now, when her pussy was still experiencing jolting aftershocks from her fifth.

She was lying on her belly on Robyn's mattress, her head turned to the side and her mouth open as she took in deep breaths of air.

She felt a kiss on her shoulder a moment before Robyn rolled off her back.

"Real talk," Robyn began breathlessly, "now *I'm* ready to do anything else."

"What bloody time is it?" Tamsin croaked.

There was a moment's pause as Robyn evidently searched for the answer to that question.

"Just past eleven," Robyn told her.

"A.m. or p.m.?" Tamsin quipped. She was knackered, her entire body felt drained of all superfluous energy, leaving her only what was needed for basic life support.

Little wonder, really…

What she had just experienced was new to her. Even when she masturbated, she usually stopped after one orgasm. If she was *incredibly* horny, she might get herself off twice, but that was it. Then it was time to move on, do something else.

The three times Robyn had made her come last night—their first together—had been novel enough. To her recollection, that had never happened before, or if it had, she'd forgotten it, though she couldn't see how that was possible.

Tonight, Robyn had taken her even further…and it had been a blissful journey to higher planes of sexual pleasure she had never once visited. What was remarkable about that journey was that at no point did her mind say *Time for something else;* nor did her core shut down after her first orgasms, the way it typically did, having been satisfied and ready to yield to whatever else her mind wanted to do other than continue having sex.

In short, Robyn was making her feel as if she didn't know who she was anymore.

She had felt herself losing her grip on reality when she came the fourth time, as if she was on the verge of hallucinating.

The fifth one shattered her, making her yell like a banshee as it pummelled her core, the orgasm syphoning any remaining energy in her body, in order to sustain itself for the longest amount of time. She remembered screaming Robyn's name and clawing at the bed sheets until the fitted one came loose from one of the mattress corners.

Now, that climax was done, save for the frequent post-coital tremors which still roiled her vagina and surprised her with their intensity. They were like mini-orgasms in their own right, and made her feel blessed to be able to simply lie here and enjoy having her pleasure extended in that manner.

So this is what I've been missing…

She had to admit, this was amazing. It was as if even more of her womanhood had just been unlocked by Robyn, as if her new girlfriend had invited her to a secret club that, in reality, was not so secret; all that had been required was for her to step inside it.

Would nights like this happen again, she wondered?

Was she now a "changed" woman, always up for shagging well into the night and having so many orgasms her blood vessels felt ready to burst?

Maybe, maybe not. Who knew? After all, she was still a woman who had lofty goals for the business she ran with her uncle, and which would one day be hers alone. That kind of drive and ambition doesn't just get switched off because a new lover has come along who had just made her wonder if it was possible to die from too much pleasure.

"Penny for your thoughts," Robyn said.

"Is it possible to die from too much pleasure?" Tamsin answered, not bothering to turn her head to face her. She felt too physically drained for even that much effort.

"Want to find out?" Robyn asked snarkily.

"Maybe tomorrow," Tamsin quickly told her. "Or maybe not," she hurriedly added. "I mean…"

"I get it, babe," Robyn said. "You do realise that your motivation to get a lot of shit done each day is one of the reasons I'm attracted to you, right?"

"Is it?" Tamsin asked.

"Mm-hm," Robyn hummed. "Well, that and the fact that you're a smart-arse and not afraid to speak your mind.

Tamsin smiled.

"That makes me happy," she said. "I'm attracted to you for the same reasons. I like a woman who isn't afraid to show some attitude. Plus, you have really, really nice boobs."

Robyn laughed.

"You should see me in a bikini," she said.

Tamsin chuckled.

"You should see *me* in a bikini," she replied.

"Mmmmm, I bet that's a sight," Robyn returned. "In fact, if I ever did see that, sex on the beach would not just be a cocktail.

"Oh god," Tamsin whined. "You're not about to tell me about having sex on the beach in bloody California, are you?"

Perhaps that was why Tremont had lost out to Carlsbad in the category of "Most Lesbian-Friendly Destinations:" their beaches could serve as sets for lesbian porn vids.

"You know what?" Robyn said. "I've decided something."

"You want to come again?" Tamsin quipped.

"No," Robyn said. "Well, I mean, yeah…like, always, but that's not what I'm talking about. I've decided that if we are still together in six months, we're going on holiday to California. You'd *love* it!"

Now, Tamsin *did* turn her head to look at Robyn.

Initially, she had wanted to say something caustic about California because by now it was an ingrained habit. But as soon as she looked at the woman lying next to her, something else came out of her mouth.

"You'd be the first, you know."

"The first what?" Robyn asked.

"The first girlfriend I've had who's lasted six months," Tamsin told her.

Robyn smiled.

"Ooh, I rather like that!" she said. "Guess I'd better make sure I don't bollocks this up, huh?"

Tamsin scooched over closer to Robyn so she could kiss her deeply, affectionately.

"You and me both," she whispered.

Chapter 26

Nearly a week went by, and on Friday, Robyn had a lot to do at the gallery.

A lot.

They were now one week away from the vernissage for Sasha's show, and it looked like it was going to be quite the event in Newquay.

For starters, the mayor had accepted the invitation to the party, as did the entire town council, as well as the mayor of Truro, which was Cornwall's county town and centre for administration.

Robyn had also gotten acceptances from the biggest business leaders in Newquay, as well as from a handful of well-known (and financially well-endowed) art collectors in Cornwall.

She had informed no less than three influential art critics in England of Sasha's show, inviting them to attend the vernissage, knowing that Sasha's reputation was growing even though she'd not yet had a one-woman show. She'd heard back from none of the critics, but that was no surprise. That was the way critics operated. In fact, if she had heard from any one of them that they *weren't* able to make it, that would have told her not to expect that person. Silence, on the other hand, in this business anyway, was as good as an acceptance.

Then, to top it all off, Victoria Linden was going to be there. The woman who had hired her and given her a gallery to run would be showing up to see just how well she was running that gallery. This, above all else, caused her the most anxiety about next week's event, and due to this, she needed to be sure everything was perfect, and she had *wanted* to do much of it today before the weekend.

For example, having decided that the lighting in the space did not meet her needs for Sasha's show, she had arranged for new fixtures to be installed, and she needed to work closely with the lighting company to ensure that the installation met her requirements.

Additionally, she wanted to talk with Tina on ramping up their social media strategy for the gallery. Robyn had some ideas that had come to her over the past couple of nights at home, while decompressing, and she wanted Tina to advise her on how best to utilise them. Moreover, Lucien had come up with a notion that the three of them could produce an advert of sorts about the public opening of Sasha's show, to post on TikTok, and she wanted the three of them to discuss that. And that was just the tip of the iceberg. There were dozens of things to do, all of them important.

With luck, she'd be able to get to most of them today. The lighting company wasn't due until half two, and she could chat with Tina and Lucien at any time.

But first…she had an artist to murder.

This was why she was on the A3075, heading to Portreath, of all bloody places. Sasha Hoffman lived in Portreath, and Robyn had watched enough true-crime shows on telly to know that if you want to murder someone, their house is often a pretty convenient place to do so.

Just over an hour ago, she had phoned Sasha to inform her of a change in the pick-up schedule for the pieces that would be featured in the show. Turns out that the art delivery service— specially hired from *London*, because Robyn didn't want to risk trusting a Cornish service to do this for such an important show— would be able to arrive at her studio a couple of hours earlier on Monday than originally expected.

Which was when Sasha had one of her panic attacks.

And this one was a whopper.

"Oh god, can't we just cancel the whole thing?" Sasha had asked in a pleading tone.

Robyn had taken a deep breath and counted to five before answering.

This was typical Sasha, and all she needed was to be talked off the ledge. Robyn had done it countless times before with this particular artist.

"No, Sasha," she had replied calmly, "we can't cancel the whole thing. This show is your big moment, and so many people are looking forward to seeing your work, and you, in person."

"But I'm such a *frawwwwwwwd!*" Sasha had whined. "Who wants to look at this stuff?"

That was when Robyn had known that this was going to take more time than usual.

However, thirty minutes later, she had still been at it, trying to convince Sasha that everything was going to be just fine, if she would only relax and look forward to sharing her fantastic art with the good people of Cornwall.

At the end of all that, Sasha had simply told Robyn, "Nope, nope, nope! Can't do it! Get *anyone* else! I don't mind being an unknown artist. In fact, I'm going to recommend it to all my artist friends! Stay unknown! Avoid the possibility of any chance of a complete and utter public humiliation! Life is so much simpler that way, don't you think? Anyway, sorry! I'm going to bury all my art and then go live in a cave in Tibet. Bye!"

And she had hung up! Which was why Robyn was now heading to Portreath, trying to decide how to murder an artist, while making it look like some kind of horrible art accident.

"Turn left onto Sunnyvale Road," her car's satnav instructed her once she had gotten off the A3075 and had been navigating the Portreath streets for a few minutes. "Your destination will be on the left in five-hundred yards."

Sure enough, her car announced that she arrived when she pulled into the driveway of a neat, two-storey home that was painted white and had a brown asphalt tile roof.

Robyn had been here before, during the discussions she'd had with Sasha about having the artist's first solo show at the Linden Gallery Cornwall. She knew that almost every square inch of Sasha's house inside was given over to the craft of painting, and that out in the back was a separate building which was used as her studio.

Once out of her car, she marched up to the wooden door and started hammering on it.

"Sasha!" she called out. "Sasha! It's Robyn! I know you're in there! No one can possibly leave for Tibet that quickly!"

Robyn stopped hammering and counted to ten. If Sasha didn't open the door, she was more than ready to scale the low white wall which surrounded the artist's property and seek her out.

Fortunately, wall-climbing was averted when Robyn's count reached *six* and the front door was cracked open.

"Robyn?" a voice asked from the crack.

"Sasha, open this door!" Robyn commanded.

Sasha did as she was told, revealing herself to her unexpected visitor.

The artist was tall, with raven-black hair which was showing streaks of grey, and she was dressed as Robyn had always seen her dressed…in paint-splattered dungarees and a black t-shirt. She had an incredible figure, and was more of a handsome woman than pretty, with an aquiline nose and thick eyebrows common among people with Mediterranean ancestry. She was also barefoot, and her hair was tied up in the messiest of messy buns. At no other time in their—albeit brief—association, had Robyn seen her attired any differently. It made her wonder what Sasha would wear for the vernissage next week. She was all for everybody having the right to express their own personal style, but she couldn't possibly have Sasha showing up looking like the janitor to the art world.

But that was a battle for another day.

"May I come in, please?" she asked.

"Sorry! Of course!" Sasha replied, standing aside.

Stepping inside, Robyn almost tripped on what looked like a bolt of canvas on the floor, and then almost tripped again when she bumped into a stack of hardcover books, also on the floor.

"Sorry!" Sasha said. "The place is a bit of a mess."

Robyn smiled. Now that she was inside, face-to-face with Sasha, she decided that tact and diplomacy was what was called for.

"You're an artist," she said pleasantly. "The act of creation is messy. Think nothing of it."

She then looked up into Sasha's eyes, giving the older woman her best steely gaze while also maintaining a smile on her lip.

"Listen to me Sasha," she began. "Invitations to your big night have already gone out. People have RSVP-ed. Very important people. You are *going* to be there, and you are *going* to be fabulous. Now…why don't you tell me what's troubling you?"

***

"So what was it?" Tamsin asked that evening, staring at Robyn over the dinner they were having at Robyn's cottage, evidently enjoying the story her girlfriend was telling.

Robyn rolled her eyes.

"A story as old as time, innit?" she asked. "She and her girlfriend split up."

Tamsin scoffed.

"That's a shame, sure," she said, "but hardly a bloody good reason to torpedo your big opening night. If I acted like that each time me and a girlfriend broke up, I'd not be able to pay my bills."

Robyn smiled.

"*Love* that you consider it *my* big night," she said, "but it's *her* big night, and I can see your point, but Sasha is one of those souls who *needs* someone in her life, like at all times."

"So what did you do?" Tamsin asked.

"Oh, I told her I'd loan you out every now and then," Robyn answered. "Do Tuesdays and Thursdays work for you?"

Tamsin smirked and then sliced a morsel of the skirt steak Robyn had cooked for dinner.

"A bit of a break from you *does* sound nice," she said. "In fact, can we make it Tuesdays, Thursdays, *and* Saturdays?"

Robyn waggled her eyebrows.

"Done," she said. "Which means I get you *tonight*, and trust me, I'm incredibly horny, so if you'll be satisfied with just one for yourself, you'll have to work to earn it."

Tamsin smirk got smirkier.

"Have I ever disappointed?" she prodded.

No, she hasn't, Robyn thought.

They'd been lovers for only a week, but so far this was one of the most satisfying sexual relationships she'd been in. And yes, there had been nights when Tamsin had been truly finished after having one orgasm, but before getting to that point, she always fucked her until Robyn's vision went blurry and she lost all feeling in her cheeks.

"So what did you *really* do to help Sasha get over herself?" Tamsin asked.

"I created an account for her in that new lesbian dating app, Lez Meet," Robyn told her. "By the time I left, she had gotten three tickles and four licks."

"Sheesh, when I get four licks I'm expecting a woman to finish me off," Tamsin quipped.

Robyn laughed.

"I'll keep that in mind," she said. "Anyway, Sasha seemed to have levelled off by the time I left. I'm hoping she won't give me any more trouble between now and next week, but just in case, have bail money ready in case I end up in the nick for trying to kill her."

"Well, wait a minute," Tamsin said. "You can't try to kill her on a Tuesday, Thursday, or Saturday, remember. She's *my* girlfriend those days, so you'll have to get by me first, and I know karate."

Chapter 27

The next day, at Xplr, Uncle Richard was explaining his "brilliant" idea.

"What I have in mind," he was saying, "is we get a blow-up of that Hollywood sign they have over there, and you stand in front of it, talking about the great package deals for California holidays we have. We can even dress you up like you're one of those entertainment reporters, and perhaps we can have you pretend to interview someone who booked one of our holidays!"

Tamsin stared at him.

She loved this man, but good lord! His suggestion was making her feel ill.

"Erm…" she began, her mind racing, trying to come up with a UN-level diplomatic way to get out of this conversation. "I think you have the bones of a great idea!" she said encouragingly. "Let me…take it home and flesh it out."

More like, *take it home and toss it in the bin*, but she kept that to herself.

However, Uncle Richard seemed satisfied with her answer.

"Well, we should get on this campaign quickly," he advised. "Summer will be over before you know it, which means people here will be yearning to get to places like California. Who knows? I may even take a wee trip there myself this winter."

He then retired to his office in the back.

Uncle Richard's vid idea may have been horrid, but all that talk of California was making Tamsin think of what Robyn had said the other day, about them taking a holiday there if they were still together after six months.

She couldn't help smiling at the idea.

That in itself was odd, considering how long she had maintained a simmering dislike for that place. She had always known she was being silly and petty in that regard, but that it was also just…how she was. She had also known she would eventually get over it, but she hadn't anticipated that it would take another woman to help her do so.

But the truth of the matter was that now, she would happily travel to California if Robyn was with her. Or anywhere else for that matter.

They'd been together for a week now. Not long, unless one is used to measuring her relationships in weeks, like she was. When looked at from *that* perspective, in just a few more *days*, this romance would count as one of the longest she's had (and how sad was that?), and in only a couple of more weeks, Robyn would be able to count herself among the handful of girlfriends who stuck around long enough for Tamsin to actually have a period during their relationship.

She blinked.

Goodness…

She had just realised that she had never had *two* periods with the same girlfriend.

It was such a silly bit of personal trivia that it made her laugh out loud. She wondered if Hallmark made a card for such an occasion.

Happy 12th Period-versary!
Our love has lasted through approximately 480 tampons!
Here's to another 480 more!

A chirp from her mobile interrupted her reverie.

Could use your help at the gallery when you have a moment,
but only if you're free for a bit.

It was from Robyn. Despite it being Saturday, Tamsin knew she was at the gallery today, along with her two assistants, continuing to make preparations before what Robyn described as the "chaos of next week."

Tamsin wondered what on earth she could do for them.

They must need an extra hand moving something from Place A to Place B.

Though she believed she was *not* put on this Earth nor constructed to do physical labour, she was fine with lending a hand, so long as she didn't have to bend down too much or climb a ladder. She had chosen a particularly short skirt to wear today, the kind a woman chooses when she does *not* expect to be doing *needs-a-union-card-type* work.

As for *being free for a bit*, she was, at the moment. It was late morning—approaching lunchtime—and she was between clients. Her next one wouldn't be showing up until one o'clock. If Robyn needed her non-bending and non-ladder-climbing help, Uncle Richard could man the agency to handle any phone calls or walk-ins for a little bit.

"Uncle Richard," she called out, locking her handbag in the largest of her desk's drawers, "I need to pop down the street for a few minutes. I'll be back shortly."

"Fine, luv," her uncle called back. Tamsin then silently mouthed his next words as he said them. "I'll hold down the fort."

Taking her mobile with her, she walked out of the agency and headed in the direction of Robyn's gallery. She had yet to be inside the place, which still had kraft paper covering all the windows.

When she reached it, she knocked on the door, feeling like something of a git because everyone else walking past her on the street was seeing her trying to gain entrance to an establishment that was obviously *not* open for business.

Fortunately, Robyn opened the door quickly, and now Tamsin felt less like a daft git and more like someone privileged who was gaining access to a super-secret club.

"Wow!" she exclaimed when she stepped inside. This had less to do with Robyn and how cute she looked (though she did look cute in a *hot-lesbian-doing-DIY-projects* kind of way), and more with the space she had just entered.

Though there was no art on the walls yet, the gallery looked fabulous, like something out of a magazine advert.

All of the walls were pristine white, except for one that was painted a striking indigo colour which made Tamsin think of a clear, darkening sky at twilight. She half expected to see stars shining in it, in fact.

The floors were of a gorgeous blonde wood, without a single scuff mark on them, and throughout the space were pieces of ultra-modern, very expensive-looking Scandinavian-style furniture consisting of two sofas, several accent chairs, and a couple of coffee tables. They were the type of pieces one would expect to see in a listing for a luxe Airbnb in Norway or Sweden.

Despite the furnishings, however, there was so much open space, exactly what a proper art gallery should have, Tamsin considered…room enough for patrons to move about, examining the works of art from up close or from afar.

"This place looks amazing!" she told Robyn. "I can't wait to see it when there's art in here!"

"Thank you," Robyn said, pressing herself against her and wrapping her arms around her waist.

"So what do you need my help with?" Tamsin asked. "I'm not climbing any bloody ladders!"

"Oh, I need your help on something very important," Robyn said, giving Tamsin a quick kiss. "I'm doing a study, you see…" She gave Tamsin another quick kiss. "…on how quickly I can make a ginger come in an empty art gallery."

Tamsin, her clit beginning to pound and her nipples already tightening to hard points, cocked an eyebrow.

"Is that right?" she asked. "Erm…where are your minions?"

Before answering, Robyn started stepping forward, which forced Tamsin to step backwards until she felt herself bump up against a wall.

"Tina and Lucien are on their way to Perranporth," Robyn said. "They just left ten minutes ago. There's a supermarket there having an outrageous sale on Champagne, and I've ordered them to buy up as much of it as they can for Friday."

Tamsin took a deep breath. Perranporth wasn't terribly far but it also wasn't exactly down the street. Such an errand would take time.

She gasped when she realised how Robyn wanted to spend that time.

Her girlfriend had brought her right hand to the front of Tamsin's skirt and snuck it up underneath it, rubbing her sex over her knickers.

"Nice skirt," Robyn purred. "Short. Exactly what I like to see you in."

Tamsin, already breathing raggedly, said, "Glad you approve."

"Open!" Robyn demanded.

Tamsin widened her stance and Robyn properly cupped her pussy over the underwear.

"These have to go," Robyn stated, before kissing the pulse point on her neck.

Due to how short her skirt was, and because of how often things like breezes and dropping pens occurred, Tamsin had protected her modesty today by wearing basic black full briefs which would reveal nothing. But Robyn was right, they needed to go.

"Do the honours," she instructed.

No sooner were the words out of her mouth when she felt Robyn take hold of the waistband of her knickers with both hands and start pulling them down forcefully, letting them drop to the floor when they were past her upper thighs. Tamsin then dutifully stepped out of them and immediately wrapped her arms around Robyn's shoulders, and her right leg around her waist, opening herself to whatever Robyn wanted to do.

"*Unnngh!*" she grunted when Robyn's fingers started pulling on her pubic hair.

"Look at me!" Robyn hissed, breathing hard.

Tamsin met her eyes.

"If you *ever* shave this off, I swear to god I will break up with you," Robyn told her.

That made Tamsin's clit pound harder, and her pussy became even wetter. The bossiness of it. The threat. The fact that it made it seem as if Robyn was already laying proprietary claim to bits of her. It excited her.

"Like it that much, huh?" Tamsin breathed.

"It's so fucking hot," Robyn answered. "I fucking fantasise about it."

Starting to become overcome with desire, Tamsin kissed Robyn deeply, ramming her tongue into her mouth, moaning into the kiss when her girlfriend's fingers began stroking her vulva.

Robyn pulled her mouth away.

"You're so fucking wet already," she mewled. "I fucking love it…"

"Oh *fuuuuuuck!*" Tamsin growled. Robyn was rubbing her clit now, using firm strokes, making the walls of her vagina flutter more strongly. She was already starting to feel her arousal on her left thigh, dripping out of her opening. "Fuck me!"

"Mm," Robyn hummed. "You can do better than that. You want to be fucked, *tell me* you want to be fucked!"

"Fuck me!" Tamsin said forcefully, putting an edge to her voice. "*Now,* Robyn! *Fucking now!*"

Fingers entered her and she surrendered to Robyn, who started taking care of her fast and hard up against the wall.

She loved this. Spontaneous sex outside of the home was a big turn-on for her, and it excited her to know that it was something Robyn was into as well. It bode well for their future together.

Just a few minutes ago, she was at her desk at Xplr, having just listened to her uncle's frighteningly horrid idea about a California promotional vid. Now, she was in this empty art gallery, and a stunning woman was fucking her up against a wall, rocketing her to super-quick orgasm.

"I'm going to taste you after you come," Robyn told her, ghosting her ear with her lips.

"*Mmmph...yes!*" Tamsin replied, knowing that wouldn't be long now.

"I can't wait," Robyn went on, continuing her thrusting into Tamsin's pussy, her hand slapping against her clit with each inward motion, "because you taste so good."

"Oh god..." Tamsin squealed. "Oh god..."

Deep in her mound, tiny detonations began, while in her vagina, the walls of her passage started vibrating rapidly.

"Look over my shoulder," Robyn said, "and then look up."

Tamsin had no idea what this was about, but she opened her eyes and did as she was told.

"*Oh fuck!*" she exclaimed, her mouth and eyes opening wide with surprise.

She was looking at a security camera that was pointed directly at them, watching her submitting to what another woman was doing to her.

"*Oh Jesus fuck!*" she gasped, the sensations in her pussy ramping up, bringing her even faster to the abyss.

"Like that, baby?" Robyn asked. "Maybe I'll bring home today's footage so we can watch ourselves later. Or..."

"Or what?" Tamsin squealed.

"Or maybe I'll show it here in the gallery," Robyn told her. "Let the world see how beautiful two women fucking is."

Tamsin's mind felt as if it was coming unmoored. What Robyn just described...it was so subversively sexy.

She actually wanted it to happen.

"Oh fuck, I'm about to come!" she gasped.

"Come all over my hand, baby," Robyn urged her. "Make me feel it! Give me lots to taste!"

That pushed Tamsin over the edge.

"*NNNNNNGH!*" she grunted as her release began, keeping her eyes on the camera. "*I'm coming! Bloody hell, I'm coming!*"

If they were at one of their houses, she knew she would have screamed that bit, but as they were not, she merely spoke it urgently, her voice strained with the power of the orgasm that was now bursting throughout her entire centre.

"Oh my days, you *are* coming!" Robyn purred.

Tamsin knew her girlfriend could feel the intensity with which her pussy was clutching at her fingers, and how come was streaming out of her, onto her hand.

Robyn kept her pressed against the wall for a few moments longer and then pulled her fingers out and dropped to her knees.

Tamsin lowered her right leg and then leaned back against the wall, pushing her pelvis out so Robyn could reach it more easily.

"Oh my fuck…Oh my fuck…" she exclaimed as she felt Robyn's mouth on her still-climaxing vulva, her tongue seemingly everywhere, licking up her effusions. What she didn't catch, rolled down both of Tamsin's thighs.

She took hold of Robyn's head with both hands, working her fingers deep into her hair, which was set in a sensible ponytail. Looking down, the visual of this awakened something in her, something carnally animalistic.

She needed to be getting back to Xplr, but she decided she wasn't going back just yet.

"Make me come again!" she commanded. "Fucking make me come again!"

When she felt her clit captured in Robyn's lips, she leaned her head back against the wall, stared up at the camera, and smiled.

Such an obedient girlfriend…

***

Less than twenty minutes later, Tamsin was walking back to Xplr on legs that felt rubbery. It didn't help that she was wearing espadrille wedges. Normally, she was an expert at walking in any kind of heel, no matter the type, but goodness did her legs want to wobble as she walked! It was only because of her natural inclination to avoid looking like a fool that she was able to maintain a normal stride as she moved, willing her body to keep its composure.

She had come a second time on Robyn's face, and it had happened quickly, making her shout out before coming to her senses and clamping her teeth down on her hand to muffle her cries of pleasure. And as with the first orgasm, she had stared into the camera's lens as her pussy enjoyed its intense pleasures.

Afterwards, she was a mess between her legs. Robyn hungrily helped clean her up, much to Tamsin's delight, but eventually she rose from her knees, took Tamsin's hand and led her to a loo in the back of the gallery. In there, Tamsin finished what Robyn couldn't and then went back out to the front to find Robyn holding her knickers out to her on the tip of her forefinger.

After she had put the underwear back on, she pulled Robyn to her and asked, "What's gotten into you today? Mind, I'm not complaining."

Robyn had smiled.

"I'm alone in an empty building," she had said, draping her arms on Tamsin's shoulders. "Four—no *five*—doors down is the sexiest woman in the UK who also happens to be my girlfriend." She smirked. "What else was I supposed to do?"

Tamsin's heart had soared at those words, but she quickly reminded herself to keep her expectations tempered.

"You're amazing," she had said.

"Better keep me around then," Robyn quipped, cocking an eyebrow. "Now…get back to work, slacker! But kiss me first."

Though Robyn had somehow managed to clean her face of Tamsin's arousal, Tamsin still tasted herself on her lips, and it got her heart pumping again as her nipples hardened once more in her bra.

But in the end, she left the gallery, knowing she'd see Robyn tonight in Tremont.

Now, her vulva was *still* twitching in her knickers as latent jolts of pleasure from her orgasms continued to delight her while she walked. Her underwear was already wet again. No surprise. She knew the cleaning-up she had done in the gallery's loo had only been a stopgap. Robyn had gotten her so turned-on and had made her come so hard that she was going to be leaking for a while.

She tried to remember if she had spare underwear in Xplr. She usually kept at least one pair in case her period snuck up on her one month, but she was sometimes careless in replacing them for the next *just-in-case* moment.

Oh well…

If she didn't, there were worse things than spending the rest of the day in wrecked knickers because she had just been fucked rather well, four—no *five*—doors down from her job.

Chapter 28

That night, Mr. Trelawny, a pensioner with the bushiest eyebrows Robyn had ever seen on a human, peered at her from across the table.

"You're the one with the posh car," he stated.

Robyn, maintaining her smile, sighed through her nostrils.

"It's really not a posh—" she tried to explain.

"*Ohhhhh!* You're the one with the posh car!" Mrs. Kelly, another pensioner at their table said, interrupting her.

"What type is it again?" Mrs. Trelawny asked her husband.

"BMW," Mr. Trelawny answered. "Jerry car."

Robyn raised a finger.

"I don't think we're allowed to call them Jerries anymore…" she protested.

"Oh, that *is* posh!" Mrs. Trelawny stated. She raised her eyebrows and regarded Robyn anew. "Bloody duchess sitting at our table."

Robyn chuckled nervously.

"Believe me, I am *so* far from a duch—"

"Oh, would you lot leave her be!" Tamsin demanded. "She may have a posh car, but she doesn't deserve the bloody third-degree!"

Robyn looked at her.

"Again, it's *not* a posh car," she told her girlfriend. "Anybody at this table could probably buy the model I have."

Mr. Trelawny scoffed and crossed his arms.

"As if I would buy a Jerry car," he said with a huff.

Robyn blew out a frustrated breath.

"Once again, sir, *Jerry* is no longer an appropriate thing to say!" she declared.

She and Tamsin were at the Ladle & Spoon, Tremont's local, for trivia night. Robyn had insisted they come because she wanted a night out, wanted to spend more time with Darcie and Rylea—who were also here—and also wanted to start making herself more visible to the denizens of Tremont, and perhaps work on dispelling any rumours that she was a cat burglar.

So far, during her brief residency in this charming village, she had been very hermit-like, often choosing to stay in after reaching home following a busy day at the gallery. And that was *before* she and Tamsin started seeing each other. Once *that* happened, her hermit-like ways had continued, except with sex.

Now, however, even though she wanted the sex to continue, she also wanted to start getting out more, and trivia night at the pub seemed like the perfect opportunity to begin making her face known.

Fortunately, further discussion about her car or whether or not she was a duchess was avoided when Mrs. Trelawny started berating her husband for something silly he had just said.

"They're harmless," Rylea, who was sitting to her left, whispered to her. "Can you imagine how bad it would have been if you drove a Mercedes?"

Robyn laughed.

"Christ," she whispered back, "I'd probably be accused of having orchestrated the Blitz."

"On the bright side," Rylea said, "you'd be promoted from duchess to princess."

"Well, my father always told me I was a princess," Robyn said. "He'd love to be proved right."

"Better pay attention," Tamsin whispered on Robyn's other side. "Game's about to start, and Mr. T. doesn't appreciate a lack of focus."

Robyn wanted to guffaw, but worried that Mr. Trelawny would interpret that as a lack of focus.

She was having such a great time. The pub was a lively spot and everybody she'd been introduced to so far had been friendly and welcoming. Based on the subset of the Tremont residents who were in the pub to play trivia, she deduced that the village was an eclectic mix of individuals. She was especially delighted to see that there were several black people in the crowd. Tamsin told her that was a somewhat new development in Tremont, one which she was happy for herself because, in her words, the village had long had "too many bloody white people."

Moreover, being in such a crowd of Tremont denizens, Robyn could finally understand why Tamsin had referred to this hamlet as "lesbian central." It was very clear that many of the women who were in the Ladle & Spoon tonight were paired up, and though she hated being presumptuous, it was also quite obvious that many of the women who weren't paired up, were gay, as much as she loathed such classifications being made based on appearance alone. However, if the plaid shirt fits…

She didn't detect any covert hostility among the locals towards all this sapphic energy, nor did she overhear any snide comments along the lines of "Look at *those* women over there!" or "What a pity *those girls* can't find decent men!"

Even Mr. Trelawny, despite his insistence that Germans were "Jerries"—even though he was too young to have been anywhere near World War II—had seemed genuinely happy that Tamsin had a new girlfriend.

In short, she felt comfortable in this pub and was glad she had insisted they come out tonight.

Being in such a relaxed state helped her contribute to her team's scoring during the trivia contest. Tamsin had warned her before they came here that Mr. Trelawny would consider Robyn on probation during the game, at least until she proved to him that she had the smarts to become an official member of The Geezers and the Girls—their team name.

No questions about art came up; nonetheless, Robyn felt particular satisfaction having been able to supply the correct answer to *Who was the first woman to win a Nobel Prize?* (Marie Curie). And *What are the first 22 cards in a tarot deck called?* (The Major Arcana).

"Can we do that again?" Robyn asked now, as she and Tamsin walked home from the pub following the game. This was another thing she loved about Tremont, the fact that everything was within walking distance, which meant that strolls like this—holding Tamsin's hand under a moonlit sky—could happen frequently. "I had such a good time."

"Of course we can," Tamsin said. "I should probably confess that tonight was a test. If Mr. Trelawny didn't like you, I would have had to break up with you."

Robyn laughed.

"Well, I know I was on the bubble there for a bit because of my Jerry car," she quipped.

"I actually wondered if *I* wanted to date you because of that also," Tamsin replied, chuckling. "Anyway, what do you want to do with the rest of the night?" Tamsin then asked.

"Spend it quietly," Robyn answered. "Young Kim Cattrall is in one of those *Star Trek* movies. Let's watch that."

"Your place or mine?"

Robyn considered that question. The answer didn't matter, quite frankly. She was equally comfortable staying at Tamsin's cottage as she was having Tamsin stay at her cottage. They had already gotten that comfortable being together in either home. In fact, as she pondered the question, she couldn't help but wonder if one day it would no longer need to be asked. If one day, the only possible answer to where they would watch a young-Kim-Cattrall movie would be, *Home.*

She blinked rapidly.

It's only been a week... It's only been a week... It's only been a week...

She *really* liked Tamsin, but she was far too sensible to fall arse over teakettle in love with somebody this quickly.

At least…she thought so.

"Your place," she said quickly, to get her mind out of the clouds.

***

This is getting ridiculous, Robyn thought.

If this kept up, she would never be able to watch Kim Cattrall in so much as a toothpaste commercial without getting aroused.

At Tamsin's cottage, when they had started watching that *Star Trek* movie the young Kim Cattrall was in, Robyn had been dressed in her pyjamas, reclining on the sofa with her head in Tamsin's lap.

Now, her pyjama bottoms and knickers were off, and her top was hiked up, exposing her breasts. Her head was still in Tamsin's lap, but now she was breathing rapidly as she recovered from another orgasm Tamsin's fingers had just given her.

What she loved was that Tamsin was still possessively holding onto her pussy, with her middle and ring fingers curled inside her passage, and her palm still pressed down on her clit. It was as if Tamsin was silently telling her, "I'm not done with you yet."

Meanwhile, the movie was still playing, though Robyn had lost the plot long ago. Being fingered to three orgasms was not particularly conducive to following the story of a film.

"Goodness," Tamsin cooed, "that was a strong one, wasn't it? You're *really* squeezing my fingers!"

Robyn could only nod. It *had* been a strong one! Tamsin was just *so* fucking good with her fingers! More so than any of her past lovers. Robyn couldn't figure out what it was that she did differently, however, without getting mystical about it. But it was hard not to venture down that path. The fact was, when Tamsin touched her sex, it was as if her fingers were able to communicate with her pussy through more than just touch. Her fingers just seemed to *know* when and where to apply the appropriate amount of pressure. When to stay outside on her vulva or when to penetrate her. When to circle her clit lightly or when to rub it furiously with focussed attention.

She was an expert at using her fingers to construct a first orgasm from the ground up, building the pleasure like a bricklayer stacking bricks, sometimes taking her time with it and keeping Robyn waiting, other times letting her come quickly—like tonight— and then using the pleasure from that first climax as the foundation for the next one, and so on.

Robyn gave a little grunt when she felt Tamsin remove her fingers from her vagina.

"Clean," Tamsin instructed.

That was tonight's game. Every time Tamsin made her come, she also made her clean off her fingers.

Robyn took hold of Tamsin's wrist and brought the wet digits to her mouth, starting to suck them clean of her own essence, an act which only made her want to be played with more.

"Another one?" Tamsin asked.

Robyn, the fingers still in her mouth, nodded.

"Yes, please," she said when she was done with her task and had relinquished Tamsin's hand. As far as she was concerned, Tamsin could keep doing this until she was too sensitive and sore to continue. "*Unnnnnnngh!*" she grunted as her swollen and buzzing clit was once more edged by one of Tamsin's fingers.

"Mm," Tamsin cooed. "My sweet girlfriend is *so* turned-on!"

Robyn nodded rapidly. That was an understatement.

"Well, you're going to have to be patient this time," Tamsin continued, speaking gently. "I've been spoiling you so far tonight. You're really going to wait for this next one."

Robyn mewled helplessly but did not give voice to a complaint.

"I'll be good," she said instead.

"And then afterwards, are you going to fuck me?" Tamsin asked.

"*Fuuuuuck!*" Robyn squealed, and then started chuckling. "You can't talk like that while you're doing what you're doing!" She squeezed her eyes shut and bit her bottom lip. She was already on the edge again.

Tamsin's finger left her clit and started caressing her opening, playing with the come that was still streaming out of it. It allowed Robyn to walk herself back from the precipice, but only by a little bit.

"You haven't answered my question," Tamsin reminded her.

Robyn let out a breath she didn't realise she had been holding.

"Yes, I'll fuck you," she gasped out. "You have no idea how much I'll fuck you!"

"I should have had you bring over that suction vibe you were telling me about," Tamsin said ruefully.

Robyn was biting her knuckle because her girlfriend was now playing the tips of her fingers on her sex in the vicinity of her clit, but not quite in the neighbourhood of it.

"You'll love it," she finally managed to squeak. "It fucking changed my life."

Tamsin laughed.

"Well, shall I send you home to get it then?" she asked.

"As if I'm going to be able to walk after you get done with me," Robyn quipped.

"Good point," Tamsin answered.

Robyn had no idea how long it took. She guessed she was made to wait at least forty minutes. Forty minutes of caring and gentle stimulation from Tamsin's exquisite fingers that kept her centre on fire and her passage flooded no matter how much of that arousal flowed out of her.

It never got boring or made her feel impatient, the way something like that could do when being done by a lesser-skilled woman. Instead, her girlfriend was so masterful that Robyn was happy to wait. At times she even wanted to beg to keep it going all night because no one should ever *not* feel like that.

When Tamsin finally granted her release, she came as hard as she ever had before. It was a titanic orgasm that made her scream and was so intense that Tamsin had to use her other arm to help keep her from falling off the sofa because of how strongly she was bucking as the climax tore through her.

When it was over, and she was lying exhausted on the sofa, with her head still in Tamsin's lap, she knew she had been right earlier.

There was no way she'd be able to walk to her place to get that suction vibe.

Chapter 29

The next morning, Tamsin offered to cook them breakfast.

"Something light, please," Robyn said. They were upstairs in the bedroom, getting dressed after taking a shower together. Oddly enough, Tamsin had been pleased that the shower had been just that…a shower, as opposed to sex with running water, and because it had just been the act of two women cleaning themselves before starting their day, it gave her a feeling of comfort and familiarity that was a bit unsettling. Normally, it took longer than a week before words like "comfort" and "familiarity" became associated in her mind with a particular woman. Those words felt like *home* to her…

"Are you on a diet?" Tamsin asked, pulling on an olive-coloured slim-fit vest.

"Not as such," Robyn answered. She was pulling her still-damp hair into a ponytail. "But you should see the dress I've chosen for the vernissage on Friday. It is *unforgiving* and will not allow an excess calorie to take up residence in my body."

"Now that you mention it…" Tamsin said, but didn't finish, knowing that Robyn got the gist.

She had also put some thought into the dress she was going to wear to that exclusive gallery-opening party, and like Robyn's, it would also be unforgiving. She'd need to mind what she ate this upcoming week—sensibly, of course—and be sure to exercise. After all, she was twenty-five and no longer young!

Downstairs, Tamsin prepared them a simple meal of scrambled eggs and some diced fruit. She also put the kettle on for tea for herself and made Robyn a cup of coffee.

As they were eating, Robyn cleared her throat.

"So, I've been thinking," she began.

"Yes?" Tamsin prodded.

"One of my assistants at the gallery is Tina," Robyn went on. "She's actually quite a talented artist."

"Nice," Tamsin said, spearing a cube of cantaloupe with her fork.

"Seeing her work gave me an idea," Robyn said. "In between major exhibitions at the gallery, it might be fun if I ran a multi-artist showcase, featuring Cornwall artists. You know, Newquay, Port Isaac, Truro…*Tremont.*"

Tamsin nodded.

"Sounds like a great idea," she said.

"Excellent!" Robyn exclaimed, picking up her coffee mug. "Glad you're agreeing to participate with your paintings. So…I'm assuming you have some Xplr work you want to get done today, right? But what do you want to do afterwards?"

Tamsin blinked.

"Wait a minute," she said. "Rewind the past thirty seconds. What do you mean I'm agreeing to participate with my paintings?"

Robyn put a *Just what I said* expression on her face.

"Just what I said," she then vocalised, in case Tamsin had trouble reading her face. "We'll put your paintings in the show."

Aargh!

Tamsin wondered why people just couldn't leave her alone about her paintings. Fine, she was great at it, but she *wasn't* trying to be an artist at this point in her life.

She crossed her arms and sat back in her chair.

"So…A: I didn't *agree* to do anything of the sort! And…B: what if I don't want to include my paintings in this show?"

Robyn laughed.

"Oh my days, you are just too adorable!" she stated. She then also crossed her arms and sat back in her chair. "So, I will rebut each of your points in order.

"A: As a woman, I reserve the right to interpret you telling me that my idea was a good one, *after* I hinted that I wanted a Tremont artist in the show—which obviously meant *you*—as agreeing to include your paintings."

"That is a load of bollocks!" Tamsin protested, but Robyn cut her off from further discussion by raising one finger.

"And as a woman you should have known that," Robyn pointed out. "And…B: As your girlfriend, I am demanding that this happen, and I will use every tactic the Girlfriend Laws provide me. I will cajole, I will cry, I will seduce, I will withhold affection until you finally break down and give me what I want."

"*That is also a load of bollocks!*" Tamsin hissed.

"Be that as it may," Robyn began, "but if you want someone to date whom you can bend to *your* will, start dating men. They're idiots."

Tamsin huffed.

Robyn leaned forward with her elbows on the table now.

"Sweetie," she said softly, "give me your hands."

Tamsin had a mind to refuse, but she also leaned forward and now they were holding hands over the table.

Robyn kissed her knuckles.

"I'm not asking you to paint anything new," she said calmly. "All I'm asking for are the paintings you already have!"

Tamsin rolled her eyes.

"No one is going to like them!" she insisted. "They are so derivative!"

"They are not!" Robyn said indignantly. "You have taken formal-style portraiture and applied a very contemporary take to it."

Tamsin appreciated what Robyn was telling her, it certainly made her feel good to hear it from someone so deep in the art world, but she had never shown her work publicly before. She painted—*when* she painted—because she enjoyed it and loved the feeling of using a talent she knew she had to create something.

"So, is that what you're really afraid of?" Robyn asked, giving her knuckles another kiss. "That no one will like them?"

Tamsin shrugged.

"Eh," she said. "I'm too smart for that. I know how subjective art is, and so I know some people will like them, some people won't."

"And bollocks to the ones who don't," Robyn told her.

"Right."

"So, can I ask a question?" Robyn prodded.

Tamsin made a face.

"As if I would be able to stop you?" she commented.

"Good point," Robyn said. "So…the women in your paintings…are they exes?"

Tamsin shook her head.

"No," she declared. She then explained that she had known better than to use girlfriends as models because, all too often, girlfriends become ex-girlfriends.

"And I didn't want to look at one of my paintings," she said, finishing her story, "and see bad memories."

"That makes sense," Robyn said. "And good…because they're not of your exes, I don't need to have you burn the paintings, so, yay for art preservation!"

Tamsin could only howl with laughter.

***

On the following Friday evening, Tamsin came down the stairs in her cottage.

"Bloody hell!" Darcie exclaimed upon seeing her.

"Yeah, bloody hell!" Rylea reiterated, staring at her.

Stopping three steps up from the bottom, Tamsin looked down at herself, trying to spot something amiss.

"What?" she asked, worried when she couldn't see a stain, a tear in the fabric, or a hole. "What's wrong?"

"Sweetie, nothing!" Darcie told her. "You look *stunning!*"

"Really, Tams, you do," Rylea added.

At the bottom of the stairs there was what Tamsin called her *Last Look* mirror. It was identical to the full-length First Look mirror in her bedroom, but down here it gave her a chance to always give her outfits a last look before walking out the door. She stepped in front of it now and gave herself another once-over.

"Are you sure?" she asked. "I mean, do I look like the girlfriend of a successful gallery manager?"

Her cocktail dress was a black pencil number with a deep V-neck, which ended just above her knees. It was classic and classy and because it fit her so amazingly well, sexy.

She had accessorised it with a platinum vertical bar pendant necklace which she knew automatically drew eyes to her cleavage, but which she also just loved wearing, and a chunky black stone bracelet in place of her Apple Watch. A smart watch may be useful for the day-to-day, but it was *not* something a woman should wear to a formal occasion. If she needed to know what time it was, she'd either check her phone, or ask a bloke.

"What is holding your boobs up?" Darcie asked, coming to stand next to her in front of the *Last Look* mirror.

"The most amazing bralette ever constructed," Tamsin told her. It came from (of all places) California and was designed for women with larger breasts. She had discovered the company while online shopping and came across one of the most amazingly beautiful models she had ever seen—a tall blonde goddess who practically seduced Tamsin into visiting the lingerie company's website just by how gorgeous she was.

In any case, the cut of the bralette allowed her to wear a deep V-neck dress like this, which was why she now owned three of the undergarments.

Robyn was already at the gallery, having had to be there hours ago in order to make sure everything was ready for primetime. Tamsin hadn't seen her in whatever dress she was wearing because she had left Tremont wearing jeans and a tee, carrying her dress in a garment bag to change into at the gallery. The plan was for Tamsin to ride to the vernissage with Darcie and Rylea and then, of course, come back home with Robyn in her posh car.

"Okay, I guess I'm ready," she told her friends, both of whom looked stunning in their own cocktail dresses. She put her phone in her clutch. Along with a tube of lipstick for touch-ups, her credit card and ID, the phone was about the only other thing she could fit in there.

"Look at us!" Rylea commented as they walked out of the cottage, their high heels clacking on the stone walk. "We are three fierce lesbians who look spectacular!"

Darcie and Tamsin laughed. Tamsin was really looking forward to this, especially because two of her closest friends were joining her. Rylea was right, they were drop-dead gorgeous, and being able to spend a night like this with her and Darcie, all dressed up and ready to turn heads, was making her feel like an unstoppable superwoman.

***

The vernissage started at 7 p.m., but as per Robyn's instructions the trio of friends arrived fashionably late, and so it wasn't until just before the clock struck eight that they walked into the gallery.

Tamsin gasped.

The space had undergone quite a transformation since the last time she was allowed in, the day Robyn fucked her against…

She turned to find the right spot.

…that wall right there. She then turned her head and found the security camera that had watched them. She cocked her eyebrow at it, as if to say, *Me again…*

She forced herself to look away as her clit started swelling, remembering, and she was *not* outfitted tonight to be aroused. The knickers she had on beneath her dress were so tiny they could accidentally be swallowed.

In any case, the gallery was now full of Sasha Hoffman's art…paintings—some of them as large as entire walls—full of colour and geometric shapes. Tamsin was looking forward to examining each work more closely.

The gallery was also full of people, and they were clearly from the toffee-nosed set. Men in expensive suits, women in even more expensive dresses. On the whole, it was more of an older crowd, though there were several people who looked to be in their early thirties. The fact that the crowd was older didn't surprise Tamsin. This was Cornwall, not London. The people who had the money and the influence enough to be invited to an event like a vernissage (let alone who knew what a vernissage was) would always be at least a generation older than herself.

She spotted Robyn and her heart melted.

That's my girlfriend…

Tamsin knew that this gallery could be filled with all the works of Bouguereau, Vermeer, and Sargent, and yet she would still only want to look at this woman who, in such a short time, was stealing her heart.

"Christ almighty," Rylea muttered. "She looks…amazing! She dates *you?*"

"Shut up!" Tamsin hissed.

Robyn was wearing a sleeveless 1950s-vintage-style cocktail dress with a swing hem. It was a beautiful floral pink colour and in a gallery full of dark suits and dresses this meant that Robyn stood out, as if she was the bright summer season personified.

She was currently talking to a woman Tamsin recognised as the mayor of Newquay, and her husband, and it was clear that Robyn was in her element, Tamsin noted. Even from halfway across the room, Tamsin could see that the mayor and her spouse were completely charmed by her.

When Robyn turned her head and spotted her, she beamed, and Tamsin sucked in a deep breath.

"You're here!" Robyn squealed a few moments later after Tamsin had watched her excuse herself from the mayor. She gave Tamsin a hug and then did the same to Darcie and Rylea. "I'll introduce you all to Sasha in a bit," she said, "but first…" She took hold of Tamsin's hand. "…excuse us, ladies, but I want to say hello properly to this one! Have some Champagne!"

She started leading Tamsin away as Darcie and Rylea laughed.

Tamsin found herself being taken into the back and then into an office, the door to which Robyn immediately shut. The next thing Tamsin knew, Robyn was embracing her tightly.

"I want to kiss you so badly," Robyn murmured against Tamsin's neck, "but I'm afraid I won't be able to stop if I start."

"I know," Tamsin told her, murmuring against *Robyn's* neck. "I just want you all to myself now."

"As crazy as today's been," Robyn said, "I missed you so much."

"I've missed you too," Tamsin replied, "even though I was *super* busy at work today!"

This was true. Yet despite how busy she was, Robyn had always been in the back of her mind.

Robyn pulled away just enough to look Tamsin in the face. Tamsin's eyes immediately went to her girlfriend's lips, which were painted with cranberry-coloured matte lipstick.

"Okay," Tamsin said, "let's allow ourselves one kiss. One tiny kiss."

Robyn nodded.

"One tiny kiss," she repeated.

"And we can both fix our lipstick before we go back out there," Tamsin added.

Again, Robyn nodded.

"Totally," she said.

With that done, they wasted no more time.

It turned hungry and aggressive very quickly, both women groaning as their lips moved together and their tongues duelled. Between her legs, the fire was well and truly lit in Tamsin's core, and her molten essence began sliding down her vagina's throbbing walls to her opening.

She surrendered to it; it felt far too good to do anything to stop it.

From the muffled whines Robyn was making, Tamsin knew she was also yielding to pleasures in her centre, and also wanted this kiss to go on far longer than it should.

Simultaneously, each woman tightened her grip on the other. By now, Tamsin was *wet*, but she didn't care. That was a problem to solve later…

***

Later came after midnight, at Robyn's cottage, well after the vernissage was over.

Tamsin, straddling Robyn's face, tilted her head back now, her eyes squeezed shut but her mouth opened wide.

She was coming again, for a fourth time, a colossal orgasm that was making her scream out to the goddesses she believed were above, the ones who had brought her Robyn.

As the pleasure throbbed intensely through her pussy, as her come sprayed out of her into Robyn's waiting mouth, as her vagina contracted so strongly it almost made her double over, she started crying.

Rylea had been right…it *hadn't* been her! It had been *them!* It was all the women who came before this one—this one who told her that there was nothing to fix, that it was fine if she only wanted one orgasm a night because there was nothing wrong with that. Nothing at all.

This one who understood that she was fine just the way she was.

But as she continued coming and tears continued streaming down her face, Tamsin was glad that she hadn't remained just the way she had been. What Robyn had unlocked in her over the past two weeks was too good to ever deny herself.

And she knew now that she only ever wanted to experience it with her.

Chapter 30

Summer turned to autumn. Alone in her cottage, Robyn stroked Empress's fur while sitting on the sofa.

"What do you think?" Robyn asked the cat. "I'm willing to bet that she will pretend as if we have never had the conversation."

Empress, purring, slowly shut her eyes, which Robyn interpreted as agreeing with her.

"What shall we bet, huh?" Robyn asked. "Tell you what…if *I* win, *you* have to clean your litter box for a whole month. Deal?"

It was Tuesday evening. Robyn had been home from the gallery now for about an hour, but Tamsin had told her that she needed to stay at Xplr later than usual today. Something to do with booking an enormous tour group on an eco-tourism voyage to Antarctica. Apparently, it was going to bring in quite a bit of money to the travel agency, and Robyn was glad.

"Oh, she's here!" she told Empress. Even the cat's ears had perked up, detecting Tamsin's arrival by the sounds coming from the front door.

By now, Tamsin had carte blanche to enter her cottage whenever she wanted. If Robyn was expecting her, she kept the door unlocked and simply waited for her girlfriend to walk right in.

"Hey, babe," Tamsin greeted Robyn. "Sorry I'm so late."

"So, am I dating a millionaire yet?' Robyn asked.

Tamsin laughed.

"Not quite," she said, placing her handbag on the entryway table, taking off her high heels and then padding to the sofa on bare feet. Sitting down, she immediately kissed Robyn. "It smells good in here," she added. Before Robyn had a chance to respond to that, however, she captured her lips for another kiss, which lasted longer than the first.

Empress, apparently not interested in seeing the humans doing this any longer, jumped off Robyn's lap.

"Mm, you're frisky," Robyn said when the kiss ended. And now she was as well.

"Making money turns me on," Tamsin told her. "Now tell me what smells so good."

"Dinner," Robyn told her. "It's still got another forty minutes or so before it's ready."

"Perfect," Tamsin said. "That gives me plenty of time to change. I swear to god, I've had it with this old bra! It bloody sucks! I think I've owned it too long."

Robyn licked her lips.

"So…tossing it in the bin, are you?"

Tamsin nodded.

"Definitely," she said. "Today is officially the last day I wear this old bugger."

"Wait right here!" Robyn instructed, standing up and hurrying to the kitchen, her heart thumping.

She found what she was looking for quickly and walked back to the living room, hiding what she was carrying by cleverly concealing it with her palm and wrist.

"Stand up," she instructed her girlfriend.

Tamsin quirked an eyebrow.

"Why?" she asked.

Robyn raised her own eyebrow.

"Do you really want to know, or would you rather be surprised?" she asked. "I mean, it's fucking Tuesday, Tams. What other exciting things are going to happen?"

"Fair point," Tamsin said, standing. "Okay, now what?"

Robyn tilted her head.

"Up against the wall," she said, meaning the entryway wall at the bottom of the stairs.

Tamsin padded over there.

"Hands behind your back," Robyn told her. When Tamsin had complied, she then added, "And keep them there."

"What if I don't?" Tamsin asked, her voice a bit huskier now.

Robyn smirked.

Very carefully, making sure Tamsin did not see it—or that she didn't hurt herself with it—she placed the item she had brought from the kitchen in the pocket of the pyjama pants she had changed into after getting home. She then reached up and removed the scrunchy that was holding her ponytail in place. She gave her head a couple of shakes to let her brown locks fall into place around her shoulders.

Reaching behind Tamsin, she slipped the scrunchie over her wrists, doubling it.

"Not exactly a copper's cuffs, but you get the idea," she whispered in Tamsin's ear.

"Mm…" Tamsin hummed. "I feel helpless."

"Mm…good," Robyn stated. "That means…I can do this, without you stopping me…"

She started unbuttoning Tamsin's white blouse. She did it slowly, feeling herself getting wetter as the swells of her girlfriend's breasts came into view.

The "old" bra Tamsin was wearing was white, with scalloped-edged cups. Robyn could tell that it was a long-time veteran in the cause of supporting Tamsin's girls. Parts of the bra's material was frayed, and she could see that the ends of both underwires were poking through their…whatever the thing that holds in underwires is called.

When she had the blouse completely unbuttoned, she opened it wide, exposing Tamsin's chest, her breath becoming ragged at the sight. They were coming up on three months of being together, and she was nowhere close to being tired of seeing Tamsin in a bra, knowing what treasures were contained within it.

She took hold of Tamsin's chin with her fingers and met her eyes.

"Stay perfectly still," she instructed.

"Yes, ma'am," Tamsin said.

From the pocket of her pyjamas, she carefully extracted the chopping knife she had brought from the kitchen and held it up for Tamsin to see.

"Ooh!" Tamsin said, letting out a slow breath. "What are you going to do with that, ma'am?"

Robyn rubbed the flat of the blade over the cup concealing Tamsin's left breast. The bra was lined but she could still see where the nipple was pushing against the fabric.

"You don't get to ask questions," she hissed.

"Yes, ma'am," Tamsin said.

"Why on earth are you wearing this silly bra?" Robyn demanded. "I thought I told you I want these uncovered at all times."

"I'm sorry," Tamsin said in the voice of a damsel in distress, "but I'm required to wear one at my job."

"Well, let me show you what I think of that," Robyn said. She slid the knife blade under the left strap of the bra, near where it joined the cup, and with a flick of her wrist, sliced through it.

Robyn's clit pulsed hard as the knife did its job, that one cut completely wrecking the bra. She'd always wanted to do something like this: tear off a woman's clothes, cut off her bra, free her body from her clothing enough to be ravished by her—consensually, of course.

But it was hardly a vanilla request, and Robyn had always been a bit worried that her various lovers would have thought she was an aspiring serial killer.

Tamsin gasped.

"Ma'am!" she exclaimed.

Robyn peeled away the fabric of the cup, stopping just before the nipple was exposed. She licked the flesh thus revealed, delighted when she became aware of Tamsin trembling.

"Your only *job*," she whispered, "is to do what I tell you to do."

"Yes, ma'am," Tamsin breathed out.

"And I never want to see this thing on you again!" Robyn went on.

This time, the knife blade was brought under the remaining strap and with her clit pounding rhythmically now, Robyn sliced through it, grunting as a spasm of pleasure rocketed through her pussy at the further destruction of the bra.

"Oh, fuck yes…" Tamsin gasped. "Finish it!"

"You've learned your lesson?" Robyn asked.

"Yes, ma'am," Tamsin said, giving Robyn faux puppy dog eyes.

"Good," Robyn purred. "Now…stay…perfectly…still!"

She grabbed hold of the front of the bra and very carefully poked the tip of the knife into the bridge, between the cups. On Tamsin's bras, this was a pretty substantial piece of fabric. After some slow twisting, the knife tip finally poked through.

"Do it!" Tamsin commanded huskily.

"Put your head back," Robyn instructed.

When Tamsin had tilted her head back so far that she was looking up at the ceiling, Robyn sliced upwards rapidly but in a controlled manner, completely cutting through the bridge and separating the massive cups.

Tamsin's breasts spilled out, her pink nipples long and erect.

Quickly, Robyn tossed the knife onto the entryway table, cupped both breasts in her hands and bent her head to the right one, sucking the nipple deep into her mouth.

When Tamsin moaned, it fuelled Robyn's lust even more and she raked her teeth along the nipple before biting it, making her girlfriend moan even louder.

While keeping her teeth's grip on the hard nub, Robyn worked her left hand under Tamsin's pencil skirt, pushed aside the damp crotch of the knickers she encountered, and easily entered Tamsin's wet pussy with her middle and forefingers.

Releasing the nipple, she kissed Tamsin, who now wrapped one of her long legs around her waist and started fucking her.

The kiss never broke. They kept at it until Tamsin squealed into Robyn's mouth, and Robyn felt her fingers being clutched tightly and rhythmically by Tamsin's vagina. This was then followed by splashes of warmth falling onto her hand.

Robyn smiled against Tamsin's lips.

Now, this is how you make Tuesday interesting…

***

"By the way, Empress and I were talking," Robyn said later while she and Tamsin ate dinner.

Tamsin looked at her.

"So…does the cat actually *talk* during these conversations?" she asked. "Or is this a conversation that happens more in your head?"

Robyn narrowed her eyes.

"You know, you're pretty snarky for someone who was just given the gift of an orgasm," she said.

Tamsin shrugged.

"Such are the perils of satisfying your woman," she replied.

Robyn rolled her eyes.

"*Anyway…*" she began, "Empress and I were talking, and I was telling her something interesting." She took a bite of the chicken she had prepared, chewed a few times and swallowed it. "It turns out

I have a two week gap at the gallery between the end of Sean Truman's show and the start of Louise Adler's. So…I plan on filling that gap with…drumroll, please…a multi-artist showcase, featuring the works of one Tamsin Tregurrian."

Tamsin groaned and Robyn laughed, having expected that reaction.

"Now this is where you say," Robyn went on, "that you have no idea what I'm talking about, and you cannot recall us ever having this conversation. Well, Empress and I already anticipated that, and you are full of shit. Not only do you remember us having this conversation but as I am even *more* your girlfriend now than I was back then, you're *soooooo* out of luck! Your paintings will be in the show."

Tamsin looked at her.

"I'm going to lose this battle, aren't I?" she asked.

"You may as well not even *attempt* to fight this battle," Robyn told her.

She suspected Tamsin would indeed attempt to do just that, though. Her girlfriend was a headstrong woman, not afraid of kvetching about things she wasn't one-hundred percent on board with.

Surprisingly, however, Tamsin shrugged.

"Fine," she said. "You know I love making you happy, and it's obvious this will make you happy."

Robyn narrowed her eyes, sensing a trap.

"What's the catch?" she asked.

Tamsin laughed.

"No catch!" she exclaimed. "I know how important this is to you, and if I'm being totally honest, I love how supportive you are of my art."

"Well, your art is amazing," Robyn told her. "I just want to share it with others."

Tamsin stared at her for a few moments.

Finally…

"And I love that you want to share my art with everyone," she said. "And I love you."

Robyn gasped, her eyes going wide.

"Oh my god, babe," she squealed, "I love you too! Like…so much!"

Personally, she had been ready to say those words a couple of months ago because she had fallen *hard* for Tamsin, and she wanted to ask her now if the same was true for her. But she decided it didn't matter. Tamsin was in love with her *now*, and that's all that mattered.

And this felt right.

I've been searching for this…

"Took us long enough," she quipped.

"Right?" Tamsin said, humour in her voice. "What kind of lesbians are we?"

"The slow kind, apparently," Robyn supplied.

Tamsin quirked an eyebrow.

"Well, since you love me so much," she began, "you won't mind if I *don't* participate in the art show."

Robyn laughed.

Looking back down at her plate and spearing another piece of chicken with her fork, she shook her head.

"Oh my love," she muttered, "you are just *so* funny."

Chapter 31

The next day, Tamsin kissed Robyn goodbye. Robyn was leaving earlier than she was for Newquay because, in her words, "I have so much to do to get ready for that show you're going to be in!"

Once Robyn had left, she finished getting ready for work herself. As she was selecting a skirt from the small collection she had started keeping here at Robyn's place, she winced when a couple of mild cramps struck her core. Her period was on its way.

This time, however, the imminence of that monthly discomfort made her do something she had never done before when thinking about it.

She smiled.

This was going to be her fourth period with Robyn.

A personal best. By far.

She started laughing in Robyn's wardrobe.

Of all the silly milestones to use to mark the length of a relationship, the number of periods she'd had while dating the same woman had to be the silliest, but she couldn't help it. There were so many *firsts* she was experiencing with Robyn that each one—no matter how odd—stuck out in her mind…

The first time she had kept clothes at another woman's house.

For that matter, the first time she had kept a toothbrush, makeup, hair products, and her favourite tampons at another woman's house.

For *that* matter, the first time another woman had kept those things at her house as well.

The first time a woman never made her feel as if she was some kind of sexually-stunted oddball whenever she was done having sex after one orgasm.

Yet on the other hand, the first time a woman had ever made her demand a fifth orgasm…or a sixth, or a seventh…

And, of course, the first time she had ever said "I love you" to another woman.

And, even better, the first time another woman had said it back.

She selected a skirt and then paused, realising that she wanted to do something important before she drove to work today.

After choosing a blouse, she laid both garments on the mattress and picked up her phone from the nightstand on her side of Robyn's bed.

As much as she preferred texting *anyone*, unfortunately there was a subset of individuals in her life who, if she texted them, she might as well have sent the message directly into a black hole.

Uncle Richard was one of them.

"Hi luv," he said, answering her call. She could tell that he was driving, presumably to the agency.

"Hi Uncle Richard," she began. "Listen, I might be a little late arriving today. There's a stop I need to make on my way to Newquay."

"No problem, take your time," he told her cheerily. She then mouthed his next words as he said them. "I'll hold down the fort."

"Thanks, Uncle," she told him.

She dressed quickly and then started on her makeup, which today she felt like keeping minimal.

"Bye girl," she told Empress as she opened the front door and exited the cottage.

At the end of Penhallow Lane, she turned left instead of right, heading to the high street.

Walking into The Bean a few minutes later, she was glad to see that although there were several people in the shop, including three people in the queue, it was manageable. Besides, even she knew the orders of the trio of pensioners waiting. They would all take herbal tea, with Mrs. Bronwyn-MacDougall wanting honey in hers. In short, it was nothing Bridget couldn't handle by herself for a few sodding minutes.

"Smarten up, Bridge," Rylea said, spotting her. "Soon-to-be-famous artist in the house!"

Tamsin blinked, wondering what Rylea was on about, but then realised that Robyn must have stopped in here on her way to work and mentioned the art show.

Rolling her eyes, she gestured towards the back of the coffee shop as she walked towards Rylea. Her friend nodded.

"Take over for a few, Bridge," Rylea said.

"Sure, no problem," Bridget responded.

Tamsin pushed through the little swinging door which separated front-of-counter from back-of-counter and then followed Rylea to the store room in the rear of the shop.

Alone now, Rylea looked at her and Tamsin could see the worry on her face. She knew that her best friend probably assumed that Robyn had broken up with her, that although this one had lasted longer than all the others, she had once again been dumped, deemed not worthy enough.

"So…what's going on?" Rylea asked tentatively.

In answer, Tamsin smiled and flung herself at her friend, hugging her tightly.

Rylea embraced her back but didn't say anything. Once more, Tamsin guessed she was expecting the worst, and so she decided to let her off the hook right away.

"I'm the happiest I've ever been in my life," she said, still holding on tightly to Rylea. She felt her eyes watering. Sure enough, tears fell from both of them.

Rylea let out a sigh of relief and gripped Tamsin closer to her.

"Oh, thank god," she said, her voice wavering. "Oh my goodness, sweetie, I'm so happy for you!"

"We're in love and I never want to lose her," Tamsin told her. "She gets me."

"I knew someone eventually would," Rylea whispered. She sniffled, and Tamsin knew she was also crying. "Hold onto her, Tams."

"I will, Rye Bread," Tamsin promised.

"And I'll be sure to threaten to break her kneecaps if she hurts you," Rylea added.

"By the way, you were right," Tamsin said after taking a moment to gain control of her voice.

"Right about what?" Rylea asked.

"She was my exorcism," Tamsin told her.

Epilogue
Three months later

Robyn showed Tamsin her phone's screen.

"It's seven degrees in Newquay right now!" she said. "That's what we could be enduring if we were there!" She suddenly gasped and dropped the phone. The device landed on her pelvis, just above her shaved mound, making her gasp again at the slight pain it caused. *"Holy fucking shit!"* she exclaimed as her clit was captured by Tamsin's lips and sucked on forcefully.

Tamsin had just come out from the en suite in their hotel room here in California, after taking her morning shower. Robyn had been waiting for her on the bed, having showered earlier. While waiting, she had caught up on things back home…checking emails from Tina about how things were going at the gallery, and DM-ing with Darcie on Instagram about how Empress was doing.

While they were on holiday, Darcie's daughter Cleo was stopping by Robyn and Tamsin's cottage—formerly just Tamsin's cottage—to check on Empress and to play with her and make sure that she hadn't eaten *all* of the food in the automatic feeder they had bought for her. Cleo was also being a dear and taking photos of the cat, which Darcie then posted on Instagram. In each photo, Empress seemed as if she was sending transatlantic death threats to Robyn for plaguing her with the presence of this smaller human.

The last thing she had checked on her phone before Tamsin emerged from the en suite was the weather. Not surprisingly, in typical November fashion, the temperature in Cornwall was bleak, making Robyn that much happier that she was currently in a US state where winter temperatures during the day were warm enough to wear shorts and a vest.

Tamsin released her clit.

"Do I have your attention now?" she purred from between Robyn's legs.

Robyn, her head back on the pillow, nodded.

"Yes," she exhaled. Then, *"Ohhhhhhhhhhhhhhhfuckyesssssssss!"* as she felt her opening stretch to accommodate the three fingers Tamsin was inserting.

"Good," Tamsin said. "Now, I don't care about the sodding weather back home. All I care about is making you insane right now."

"I'm on board with that," Robyn insisted.

"This will just be a warm-up," Tamsin advised, moments before she again wrapped her lips around Robyn's engorged button, sucking on it while swiping it with her tongue.

Robyn's back arched and she grabbed her breasts, squeezing them tightly. Her pussy's walls fluttered around Tamsin's fingers as her girlfriend's mouth brought her closer to release.

Robyn surrendered to it, feeling even more sexually charged up because it was the woman she loved doing this to her. That fact had made their sex life more potent, in her opinion. Tamsin being her person, the one she truly felt she was meant to be with, made every touch, kiss, lick, thrust, whatever…that much more exciting.

Because of this, it wasn't long before Robyn felt herself fast approaching the edge.

Apparently, Tamsin sensed this, and also apparently—Robyn deduced—*this* was not how she was meant to come.

The fingers filling her were withdrawn, and the mouth was taken away from her sex. Robyn whimpered at their abrupt absence, but she growled lustily when Tamsin quickly sixty-nined her.

Suddenly, Tamsin's gorgeous pussy was right above her face, and that spectacular ginger-covered mound was within reach.

Robyn grabbed her girlfriend's hips and pulled Tamsin's haunches back far enough so she could open her mouth and bite down on that mound, relishing the feeling of that hair on her lips, on her tongue, against her teeth. She still found this unshaved bit of Tamsin such a turn-on. Even just glimpsing it while watching Tamsin get dressed for work or stepping out of the shower, made her clit pulse, and she knew it would always be like that.

Meanwhile, Tamsin's mouth was working fast and hard on her own sex. Robyn knew she should be reciprocating, that's what sixty-nining was all about, but she decided *this* was how she wanted to come: with that ginger mound in her mouth, her tongue licking the hairs in time with Tamsin's tongue licking her clit.

Soon enough…

"*Nnnnnnnnnnnngh!*" she moaned against the prize in her mouth as she started coming. She repeated the sound when she felt her pussy convulse *hard*, pushing out her arousal in a thick stream which Tamsin started licking up immediately.

Finally pulling her mouth away from her girlfriend's mound, she let out a cry of delight. Everything below her waist was detonating with pleasure, but she still had the presence of mind to realise that she'd been selfish so far.

Adjusting her hold on Tamsin, she brought her mouth to her pussy and began eating her out while still moaning and squealing from her still-continuing climax.

It didn't take long.

Tamsin's pussy burst like a dam. Robyn would have thought the woman hadn't come in days, which she knew wasn't true. So far, their holiday—which had started in L.A.—had lasted four days, and they had fucked during every one of them.

But Tamsin must have been exceedingly turned-on this morning because when she came now, she started shaking, forcing Robyn to tighten her grip on her hips to keep the throbbing vulva right where she wanted it, and her mouth and tongue had to work especially fast to keep up with the flow of come streaming out of the ginger's opening. Even so, she missed quite a bit and some of it dribbled down her chin and onto her throat.

She didn't mind. In fact, the feeling made the intensity of her lust that much stronger, and she started humming with delight as Tamsin's taste filled her mouth.

***

"You have to admit, this is such a lovely town!" Robyn exclaimed about half an hour later. They had cleaned themselves up and gotten dressed, in preparation to go out and explore. Robyn was standing on the balcony of their hotel room, looking out over the Pacific Ocean and the beach which edged it.

When she turned her head to the right, she could make out a long pier, appearing hazy in the distance. They had been told that was in Oceanside and that there was a diner-type restaurant at the end of the pier, over the water. They had plans to walk along the beach later to reach it and have lunch.

From just inside the room, she heard Tamsin—who was rummaging through her suitcase for something—sigh.

"Fine," Tamsin said. "This is a lovely bloody town! But I'm not putting that in writing!"

Robyn laughed and continued surveying the ocean and beach.

They were in Carlsbad, a town north of San Diego. Some time ago, Robyn had finally learned that Tamsin had a silly one-sided rivalry with Carlsbad because it had come in tops on some *Best of* list that Tamsin had conceived, while Tremont had come in second. Something about top destinations for lesbians.

Well…

They had arrived last night, driving down from L.A., and from what Robyn could see even then, this town was a gay woman's dream destination. This was only confirmed by the view from the balcony right now.

Back home in Cornwall, the women—like everyone else—were covered up daily against the cold weather, which in some areas was more biting because of the frosty winds coming in off the Atlantic. Many of those women were putting on winter pounds, figuring why bother keeping them off? With the layers of clothes and the spring weather months away yet, diets and extra treadmill time could wait. Similarly, many of those women had stopped shaving their legs, at least regularly. Again, why bother? Who was going to see their legs until after Easter or later?

Here in Carlsbad, however, the weather allowed the women to walk around with short skirts, skin-tight athleisure wear, denim cut-offs, and crop tops, showing off long legs and taut midriffs, beautiful shoulders and toned arms—all of which were tanned from a sun that never seemed to disappear except at night.

It was definitely an…*enticing* population, Robyn thought, and although she was perfectly happy with the woman she had chosen to be her mate, she was looking forward to spending a day out in this beachside town, enjoying the eye candy.

She and Tamsin had come on this holiday in order to fulfil Robyn's promise to her that if they were together for six months, they would visit California. Tamsin booked the trip, only occasionally complaining that of all the places in the US to visit, why California?

But by now, Robyn knew how to get her way with Tamsin. She personally loved this state, which meant that her girlfriend was going to learn to love it as well.

And so far, they had been having a great time, with Tamsin even seeming to forget her ridiculous resentment of the place.

And here in this particular town, they had amazing accommodations. The hotel they had chosen was hard by the beach. They could literally walk out of the building and have sand under their feet right away. What's more, their room was a spacious suite, not a tiny shoebox with barely space enough for the bed.

This had all been paid for by Tamsin.

At the multi-artist showcase, the three paintings Tamsin had (reluctantly) entered had all sold, earning her close to twenty-five hundred pounds, which for an unknown artist was incredible, a fact which Robyn had lorded over Tamsin for at least a fortnight following the show.

Despite that success, her girlfriend still wasn't painting, though.

Robyn facetiously blamed that on Uncle Richard, who had finally decided to retire, handing over the reins of Xplr to his niece, who was now more focussed than ever on ensuring *her* business succeeded.

At times, this manifested itself as Tamsin being ready to begin working on other things after a quick shag.

At other times, this manifested itself as Tamsin needing orgasm after orgasm after orgasm in order to relieve the stress she was putting on herself.

At still other times, this manifested itself as Tamsin needing a cuddle on the sofa, with Robyn cooing *I love you* or *You got this* in her ear.

At no point, alas, did this manifest itself as Tamsin needing to create—to lose herself in painting a new picture.

However, there had been an encouraging sign a few weeks ago…

While the two of them were shopping at The Range, in Truro, Tamsin had wandered off while Robyn had been looking at a new duvet she possibly wanted.

Ten minutes later—after deciding the duvet wasn't quite right for the bedroom—she had found her girlfriend in the Arts & Crafts section, selecting tubes of oil paint.

Robyn hadn't commented on it, afraid to break whatever spell Tamsin might be under. She had simply approached her, remarked that the duvet wasn't right, but that she still wanted them to look at new cushions for her sofa.

"Okay," Tamsin had said, tossing the four tubes of paint she had selected into their trolley as if they had always been on their list of items to look for.

No painting had occurred just yet, but Robyn was prepared to be patient.

In any case, Tamsin had decided to be ironic with the money, stating that if Robyn was hellbent on making Carlsbad a stop on their holiday through Southern California, she was going to make sure they were treated like royalty.

"We're British, after all," she had told Robyn.

Thus were they in this expensive hotel, so close to the ocean that the sound of the surf would help lull them to sleep.

Turning to go back into the room from the balcony, Robyn stopped, her heart thumping and her emotions threatening to spill over into tears.

In the room, framed by the sliding glass door of the balcony, was Tamsin, standing at a mirror, fixing her red hair up with some clips.

Robyn stood still, watching her.

She was just so beautiful!

It was heart-stopping, really. Even six months in, Robyn couldn't believe it. Even more, she couldn't believe all the things she got to do with her…

Hold her hand.

Kiss her.

Give her shoulder rubs.

Snuggle with her under a duvet while watching movies.

Buy her surprise presents and watch her face light up.

Wake up next to her.

Fall deeper in love with her.

Looking at her now, she knew she'd be watching Tamsin do the exact same thing to her hair forty-five years from now, when the red had long faded to grey.

And Robyn wanted to see that sight.

Because when it came to Tamsin, the colour of the hair didn't matter, only the woman it was growing on. For as long as it stayed ginger, Robyn would love her, and when the ginger was gone, she would love her even more.

She took a deep breath to gain back control of her emotions. She didn't want to start crying and make Tamsin wonder what was wrong. Especially here in "bloody Carlsbad."

When she was calm, she stepped into the room.

"Well, come on, slowcoach," she said, patting Tamsin's arse, which was wearing—SoCal style—Lululemon yoga shorts. "You're in love with me, which means you know I need coffee in the mornings, and I've heard there's a lovely shop with a cute name just up this street…"

THE END

Thank you so much for reading *What Comes After One*!

If you liked it, please consider rating it or even writing a review on Amazon or Goodreads! Reviews are super important to independent authors, and we love getting feedback from our readers.

Follow me on Twitter at *@kanelesfic* for updates on what I'm writing next! You can also find me on Facebook at @CultOfVanessa.